THE INLOOKER

BY

TERRY TUMBLER

Copyright

Copyright © Terry Tumbler 2015

The right of Terry Tumbler to be identified as the Author of the Work has been asserted by him in accordance with the Copyright, Designs and Patents Act 1988.

No resemblance is intended to any real person, living or dead.

This book is sold subject to the condition it shall not, by way of trade or otherwise, be circulated in any form or by any means, electronic or otherwise without the author's prior consent.

ISBN 978-1-909121-80-5

www.terrytumbler.com
http://terrytumbler.blogspot.com.es/

Cover re-designed by Patrycja Pawlik
patrycja.ska@wp.pl

Vsn 2g

Dedication

Deepest thanks are extended to my patient and adorable wife, who helped me with the preparation and revision of this book.

Acknowledgements

Special thanks are extended to:
The Hungry Monster Reviews
Who have since emailed me with the following:

Congratulations!
We are proud to present you with our Hungry Monster Book Award.

Your book deserves extraordinary praise and The Hungry Monster is proud to acknowledge your dedication, writing skill and imagination.

The Gold Award is bestowed on books that we found to be perfect in their delivery of original content, meticulous development of unique characters in an organic and striking setting, innovative plot that supports a fresh theme, and elegant prose that transforms words into beautifully written novels.

Thank you,
Thomas Anderson
The Hungry Monster Book Review

Titles

Seb Cage Begins His Adventures – where Terry Tumbler's grandsons come to stay with him and his long-suffering wife, who live on the Costa Blanca, for the entire summer vacation. During this period, the elder one, Seb, experiences a number of futuristic adventures when he joins a summer campus run by a mysterious organization called *The Sombrella Syndicate*.
Series: **The Dreadnought Collective Book 1**

The Inlooker – where a presumably unique character, Thomas Beckon, realizes his paranormal talents and changes the nature of society in Great Britain, and thereafter of the World, to help shape mankind in its future development.
Series: **The Dreadnought Collective Book 2**

The Time Slipsters – A group of friends take a trip together. It is the near future, and they will be traveling on the latest type of air-road transport. Unwittingly, they are entering a world where time travel is a reality, and soon they embark on a sightseeing tour like no other they could have imagined. More than one person has a hidden agenda, as they realize when they reach a highly protected secret location.
Series: **The Dreadnought Collective Book 3**

The Deaduction Agency – witness at first-hand a group of specialist investigators, as they set up and run a new agency. They are dedicated to the resolution of criminal cases using paranormal

assistance. This will be a new and emerging brand of policing designed to protect the citizens of our country.
Series: **The Dreadnought Collective Book 4**

The Sightseers – the first recruit to the new Sightseers Agency is a remote viewer who actively seeks the resolution of events threatening world security. Both his fledgling agency and that of the Deaduction Agency belong to The Dreadnought Collective.
Series: **The Dreadnought Collective Book 5**

For those who may become interested in his upbringing, the author Terry Tumblers' childhood behavior is recounted in a mildly fictionalized autobiographical work called:

The Rough & Tumbles Of Early Years

The author himself subsequently regarded this as a potentially valuable compendium of incidents, which could be serialized in the same vein as *Just William*. Originally, it was prepared for the benefit of his family, who would otherwise have known nothing about his outrageous childhood behavior
Series: **A Wonderfully Wacky World Book 1**

Santiago Tales – where the irascible and incorrigible Terry Tumbler, based very loosely on the personality of the author, organizes a trip for himself and his cronies to travel to the sacred city of Santiago de Compostela, following parts of the St James Camino, in Northern Spain.

En route, as well as swapping stories in the same vein as those published in *Canterbury Tales* by *Geoffrey Chaucer*, they endure an interesting encounter themselves.

Conceptually, this is a semi-fictional book within a travelogue.

Series: **A Wonderfully Wacky World Book 2**

Note. Please be advised that English UK spelling is mainly used in this book.

Foreword

This is a 'black humour' science fiction story set in the near future, where a man finds that he has a very special talent. It is to take over other people's souls and thus possess their bodies as if they were his own.

As he becomes increasingly aware of his abilities, he first uses them to mete out justice to mentally warped criminals, and then to undertake sexual adventures.

Growing tired of what are, in the scheme of things, trivial pursuits, he embarks on a life of crime intent on accumulating serious amounts of money. Whilst fleecing the wealthy, he comes across an alien hiding amongst us, and is impressed by the seamless transport system on its own planet, so he decides to emulate it on Planet Earth.

With a colleague recruited from The Lockheed Skunk Works in America, he develops a vehicle based on UFO technology, and uses it as a stepping-stone to power. His motivation soon goes beyond his revolutionary and hugely successful transport system, and extends to a serious attempt at population reduction. For this he requires even more prominence on the world stage, as he battles aliens to prevent annihilation of the expanding human race.

This book charts his progress, as he strives to achieve the impossible. It also monitors the impact on his family life, where he eventually has to decide whether to opt for mortality or immortality.

If all you want to read about is sexual adventures, and cannot be bothered with the future of mankind, this book is not for you. It is intended for those who like to ponder the value of life as we lead it, and what it could be like if we choose to take up the challenge.

A word of warning: this story is initially written in the same pompous style in which the Inlooker thinks, that is to say disdainfully aloof of the people he meets. As he progresses through life and his personality becomes more worldly-wise, the style of presentation changes to match his growing maturity.

Contents

The Mirrors Karma

*When people insult you, don't take offense,
don't take it personally, but do listen to their
words.*
*They are telling you how they see the world,
and they are telling you the exact negative
qualities that they possess.*
*"The Law of Mirrors" states that one can only
see what's in them, regardless if it is what is
actually present in reality or not.*

§ 1: Unpleasant Specimens

The prison warder was beginning to nod off, which was strictly not allowed, when all hell broke loose in one of the cells he was supposed to be monitoring. His head jerked back painfully as the sole male occupant let out a series of blood-curdling screams.

"It's him again," he muttered, rubbing his sore neck. "They come in here feeling sorry for themselves, insisting they're innocent and then get all suicidal. He's an evil swine that one is!"

The prisoner in question had been tried and found guilty of murdering a little girl, presumably for sexual gratification, and disposing of her body. Pretty little thing she had been, and no trace of her was ever found, apart from blood scattered throughout his rented property.

"I'll never understand why they don't dispose of animals like him, instead of putting them in here at huge cost," he grumbled. He then thought a bit harder, and perked up somewhat *"On reflection, it's*

worth keeping him alive if it means me having a job."
He picked up the phone to call for help.

It took three of them to restrain the wild-eyed, panting prisoner none too gently, while his neighbours cursed from their cells at their sleep being interrupted. It would have been satisfying if he had shown some signs of remorse, but he was in a state of incoherent rage at being held captive, nothing more.

A male nurse who was patiently waiting nearby for the struggling to cease was finally given the opportunity to inject a sedative, before they laid him down on his bed where he was stretched out comatose.

"We'll put it in his food next time," the nurse confirmed as an aside before walking off, "so he doesn't get the chance to give us a repeat show."

"He carries on like that, and there'll be no next time," growled the original warder, more in hope than expectation of being given his wish.

Little did he realise that even in this imperfect world in which we all live, his desire was going to be granted from an unexpected source. Someone who had witnessed events at court as they were reported on television had been appalled at this loss of an innocent life, and was determined to pursue his own type of justice.

Already, murderers like the man in question had been slashed with makeshift knives by fellow prisoners, so widespread was the disgust at foul deeds of this nature, although many would have considered the life incarceration of monsters was satisfactory punishment for them.

But had the scales of justice tipped too far in favour of compassion for serious offenders?

Increasingly, revulsion had entered the hearts of people who felt loathing for these vile people, compacted by a shared contempt at the dominance of those influential citizens who regarded human rights as the prerogative of the criminals.

This was putting them before those of the victims and their families.

In the mind of one man, too much was going wrong with society to let matters continue unchecked, and he desperately wanted to do something about it. That man was Thomas Beckon, and you couldn't have wished to meet an apparently nicer person than him. He regarded himself as a godsend to the population at large, rather than a 'God Sent' individual, with all that implied.

He felt powerless to intervene in the criminal justice system, but within himself the desire to act was growing and all he needed was to find the means to do it.

He was not a Christian at heart, and moral strictures would not hold him back.

§ 2: The Inlooker Finds His Talent

All Thomas's friends referred to him affectionately as Tommy, a term of endearment that suggested someone who was obviously friendly, without a sharp edge and no threat to anybody.

People who were introduced to him warmed instantly to his welcoming smile, and saw a person that they liked, with no reservations. He could easily have been mistaken for a man of the cloth, with his meaningful, quizzical countenance, and chestnut-brown intelligent eyes. So memorable was the experience that, when Tommy was out of earshot, more than one person commented, "He's looked into my soul."

Whilst he appreciated the favourable impression he created in strangers' hearts, he knew clearly what he was really like. In fact, he realised that suspicious people of other nationalities might well have referred to him as 'Adolf' or 'Attila', and dealt with him in a more - how to put it? - circumspect manner.

You see, Thomas Beckon was a man born with rare, possibly unique skills: he could not only look into a person's soul, he could also take possession of it, gently or otherwise. It was an insidious process that he barely realised he was initiating, and not once did he encounter any formidable resistance, at least that he was aware of.

He did wonder at times if what he thought was happening did actually occur, but if it didn't then it was one hell of an imaginative experience. His suspicion of his latent abilities was aroused in the most humdrum way, with his cats of all things.

In his present incarnation, Tommy was a happily married man with a contented wife, Pat, and two adult daughters, the younger one living with them at home. Their modern, four bedroomed two story house was located in a small but growing village in Northern Essex not far from the 17th century base of the Witchfinder General in Manningtree.

Originally, the family had only two cats that they had selected as sisters from a nearby cat rescue centre. Thomas had named them Belle and Mia deliberately; they had two distinctive personalities, as different as chalk and cheese. Thomas loved it when one of the women went into their landscaped garden, and shouted, "Bella Mia!" to attract the cats back home for their evening meal.

"Bloody child you are!" grumbled Pat when he burst out laughing each time that it happened, when he was at home to witness the calling of the cats.

Tommy and Pat's older daughter, Sharon, had suffered a troubled marriage in her late teens after her weirdo husband abandoned her when she was pregnant, leaving her to bring up their baby daughter on her own.

Naturally, Pat and Thomas helped out as best they could, while their independently minded older daughter and granddaughter Rose continued living in her own heavily mortgaged Victorian terraced house until it was under threat of repossession by the building society.

For a while, she rented out rooms to young people to help make ends meet, but the costs of upkeep continued to rise ahead of income. The situation with the mortgage became critical, as was evidenced by the relentless correspondence from the building society warning that action was pending unless outstanding payments were made forthwith.

At the instigation of her father, Thomas, Sharon vacated the property and handed back the keys to the society.

He counselled, "Let *them* chase the errant husband for repayment; he's the one responsible for what's happened!"
It was a blessed relief for her and her parents, and she returned home with her precious toddler, Rose, to live with them and Sharon's younger sister, Julie. It was a big house with plenty of bedrooms. Thankfully, they never heard anything more from the mortgage provider, which had changed its tactics and was doubtlessly hounding the ex-husband.

After a year or so, she met a strapping young man by the name of Chris, and he invited Sharon and Rose to go and stay with him.

Thomas sighed, saying, "Some people never learn!" His instinct told him that her latest conquest was not to be trifled with.

Chris's current abode was a furnished house set in its own grounds, where he and Sharon were to act as live-in caretakers during the wealthy owners' long absences abroad. This meant that she couldn't take her beloved male tabby cat, Stusie, with her, so Pat and Tommy temporarily adopted it. They were sorry to see them go, in particular the irrepressibly cheerful Rose who seemed blissfully ignorant of what was going on around her.

Stusie was the dominant cat out of the three, without being vicious, and soon integrated with the family. However, one day he simply vanished, and after an anxious wait, the family accepted the sad probability that he had either been run over by a vehicle, or been snaffled by a fox in one of the nearby copses of trees.

This was when Tommy realised that Stusie's distinctive personality had transferred itself to Mia, who began behaving in ways that only Stusie would have done. He looked into Mia's eyes, who would normally have looked away shiftily, and with a shiver he recognised it was Stusie staring back at him, and extending her claws into his lap as a typical warning sign that she wanted his attention, without drawing blood.

Gradually, over the days that followed, Mia's suppressed soul (that is to say, spirit?) returned to take control of her own body and Stusie passed onto the spirit world, as Tommy liked to believe. Thereafter, normality resumed, although Sharon was naturally upset by the loss of her cherished pet in her enforced absence.

The next cat to die, through age-related illness, was Mia and it was another sad day when Tommy took her to the vet to be put down. He held her paw as the vet gave her a terminal injection and she fell asleep while he suppressed his desire to weep, it not being considered a manly thing to do.

That evening, for the first time ever, it was Mia's soul looking up at him through Belle's eyes, as she stood at the foot of his chair and leapt up onto his lap. He shivered as he realised that Belle was behaving exactly like Mia used to do, even to the extent of laying on her back for him to tickle her belly and meow contentedly.

To his consternation, he felt his own spirit wanting to enter the cat and empathise with it as far as a human being could, but he resisted the temptation to do so. After all, it *was* only a cat. However, temptation became an irresistible urge to which he grudgingly yielded, and Mia's soul resisted hard as he took possession and suppressed it. He became conscious of the probability that Belle's soul was lurking somewhere in the background, and was being suppressed by the more dominant Mia.

A shiver went through him as he looked up at himself through the eyes of the cat, almost like he was using a mirror, and he gave an involuntary shudder before returning instantly to his own body, with the cat hissing at him in fright and putting its weight on its haunches.

It made him quite upset, all this transparently obvious transference of souls, while he and Pat occasionally discussed the cats' repeated strange behaviour in the evenings that followed, until Belle resumed her normal pattern of disinterest and wandered away.

This was when Tommy's curiosity about his latent abilities to 'see into others' began to develop, and he decided instead to concentrate on people. Granted, his reasons for doing so were slim, with only the cats to guide him, but he had been sure for many years that every living thing felt emotion, from the lowliest ants which scurried away when threatened, to videos showing terrorised animals in abattoirs about to be slaughtered.

Presumably, even fish felt scared when they closed up into tight, fast circling shoals as predators attacked, and likewise he scorned the priests in Spain for blessing donkeys before the local population threw them off cliffs, with the helpless animals braying in terror.

"Cruelty beyond belief, condoned by an icon-worshipping church" was how he condemned such behaviour.

Thomas reasoned that if animals felt emotions and could move their souls from their dying bodies to other, living animals of the same species, as the cats had demonstrated, why couldn't humans do it too, only better?

The time finally came when Tommy decided to experiment on a real person as a guinea pig (or potential victim, if you choose), using someone he knew and thoroughly disliked. Naturally, it was meaningful to him, since he had chosen a person who did something profoundly bad to a member of his family.

His attitude could be regarded as that of an amoral person, who can distinguish right from wrong but is indifferent to the opinion of others on what he chooses to do with his life. As a result, it can be asserted with confidence that he knew that his actions would offend some people quite significantly.

The opportunity had presented itself when Chris revealed the nasty side of his nature and decided to knock Sharon about. Physically, Tommy realised he was no match for him, and Chris's physical superiority was proven when he got into a fight in a pub and effortlessly set about everyone with his fists who tried to give him a hiding. That was practically all those present, who were gypsies that Chris had fallen out with, and were now laying there senseless and occasionally broken-limbed.

"There's more than a touch of the gypsy about that young man himself," Tommy confided in Pat.

Immediately that Chris turned on her, Sharon made plans to exit their shared accommodation. She applied for sheltered housing with the local council, and after their officials took the child into consideration, the request was granted. Soon, Sharon made arrangements to move her belongings and child out of harm's way, forthwith.

The actual move was conducted by a local removal company, while Chris was standing to one side near the exit door, under the wary supervision of two police constables, one of whom was a woman.

Fortunately, he had decided to behave himself, having been in trouble before with the law. All went smoothly with him, the root cause of Sharon's problems, pretending to be as serene as he could possibly be, while declaring, "I still loves yer, babe!"

Anyone else might have had dreams about what they would like to do; however, Tommy took things to the next stage with determination and heartfelt venom. For practise, he imagined himself entering Chris's brain and using his eyes to look at the world around him.

Earlier, he had found where Chris was staying by casually asking Sharon where she had been living, knowing that the two of them had been 'an item'. The location was easy to find, after a cursory tour of the area by car one day, using a map.

A few late nights later, resting on the chaise-longue in his study, he detached his spirit from his body and soared swiftly to the house where Chris was found to be sleeping.

It was an ideal opportunity to try out his fledgling talent and mete out justice He couldn't know whether what he was seeing was imaginary or not, as he straddled his victim's chest. Putting aside his doubts, he concentrated instead on giving Chris a pounding headache by reaching into his eye sockets and rubbing them hard, thus disorienting his senses.

Chris's physical hands reached up to cover his eyes, but it was to no avail as Thomas's spiritual form continued to rub them aggressively. The pain must have been intense, but Chris had been down the pub and was fairly sozzled.

When he had finished with his savagery, Thomas raised himself in the air and returned in minutes to his own physical body.

The next day, feedback from his unsuspecting older daughter proved most satisfactory.

"Chris phoned and told me that he's feeling really unwell," Sharon commented. "But if he thinks I'm going back to him he's had it!" The blond-haired young man-mountain was used to doing hard, physical work and had never shown signs of ill-health at any time previously.

Tommy redoubled his efforts after this, intending to make his target feel sick and disoriented all the time, especially at the wheel of his battered old car. A short while later he was rewarded with news provided by his distraught daughter; Chris had crashed his car into a tree, been taken to hospital concussed, and was now in an induced coma.

Sharon had sobbed uncontrollably when she told Tommy and Pat about her latest misadventure, while Tommy contained his elation and showed her only compassion. Eventually Chris died, with no one at his bedside to comfort him.

"*One less evil sod to endure!*" was his callous inner thought, while he wondered if he really was responsible for Chris's demise. He remained utterly remorseless in his attitude and felt proud of what he thought he had done.

§ 3: The Inlooker's Working Life

Undoubtedly, there was one aspect to Thomas's life that was the most influential in shaping his character.

During a commercial apprenticeship with a major industrial group, he took a senior manager's advice to change employers every two or three years, purely for the sake of gaining a varied experience and to avoid getting stuck in a rut.

Thereafter, it was a natural progression for him to gravitate towards computing, and he was fortunate to be there almost from the birth of this new profession. Recruited by IBM, he participated in the sales support and maintenance of huge batch-processing computers provided by IBM. In general, only large enterprises could afford to rent them and the rewards were highly lucrative.

One of his biggest regrets was to pass the tests that IBM set for programmers but be denied access by his future line manager, who gloated as he stated, "Thomas, this is the first time that we've thwarted them. They've always managed to pinch our best candidates in the past!"

In spite of his misgivings about a lost opportunity, Thomas did well and rose to be appointed as head of the emergency supply team, where he became aware of sudden changes in technology; IBM was leapfrogging its rivals with the introduction of revolutionary components that looked unworldly to him.

Within a few more years, the vast data-crunching machines were being superseded, in the second phase of computing, by affordable mini computers. Thomas therefore decided better opportunities lay elsewhere, and chose to apply for work with end-users of them in the London area.

The fact was he didn't realize that he had already hit pay-dirt with this major employer and afterwards regretted having summarily left.

Be that as it may, he was soon riding the crest of this transition by installing and managing computers in a succession of small to medium-sized companies. These were all in the insurance services sector, where he felt that the rewards offered were greater than those that were available elsewhere.

It was at this stage of his life that Thomas was finally able to satisfy his ambition to learn computer programming. He could at last apply this skill for personal satisfaction, to the benefit of others.

During those early years he became a disciplined well-rounded computer manager, and the majority of his rough edges were lost as he interacted with influential players in the market place. He also learnt to hide his true feelings from others, being aware that his future success depended on portraying a true, professional attitude to whatever task he was currently undertaking at any one time.

There were two things he enjoyed wherever he worked; the first was the satisfaction he gained from achieving other peoples' ambitions, by providing systems that worked well. The second was the few close friendships he invariably made in each workplace.

Unbeknown to him, he was honing his skills at reading other people's minds.

At this juncture in his life, Thomas had been recruited as an Information Technology (IT) manager in the City of London. He was in his early forties and reasonably fit. Each weekday, he cycled a few uneven miles to and from the railway station linking him by commuter train to his office, where he exercised his brain by providing systems for a management team whose companionship he enjoyed, to an extent.

Part of his life was regularly spent programming, out of enjoyment, and he employed a small team of developers as well as operational staff. Frequently, he lugged a heavy, so-called 'portable' computer home, to continue working in his study during the evenings and weekends, but still managing to spend precious time with his wife and two growing girls.

Emotionally, he was well-suited to his role and usually employed cold logic in his decision-making. When he started this demanding full-time job, which proved to be his last of any substance, the few hours he spent each day travelling on the train were devoted to the resolution of practical problems requiring logical solutions.

Later on, he made friends with fellow commuters and they sat together in one compartment chatting and enjoying banter. Inadvertently, he was examining their minds without knowing how remarkably accurate his understanding of them was.

At times, he would come to a conclusion, such as, *"Oh dear, it's only a matter of time before he leaves his family!"* or, *"He's likely to lose his job soon, and he's hiding his fears from everyone!"* or, *"He hates his work, is bored by it and wants out!"*

Then he would back off, and the predicted outcomes would happen. It was occurring too often for his liking, and he began to keep his distance regularly, rather than get emotionally involved.

Some of them must have suspected that he possessed this talent for mental 'eavesdropping', when he noted that they were beginning to secretly harbour dislikes of him, He needed solitude, before the 'mind chatter' became oppressive, and reverted to doing programming during his journeys.

It was probably this preponderance of 'cold thought' that brought his talents as 'The Inlooker' to the fore. Subconsciously, his algebraic skills at defining rules to solve problems were becoming supreme.

He also had a dream one night that unsettled him; in it, he was standing in front of a long blackboard completing rows of formulae that were extremely complex. To the untrained eye, they were meaningless, but he understood them perfectly, and went back and forth with a chalk crayon, making subtle corrections to the logic; it all made sense to him.

He stood back in an instance, aware of the strange situation, and asked himself, "*Who am I, why am I here?*" As he did so, he began to awaken, and grew alarmed as his memory of the formulae faded into nothing.

From that moment on, he believed that something was blocking his memory of an academically prominent past life; he also began to question if it was his faith in Christianity that was driving him along his current path. The explanation, if his dream was an actual recollection of a past life, had to involve reincarnation as a recurring event, and that was a possibility denied by the church.

No, he needed to find a faith that was more attuned to his disturbing, credible dream, if only to give moral support in what looked likely to be a lonely passage through life.

To continue the story; it was now in the late 1980's, and in spite of his self-restraint Thomas's employers at that time were getting on his nerves. Four year earlier, all had been sweetness and light as he project-managed the installation of their first in-house computer, smoothly replacing a third-party bureau service with a more cost-effective, responsive and dedicated department for which he became entirely responsible.

The rewards were commensurate with their appreciation of his undoubted achievements, but rumblings were afoot within a few years as the senior management structure was 'adjusted', largely to cater for the ambitions of a new generation of 'rising stars' who were seeking and expecting advancement.

Primarily, this was a fresh intake of privileged 'wannabee' underwriters who, in many of their colleagues' opinions, were privileged popinjays (persons given to vain, pretentious displays and empty chatter).

Thomas watched in abstract amusement as they jostled for attention; that is, until they turned their eager attention to his department. A shrewd onlooker, who was a female ex-barrister, commented to him one day, "You mark my words, they'll be making your life hell before long!" And so it came to pass.

The groundwork for interference was laid when Thomas's kindly boss, the underwriters' principal partner, delegated responsibility for the rest of the company, including Information Technology, to his main financial accountant, who he awarded the new title of Group Managing Director.

This main board director was a tall, skinny man with an olive-skinned complexion and unkempt black hair, who devoted most of his time to staring abstractedly at a screen perched high in one corner; he was watching the performance of stocks and shares and the various financial markets in a ticker-tape style of presentation.

Unfortunately, whenever he summoned Thomas to his inner sanctum, he continued devoting most of his attention to these other activities, and was belittling of the IT function. It was an irritant to him, as far as Thomas could see.

In spite of his wariness, Thomas himself was re-titled 'Managing Director of IT', which sounded good, but was merely following the city trend of giving staff fancy titles that were supposed to impress outsiders.

"I can't quarrel with that," he smiled, as he was rewarded with a handsome pay rise and company car. A week later, at a presentation and buffet lunch organised by a supplier, he met a kindred soul who was IT manager at another underwriting group. This person informed him, "We're unique, us two! We're the only ones left who're still in our jobs; everyone else has had the sack!"

Thomas nodded knowingly, but could hardly credit what he had just been told and did not bother to follow it up. If anyone was secure, it was surely him! He should have known better, because this stranger who had given him the warning was an SAS reservist, a sergeant no less, whose sense of self-preservation had to be acute.

Then the fun started. His new boss arranged monthly meetings with Thomas and his second-in-command, and loftily announced that he too, the group MD, would be accompanied by the lead underwriters' other partner, who Thomas scarcely knew, and a female secretary who would be recording the minutes.

She was a delight to look at, being tall, smart and blond, with slim legs and big knockers, which were always threatening to burst out of the tight blouse she invariably wore. Her articulation was superb, as was evidenced by Thomas when she confided something to him; apparently his boss had offered her the chance to work for him full-time, if she was prepared to 'spread her legs and accommodate him'.

"Ugh!" was the expression they both used, and thereafter they both felt that they shared a common enemy.

At each meeting, Thomas was presented with a list of the newly promoted underwriters' naïve suggestions for system improvements. These he would painstakingly analyse, and afterwards explain, in elementary English, why they could not be implemented.

Unfortunately, neither the ex-accountant nor his companion, the obscure founding underwriting partner of the company, had sufficient understanding of computing to appreciate what was being described to them, and would leave shaking their heads in bafflement.

Thomas and his deputy repeatedly asked themselves and others, *"Can this be articulated better?"* but came to the opinion that their superiors were, in a nutshell, somewhat restricted in mental capacity. This view seemed to be shared by the secretary who also attended the meetings; in confidence, she expressed herself puzzled by the failure of either of the senior managers to comprehend what was obvious to the IT team and herself.

Years before, when Thomas was progressing through the ranks supporting Lloyds' insurance brokers, he had been advised that, "In a wealthy home containing three sons approaching manhood, the most clever would go into merchant banking, the second most clever was expected to become a stockbroker, and the least intelligent would go into insurance."

Thomas was beginning to think that he was witnessing this in practise, especially when one of the promoted, fledgling senior underwriters repeatedly failed his Chartered Insurance Institute exams, which were a compulsory requirement for becoming a Lloyd's underwriter. The young man was a dashing, highly accomplished sportsman, educated at Eton no less! But academically he was a complete airhead, much to the consternation of the main board members, who had no idea how to overcome this serious obstacle to his privileged expectations.

Thomas was worried that his computer would become overwhelmed if they were to implement the various impractical ideas being submitted, and his fears were reinforced when a Nelson-like figure, the lead underwriter who he hero-worshipped, confided in him that he would "be unable to protect Thomas, should the situation continue." He was not saying that he lacked faith in him, but that his position was becoming untenable.

Later on, his original mentor, the head honcho, became prominent by his sparse attendance of key meetings, and Thomas realised that he, the leading underwriting partner, was making himself scarce; he was essentially a weak person who liked to surround himself with an inner circle of lesser mortals. It was such a disappointment to Thomas that he began to dislike his place of work intensely.

For the first time in his working life, Thomas was floundering. His tried and tested formula for success had run its course, the second phase of computing had become entrenched and he had become settled where he was. Moreover, his age was militating against him.

To increase his misery, his new boss kept dumping unwanted staff on him, for whom he had no use. It was being done to avoid sacking people who had become unsuitable for their existing roles, and Thomas worried that eventually, it would be noted that his department was becoming an excessive burden for the group to support.

He protested at meetings and in writing that, "I don't need nor want this burden on my payroll. I could manage with no more than five in total, yet here I am with thirteen people! What is the point of it all?"

He could see where this situation would eventually lead, and it did cross his mind that it was deliberate. Nevertheless, the more he looked into matters, the more he came to the conclusion that his bosses were just dim witted rather than malicious.

Unfortunately, Thomas was incapable of saying "Yes" to people who were senior to him and who were behaving so foolishly, and they in turn devised a plan to get rid of him, for his disdainful attitude and rudeness, when he was in emotional turmoil and regularly visiting his dying father at weekends.

Curiously, Thomas never felt deep animosity towards those who were making his life hell, nor had he any desire for revenge, even though his dismissal was sudden, brutal and acrimoniously conducted by his powerful adversaries. As far as he was concerned, they were beneath contempt.

In the wilderness years that followed, spent by Thomas working in a variety of aimless jobs, he was taught by changed circumstances a sense of compassion, and the love between his wife and himself deepened as she became the main source of their mutual support.

On the surface, this might have seemed a selfish motive, but it was a big 'thank you' from her, for all the years he had devoted to supporting the family. Money was never short for them, as they had always lived well within their means with no debts to speak of. They were a team through good and bad times.

On the other hand, his previous employers were suffering a series of setbacks that would have gladdened Thomas's heart, if he had known or cared about them. However, Thomas was also fully aware that he didn't have to do anything other than wait for things to happen.

In the past, he and others in his immediate circle had noticed that dramatic events occurred whenever he was upset. These were in stark contrast to the normal failures of household electrical appliances, ranging from light bulbs popping to computers, TVs and fridges terminating prematurely, barely out of warranty.

To illustrate this at work; immediately on his departure, discontented staff began to leave in droves and the remainder had to be paid salary increases to coax them to stay. This had caused alarm amongst the senior management, who came under fire from the staff in general for their uncharitable attitude and willingness to succumb to pressure from the newly promoted underwriting board members. This reaction was understandable and could have been anticipated by anyone with an ounce of compassion in their souls.

Next of all, the central computer suffered a series of problems as its capacity was overloaded. The staff throughout the group felt a sense of outrage at the newly promoted underwriters' politicised manoeuvring, and lost little time in pouring scorn on senior management for their failure to listen to their sacked IT manager. This too was understandable, and his heart would have gone out to the people he liked, if he had been aware of what was happening.

Subsequently, in fits of pique or loss of interest, those underwriters who had caused most of the problems soon left the company for pastures new, an event that was a cause for celebration in many parts of the company, much to the embarrassment of the true, ruling partners. Not many of their subordinates liked this fresh intake, since they had always kept themselves apart from the others and had acted as belligerent outsiders who collected only a few toadies to surround them.

By coincidence (or was it?) every personal computer in the company crashed with a systemic hardware problem, directly causing the manufacturer to go out of business.

Additionally, the company secretary lost contractual support for his accounting system, after he had insisted on going his own way by choosing an unknown supplier, who went bust. This decision was taken out of petulance because he had fallen out with Thomas, who he had blamed for trying unsuccessfully to provide an all-singing and dancing accounting package that the secretary had chosen to buy for the measly sum of £85. That was all this jackass was prepared to fork out.

Longer term, after the inconvenience caused by Thomas's dismissal and the management failure to find a satisfactorily compliant replacement, the Group Managing Director succeeded in recruiting someone who said "Yes" to every proposal rather than risk being put to the sword himself. This was the cause of much comment and derision in the company, especially when he resigned after a short period of indifferent compliance.

Additionally, not too long after Thomas was dismissed, the insurance industry suffered two significant reversals that impacted nearly all the companies in that sector, and caused his former employer many a sleepless night.

The first reversal was the rising onset of a formidable wave of asbestos related claims, to which the company's profits were proving vulnerable. It was with gritted teeth that they were being obliged to pay out large sums in compensation to the victims of this scourge, of which no one could claim to have prior knowledge. This was going to hammer their returns.

It was an arduous task for the main underwriter, who was also the company founder, to identify specific threats to the survival of his company. If Thomas had known, he would have been justified in thinking, "*Serves him right!*"

The second reversal was associated with the way in which insurance business was passed between underwriting groups, where others were given the opportunity, as 'reinsurers', to share risks initially accepted by the original leading underwriters.

For convenience sake, as the risks were passed on to other willing participants, they would be bundled into a bureaucratic tangle of contracts. Hence, their initial identities became submerged and often altered. Sometimes the nature of the contract itself was changed between reinsurers, and the risks were sub-divided as individuals saw fit. It was an ill-conceived way of processing business.

Anyway, when this house of cards predictably came tumbling down, no one could work their way through the labyrinth of paperwork that every participant had created. Each group of underwriters scrambled to protect their livelihoods by trying to match references on accepted risks to the variations on those identities casually applied by the next layer of reinsurers, as quoted on several types of contracts. What a Gordian's Knot of a mess it was.

Tommy surmised, not believing that anyone else would be that stupid, "*If a system like this is used for financial transactions outside the insurance industry, then the shit will really hit the fan!*" Well, that was exactly what happened when the cleverest sons from the wealthiest families allowed contracts to be created to accumulate poor-quality sub-prime mortgages in the USA, and started passing similar contracts electronically around the world, to 'spread the risk'.

This was Thomas's short-lived experience in the bowels of the City of London, and he was determined not to continue to work in such an environment ever again. Not that he had much choice in the matter, since his reputation was busily being blackened.

"They're all as daft as brushes!" he concluded.

§ 4: The Talent Is Indulged

It was at this stage in his awareness of his emerging abilities that Thomas's attention had been drawn to the sub-human monster who was currently incarcerated in one of her Majesty's prisons. In fact, it was hardly possible to avoid seeing or hearing about him, since it was a topic that recurred regularly on the news channels and in the newspapers.

However, it was purely coincidental that the prison warder mentioned earlier was experiencing problems with this particular inmate, the sadistic child murderer.

One evening, after a long day spent doing freelance computer work on a contract basis, Thomas sat down at the meal table with his wife Pat and younger daughter Julie. As they ate, they spent valuable time together catching up on local and national events and socialising as any normal family would.

Shortly afterwards, the table was cleared, the dishes cleaned and put away by them working in harmony. Thomas excused himself so that he could go to his study and do some more contract work.

In fact, he liked to meditate in isolation, and the red velvet-covered soft padded chaise longue located there was perfect for his mind to unwind. A quick shower was taken and he changed into casual clothes ready to relax. Laying back with his arms crossed over his chest, he closed his eyes, visualising whirling vortexes over key parts of his head, neck and chest and mentally sucked them into his body.

The effect was calming to his senses, and he formed a mental picture of the shaven-headed cruel-lipped staring man that he had seen reported so frequently in the news.

He decided, "*It's time to deal with a monster!*" and felt his spiritual-self leaving his physical body, before channelling it towards the prison where the murderer was being held, much further north from where Thomas lived. He had located it on the map stored on his computer, and didn't take any notice of the countryside he presumed he was rushing over; it was irrelevant to his intentions.

The same applied to the actual prison, since he was focusing entirely on the prisoner itself; he liked to think of the target as an '**it**', since it was clearly inhuman and on a much lower plane of existence.

To his logical mind, this was not a sub-conscious attempt to justify his intentions, nor any desire to salve his conscience; it was consistent with his Hindu-based beliefs in reincarnation and the creed of good behaviour, and that he was righting a wrong. It was akin to punishing an animal that had committed too many vile acts to be forgiven.

Locating his target involved a brief time searching, as he first identified the area to be accessed by its tighter security. Next he floated into each cell for any individuals resembling the photos he had seen, and briefly sunk into their bodies one by one to examine their innermost recollections. These were transparent to him and could not be misinterpreted.

"*Come on, come on!*" he urged himself impatiently. "*There's things to be done!*"

It soon became apparent who the guilty party was from his brain activity and his features, as he relived recent events that were a recurring, poisonous cocktail of drug-induced erotic pleasures and nightmares. There was no shadow of a doubt of the guilty party from his evil recollections.

"There's still some sane part of it that feels guilt," Thomas reasoned, with satisfaction. *"The rest of its thoughts are plain disgusting."* He exited the man as he laid there, his spiritual body straddling the man's chest, and his hands reached under the murderer's skull.

He easily found the general location of the brain stem at the base of the prisoner's head, and concentrated on spiritually throttling him. With a sense of satisfaction, he found that there was a physical manifestation to his activity, which lent real power to what he was achieving.

"There's more to this than I thought I was capable of," Thomas realised, gaining further awareness of the true extent of his powers.

It gave Thomas great pleasure to look down see the monster's eyes bulge in horror and its mouth gape wide-open, as it lost its capacity to breathe and its life drained away. *"I hope that was painful!"* Thomas muttered and rose up from the recumbent corpse with its face etched in agony.

"Before I go, I should find the one who slashed him with a knife," he decided, and resumed his search for the inmate who had attacked the monster with that type of weapon.

By questioning the thoughts of a few occupants of the neighbouring cells, not much time was needed to locate the man concerned. It was revealed that the other person and its resident soul had a long record of predatory sex.

Thomas wondered, "*Is this not a case of the pot calling the kettle black? Its deeds may be lesser, but it only did it for the esteem it brings in this hell-hole.*"

Again spiritually straddling the second victim's body, he placed his fingers on the area of the occipital lobe on the right-hand side of the brain, at the rear of its skull, and concentrated on inducing burning-heat in the three-sided, pyramid-shaped area. "*That should screw up its vision most nicely,*" he reasoned. "*May its future life be spent in blinding pain!*"

To his surprise, the attacked inmate suddenly let out a series of bellowing cries, which would no doubt bring the guards running to the cell in double-quick time. Given Thomas's inclinations, it was a sore temptation not to exterminate all the inmates of the prison, but he was no indiscriminate mass-murderer and didn't want to draw any more attention to what was unnaturally occurring.

Rising up once more and standing erect, Thomas's spirit flew back direct to his own body, which was laying relaxed on the chaise longue in his study. He lay there eyes half-open, with his hands behind his neck, feeling relaxed and at peace with himself, whilst sweating because of his recent mental exertions.

Thomas Beckon might have insisted, if he was asked, that he regarded his actions as those of a man seeking justice for unpardonable offences committed by others. On the other hand, his wife would undeniably have labelled him as a murderer for seeking vengeance, if she knew what he was up to.

His justification would have been based on two opposing behavioural aspects of society: the clamour of the masses for the death sentence to be imposed on those who perpetrated certain crimes; and the refusal of their elected politicians to accede to this demand. If asked, he would have regarded it as his duty to step forward and perform the role of a public executioner on behalf of the denied wish of the masses.

Her disapproval of such extreme, anti-social behaviour was based on the premise that killing another person would have made Thomas no better than the person who committed the original crime. Hence, their views on justice were at odds with one another, and for the sake of the marriage were best left unspoken. He realised what she would think of his behaviour and was glad that she didn't know.

"*What the eye doesn't see, the heart won't grieve over,*" he reckoned.

Undoubtedly, he accepted that he was a social psychopath but couldn't care a damn about it, or what he had done. It had felt satisfying to unleash one of his baser instincts.

The following evening, after enjoying the company of his family, Thomas showered, retreated to his study, and once more lay on his chaise longue.

"*I think I'll vary my activities this time and show the loving side of my nature,*" he decided, with a smile on his face.

Another matter was about to come to the fore, and that was Thomas's view on the question of love. To clarify, it was not in relation to *love-making* with his wife Pat, since that was a deed performed lustily many times over, in earlier years. It was more to do with his attitude to the marriage remaining monogamous.

With his new-found skills, he was in a unique position to remain physically faithful, whilst simultaneously 'spreading himself around' at the spiritual level. He believed that he could do this without breaking any of the basic rules established when making his marriage vows, although he accepted that his personal commitment would be 'bent' a little in his quest for complementary sexual gratification.

It was also the case that his dismissal from his city job left him with time on his hands, and as the proverb goes, 'Idle hands find mischief'.

The first female partner he chose was a straightforward selection from a television news broadcast one evening. There she sat, with sparkling young eyes, a flawless brown skin, short hair, and shapely body; her speaking voice was attractive too, as she articulated her words with no trace of an accent, and verbally sparred eloquently with the male announcer sitting next to her.

Her only visible shortcoming was her ears, which stood out at right-angles from her petite head; that was a minor problem, however, and if there were to be a repeat visit he could encourage her to have them pinned back.

He could barely contain himself as his spirit waited for her to exit the studios, floating around by the front, swing doors near the car park. When she did emerge, with the front of her high-necked winter coat flapping in the wind, he walked unseen with her to her small saloon car and sat invisibly in the back. He disliked her taste in music, which was a form of 'rap crap' while she was shaking her head in time to the music; she even knew the words, which he found to be indecipherable.

He blended into her neat body as she stepped out of the car, and was conveyed upstairs to her chic first-floor apartment in a modern block in the suburbs, in Chiswick. There, she undressed swiftly, ready to enter her walk-in shower, and he closed his eyes in over-eager anticipation of the mobile feast he was about to experience.

In the background and more to his taste, a serene track of jazz-funk music was playing, and a table could be observed, laid romantically for a late dinner for two; clearly, she was expecting a visitor. The scene had been set, and he opened his spiritual-eyes through hers, as she was standing in front of a full-length mirror, deciding which dress to wear later. It was at this delicate moment that his desire drooped, instantly, when he looked below her waist.

She had the biggest, bushiest, pussy he had ever clapped eyes on, and it was an instant turn-off for him.

Had he chosen to wait in the other room, his personal attention would have been elsewhere, along with that of her lover. However, all he wanted to do now was flee the building and go home, regretting that his first foray had been a disaster. He obeyed his instinct at high speed and returned to his recumbent body, which was on the chaise-longue in his welcoming study.

The evening after, the second attempted seduction was conducted more shrewdly, although selection was from the same stable, if desire could be expressed so coarsely. Clearly, here also was a woman of refinement, a superb liquid-eyed, long black-haired and brown-skinned specimen of apparent Arabic descent, who appeared regularly on one of the news channels as a weather girl; he had lusted over her in an abstract way on many occasions.

Again, it was when he took possession of her body, after leaving himself laying in his study and spiritually following her home from the television studio, that he had the chance to take full-stock of her attributes. This time, he exercised prudence before pleasure, stood back from the table and waited *by* it until she and her boyfriend were ready to eat, before re-entering her body.

"*At last*," he thought as the food was served. "*I'm bloody starving!*" She unfortunately had an hour-glass figure and did not have much of an appetite. "*I hope she's hungrier for sex!*" he thought, trying vainly to appreciate and digest the dry salad she was simultaneously chewing.

He had to accept that there were drawbacks to the physical aspects of his spirit exercising partial control over the targeted, physical body, whilst temporarily sharing it with the previous sole occupant.

Frustratingly, he had to wait until midnight for them to go to bed, before he could hope to start satisfying his base desires through her body; she was content to wait for her desires to be met.

It did not take long for him to realise that once more he had made a mistake; it was solely to inhabit her, *instead* of swiftly moving on to possess her boyfriend.

The suppression of her personality dampened his male ardour, since he felt that domination of her body made him feel too aware of her normal emotions, when she was occupied by her own spirit. Unfortunately, as a male he couldn't rest easy with the reactions of the female spirit; these were new to him as a recipient.

Inconveniently, he also had to make her ask her boyfriend to rest on his elbows when they were performing, because the weight of her lover was making him feel claustrophobic.

It was only when he instinctively transferred his soul from her body to that of the boyfriend that he could begin to climax.

It was still dodgy, though, making the transition mid-act, as her spiritual self took advantage of his disappearance to start yelling for a short time like she was possessed (which she had been). To quieten her, he indulged himself by kissing her passionately on the lips.

Now that he was spiritually attached to the man's vital organs, he could instinctively savour the gorgeous young lady's erogenous zones as the love-making eventually became two-way.

Fortunately, her male partner was no longer in control to question her behaviour; Thomas was playing that role now and could ignore her orgasmic outbursts, while he eagerly distracted her as her partner's original spirit rested passively in the background.

His third ambitious conquest was a stunningly beautiful blond ice-maiden who was a newly appointed newscaster. She was also severe-looking and apparently straight-laced, and the prospect of satisfying her apparently dormant desires thrilled him to his loins.

This time, crucially, he preferred to transfer earlier between bodies. His spirit occupied her temporarily as she was driven home, remaining in the background of her consciousness, and was carried by her unaware into her detached luxury home. There they enjoyed an invigorating shower together before Thomas transferred to her husband, who had thoughtfully prepared a superb meal for the two-cum-three of them, which they enjoyed with gusto before retiring early to bed.

By now, the compliant husband's personality was totally submerged, while Thomas took full advantage of the situation to coax her into multiple orgasms. The advantage of transferring to her male partner was the unrestricted physical enjoyment it brought with it. His sensual pleasure had indeed entered the realms of ecstasy.

Gratification was hardly an adequate expression for their mounting thrills, as he ran his fingers up and down her slender, silky legs and kissed her firm, little breasts, whilst thrusting back and forth rhythmically ever more frantically. Frankly, he couldn't get enough of her.

Once or twice, he caught her studying him with eyes wide-open in wonderment at his hardly waning endurance and enthusiasm. Clearly, she was wondering, "*Who **is** this man?*" and had been accustomed until now at being the partner who called the shots in their relationship.

"*Never mind,*" she was now thinking, "*I can catch up on my sleep in the taxi service, early tomorrow morning.*"

When Thomas's spirit floated from the rumpled King-sized bed and back into his own body, his feeling was one of total satisfaction compared with Mick Jagger, who was always lamenting that he couldn't get any. Reputedly, the lead singer of the Rolling Stones was still on the prowl for that elusive state well into his dotage.

Yes, Thomas had potentially great multiple sex-lives going for him. If things carried on like this, he could rest easily and contentedly with his wife, knowing that he had never actually been unfaithful.

The truth was, he still loved her.

35

§ 5: The Mother Of Invention

One bright Saturday, the long awaited summer arrived and Thomas felt renewed desire for outdoor exercise. His weekday cycling to and from the rail station, travelling to and from his job in The City had ended on a sour note, and he was beginning to feel jaded.

There were so many things he previously had to do, managing and forward-planning his department's role, that his spare time had been severely limited. Now that the relentless pressures placed on him had evaporated into thin air, he was determined to make the effort and indulge his fancy for strolls at a fast pace.

That was to say, whenever clement weather made it possible, like this idyllic day when his desire had returned, forcefully.

"My body's trying to tell me something," he reasoned.

Money was not a problem in those halcyon days, since Pat was earning a good salary that more than covered their frugal lifestyle, while he pondered what to do next.

He had received a more than adequate lump sum from the 'Group Managing Director', grudgingly awarded to prevent him from seeking compensation via the legal system for unfair dismissal.

Later on, the same petty-minded individual had tried to claim back the VAT on a personal computer they had allowed him to take with him, so he could do contract work as a freelancer. He must have been slapped down by others on the main board for his petty-mindedness, after Thomas's rebuke was handed in.

In his spare time, walking appealed to him most, because he could also indulge in planning for an unknown future as he made his way along the country lanes, green pastures and small parks that surrounded and were within the village where he lived. When combined, the two activities, both mental and physical, were most pleasurable to experience.

Exercise like that stimulated his blood flow and made his thoughts innovative. Hence he could kill two birds with one stone! It was far more effective than using static machines in a gym to simulate rowing and cycling, which he found absolutely boring and tedious.

That same morning, he strode out of the house wearing a cotton short-sleeved shirt printed with a red-check pattern and hanging loose outside a pair of Khaki coloured shorts. His brown short socks were worn inside a pair of trekking boots laced up to the ankles; these he found to be extremely comfortable.

He had tried wearing mountain boots before that fitted over the ankles and, found that they chafed his skin, which left him hobbling within the hour.

"Never again!" he had exclaimed, and dumped them in a clothes container for charitable causes.

On his back he carried a haversack containing his small shoulder bag with identification documents and wallet, plus a small plastic bottle as used by cyclists, a few pencils, a sharpener and a notepad.

On his head he wore a broad-rimmed floppy hat and sunglasses. These were measures recommended by his hospital specialist in Dermatology, to counter the mild threat of skin cancer from which he suffered in his later years. For the same reason, factor 50 sun cream had been rubbed on the exposed parts of his body.

He also walked carrying a stout, waist-high stick with rounded handle, patting the ground in time with his pace. It was not that he needed it as an aid, but to protect himself - should the need arise - against snakes and wild animals, if confronted.

Reaching his immediate destination, which was a small, badly tended park near the local primary school that his daughters had attended, he plonked himself on the nearest of the wooden-slatted benches that were anchored there to concrete bases, placing the haversack next to him.

These benches were generally covered in deep scratches, presumably made using a screwdriver or a knife by kids, given the childlike graffiti that was sprayed in paint on the backrests.

With a sigh of regret for this mindless vandalism, he brought out the notepad and a pencil, and began to record his possible choices of action.

"*Things are shaping up nicely,*" he thought, as his ideas led him into a future otherwise filled with uncertainty.

"*This can be done!*" he asserted, filling his pad with notes to put flesh on the bones of the options.

Irresistibly, the chirruping of the birds in the trees around and the rising heat as the morning lengthened soothed his senses. His head drooped and he started to snooze in harmony with life in general.

"Wake up!" a male voice bellowed in his left ear, snapping him back into the real world and frightening the hell out of him. A lanky boy aged about fourteen, with hairy legs and the makings of a moustache on his gaunt, sneering face, raced off on his mountain bike, laughing out loud at his prank on the older man.

"Stop it!" Thomas yelled back, and the boy skidded to stop, turning the bike sideways to stare aggressively back at him. Tauntingly, he replied, "Make me!" and turned ahead to race off laughing. Thomas waved his haversack threateningly at the youngster and sat back down, feeling furious.

It was a pathetic action really, waving the lightweight bag in the air like he had, but Thomas was angry that his period of relaxation had been ruined by the bad behaviour of a total stranger. He noticed that the first youngster had been met some distance away by a second cyclist who was younger, possibly eleven or twelve years of age.

From the grins on their faces, they were going to attempt to provoke him further, so he tensed up and slouched forward, ready to take action if they dared to try.

He mused, *"Here I am minding my own business and these two louts come along, bent on aggravating me. What's the world coming to? Where are their parents?"*

Feeling nervous and distracted, he waited for the inevitable to happen while remaining motionless. On hearing a bike approach, he saw the tyre on the front wheel appear beside him as the older boy leaned over to repeat his bellowing. This time, Thomas clenched his walking stick with both hands and thrust it hard between the spokes of the wheel when it passed, and held it rigidly in place until they snapped.

Then he ducked away, to avoid the whirling spokes hitting him, as the boy screamed and was catapulted over the handlebars, with the bike landing on his sprawled body. He turned over onto his back, using his feet to push the bike to one side, before using his legs to propel him backwards along the gravel.

"*That must be painful!*" Thomas thought. "*He's ruining his clothes!*"

Out loud, he shouted, "You little sod! You think you're clever, do you?"

The boy's face was filled with fear, now that he was on the defensive. Hearing stones hitting the ground around him, Thomas looked back to see the second boy throwing them in his direction. As he turned to run after him, the first boy took the opportunity to try and flee at high speed on his damaged bike; he dropped it on its side after a few turns of the buckling front wheel and ran away on foot, with a limp.

At that moment as if by magic, a much larger group of boys came walking into the park from the opposite direction. They were all in the eleven to twelve year old age-bracket. Intent on joining the fun, they started taunting him as well and throwing stones.

Thomas shouted at them, "You're nothing but a bunch of cowards! Be warned, I'll find you wherever you live!"

Feeling stones hitting his back, he turned and saw the original two miscreants doing the same thing; he was being peppered with stones from two directions from an out-of-control pack behaving like wild animals. It would surely not be long before he was injured, perhaps seriously.

Remembering that he possessed the talent to deal with situations like this (albeit only proven against fewer numbers), an old saying sprang into his mind:

"*Necessity is the mother of invention.*"

Unleashing his instincts, he rapidly regained self-control, brushed aside his mounting panic, and asked for innermost, spiritual help. As a consequence, and as if he were a dispassionate onlooker, he was surprised by the events that started to unfold before him.

His spiritual-self seemed to leap backwards and paralyse the two nearest boys, who had, by all legal definitions, assaulted him.

At the same time, his spirit seemed to further subdivide and descend on the larger group of boys further away, as they stood there picking up and throwing stones. They stood immobile for a brief while seemingly perplexed, as if Thomas's spirit was independently influencing them in some intuitive way. Then they fixed their focus beyond Thomas and, by common consent, took it in turns to hurl their stones with increased strength high over his head. Thomas instinctively ducked as the stones accurately hit the ringleaders behind him.

The two targeted youngsters awoke suddenly when they realised what was happening and screamed at the others to stop. Their cries were in vain, as the gang continued remorselessly aiming and throwing stones. Eventually, they collapsed to the ground crying and covering their bleeding heads.

Presumably by silent spiritual command, as the two wounded boys lay on the ground barely moving, the larger group came to their senses. Clutching their remaining stones, they looked with horror on their faces at what they had done, and realised there would be repercussions for their misdeeds. Then they got angry with themselves, seeking to blame each other for starting it.

Shouting and shoving, they got angry and started to fight amongst themselves. Thomas watched them bemused, as clenched fists were thrown at each other without restraint.

"There'll be a few black eyes, broken noses and split lips before this ends!" he reckoned with grim amusement, and departed to let them all get on with it, after he was sure that all elements of his spirit were safely back in his body.

As he walked home jauntily, he wondered, *"How the devil did that happen? It must have been my natural response to danger!"*

When he opened the front door, Pat came into the hall from the kitchen opposite; he told her that he had been assaulted and briefly described the events that had occurred.

She insisted, "Go upstairs and have a shower, while I make you a cup of tea. Then sit down at your desk and write a report while it's still fresh in your mind, before you contact the police. I'm glad you came through it alright, without a scratch!" They gave each other a big hug and she went back into the kitchen and put the kettle on.

As a footnote, Thomas volunteered to accompany the police in their patrol car and drive around the village to identify his attackers. He also volunteered to go with them to the local senior school which they had to be attending from the local catchment area. Neither offer was accepted, nor did he ever receive any indication of the outcome of this case as they were handling it.

In exasperation, he took matters into his own hands and began waiting outside the local secondary school, in his car, to identify the ringleaders at the end of their day. When they emerged, he provoked them from a distance, by causing them to stumble into other boys and get into fights.

After a few days, as they became increasingly the worse for wear, he drew their attention to him, by standing by the car, in full view, and communicating with them.

"Think what I will do to you, if you ever cross my path again!" he warned them, mentally, and they ran away, leaving their satchels laying on the path, for the other boys to rummage through. This unusual form of encounter had left them frightened and confused.

Thomas wondered how common such outbreaks of violence were, countrywide, and was starting to yearn for a different style of life that wouldn't expose him to risks like he had just encountered. He didn't want it to be 'humdrum' though.

He remembered vividly what factors had governed his working life, whichever company he chose to join; one of the key ones had been rubbing shoulders with the people who occupied them, at all levels, but less so with the management teams that controlled the activities of the enterprises.

Instinctively, he didn't enjoy the politics that went on at the more senior levels, and the distortions in personality that often emanated from these power brokers. The more thrusting and ambitious they were, man or woman, the more apparent became their shortcomings as human beings.

When systems were being installed, and he spent time with the people who were expected to use them, he found great pleasure in being in their company. They were, on the whole, devoted to tasks that were within their capabilities and generally appreciated. It was easy to identify misfits and troubled souls, and not his direct responsibility to weed them out; that invariably happened in due course.

The ambition was growing in him to achieve something worthwhile in life, away from the physical aggravation he had been forced to endure.

He had progressed from relatively humble roots, and wanted to use his special talents to amass instant wealth. Not surprisingly he intended doing this unscrupulously by indulging in untraceable, self-serving theft.

Thomas could envisage using his ill-gotten gains to create a successful company, and thereafter as a springboard to public achievement. A game plan was developing to serve this ambition.

§ 6: Squaring The Circle.

Little was he truly aware of it, but Thomas was probably suffering from symptoms of Post-Traumatic-Stress Disorder after losing his managerial job. Any doctor could have told him this if he had bothered to seek help.

One minute he was filled with elation and relief, as he stood looking out of his bedroom window and enjoying a view of the bucolic countryside, realising he wasn't committed to full-time work anymore. The next minute he was reduced to utmost fits of depression as he contemplated a future unlike anything he had previously known, wondering what fate would have in store for him if he didn't act bravely.

Eventually he snapped out of it, took a fatalistic stance, and decided to adopt a positive attitude. He decided, *"I may as well do something useful."* A realistic plan that was well within his capabilities had already been quickly devised, to help generate immediate cash income. Now he had to execute it, promptly, or lose the initiative; time was of the essence and waited for no man.

He would get up at the same time as his wife Pat, and would shower, dry himself, shave and dress formally in the same clothes that he would normally have worn when he was working in The City. She had to leave the house by 08:30am to drive a few miles to a regional offices belonging to a major brewery group, where she provided clerical support to the directors.

When the routine was first set into motion, they ate breakfast together, giving her the chance to quiz him on what he would be doing that day. He sat there full of aplomb, his self-assurance totally unruffled as he nibbled at his toast, which was spread with Frank

Cooper's Vintage marmalade. Between sips from a mug of filtered coffee, he patted her hand reassuringly and said, "I'm going back to The City, and will be approaching contacts who I feel can help. I am confident that I will get what I want."

In the days that followed, as she saw a sustained change in his attitude for the better, she learnt to be less inquiring. He was always evasive when pumped for information, vaguely reassuring her that he was doing something worthwhile that was highly profitable. He never elaborated on that theme, and she in turn trusted him totally, knowing that he was no slacker. Anyway, his dress sense had become exemplary again, and she liked him looking at his best.

Uncharacteristically for a person who had held a series of reputable jobs of good standing, his planned actions were known by him alone to be criminal in nature. A person had to delve into his childhood roots to understand what was motivating him to take a risk, apart from the thrill of doing it.

His father and his grandfather were successful scrap merchants, who traded in recycling metals during and after the Second World War. They had also established a fleet of trawlers, were demolition specialists, ship and factory salvagers, and ruthless in their pursuit of questionable profits.

What Thomas had in mind would have been child's play to them, and they would have given him their belated support if they had known about it.

"Well done!", "At last!", "A chip off the old block!" They would have cried out, if they were still alive.

And what was it he proposed doing? The plan was very simple in its execution, and required him to buy

'Cheap Day' return train tickets, for use outside the specified rush-hour periods.

As stated earlier, dressed formally in his Austin Reed suit, he would travel later in the-morning to London, walk towards Leadenhall Market, and sit at a corner table in one of the nearby upmarket cafés to sip a pre-paid coffee and read a newspaper. There he would wait until any middle-aged or older business man of prosperous appearance came in on his own, sat down to nurse a coffee or tea and started leafing through paperwork stored in his briefcase.

A few days earlier, Thomas had started to concentrate on enhancing his ability to occupy another person's body, and attempting to do this while retaining a level of control over his own.

He was therefore pleased when he succeeded in taking possession of his first targeted victim, a bespectacled, plump middle-aged man with fresh red cheeks and a solemn demeanour, whilst Thomas left sufficient of his soul in his own body to be able to deal in an abstract manner with anyone who approached him.

The main part of his spirit invaded the stranger and got him to pack his documents, leave the café, and walk the short distance to a nearby cash point dispenser. There, Thomas's spirit coaxed the man to withdraw the maximum permitted personal amount on his 'gold' credit card, which in this case was a generous £500.

Communicating with his original self in the café, Thomas's physical body and residual spirit collected his belongings, and got up to rendezvous with the stranger in the street, near the cash point machine.

A jovial meeting was contrived for the stranger to discretely transfer the money to Thomas, when they embraced. Both parts of Thomas's spirit reunited, and the two individuals went their separate ways under happy circumstances, with a shaking of hands. In this decade, the use of cameras in public was rare.

The puzzled stranger was left alone and wondering where his time had gone, while Thomas chose a different café to repeat the process with someone else.

Perhaps it would be a woman, but he felt chivalrous towards the opposite sex and disliked extracting their cash. After a short day spent collecting funds in this way, he made his leisurely way home before the evening rush hour, went into his garden shed and placed that day's cash hoard in a metal box, which had been secreted in a waterproof covered recess in the concrete base.

This routine was repeated on each and every weekday as Thomas saw fit, to the extent that he got tired and fell asleep on the return journey, during which period of travel he would clutch his briefcase on his lap as if for dear life. He felt lucky that the cash machines accessed had dispensed notes of large denominations, otherwise the volume of money he was stockpiling would have caused it to bulge. In the end he tried to stay awake the whole time, rather than risk being robbed of his booty.

In a single-minded fashion, Thomas never became really curious about the lives and characters of the people whose money he was taking, and neither did he come across any newspaper reports indicating that his activities had been detected. To him, it was better to remain ignorant of these strangers and their affluent lifestyles than to become emotionally attached to them, unlikely as that was in view of their stand-offish attitudes.

He passed some of them in the streets days later, and read their minds to see if he was being hunted, and was not surprised to find that nothing untoward had registered in their subconscious. They were earning so much money that nothing he did put the slightest of dents in their measurable incomes.

Within fifty industrious working days spent in this manner, not far off £100,000 had been accumulated, and Thomas was ready to commence the next stage of his plan. Purchasing an accounting package for his PC, together with a companion self-tuition course, he setup a small trading company to market and manufacture a specialist item of clothing that was tailored to be sexy and would help combat the cold in the UK's deteriorating climate.

The products the company would supply were destined for domestic use indoors, so that people could wear garments that kept them warm, without having to switch on central heating for so long each day and evening.

He was anticipating that electricity bills would continue to rise inexorably, and reckoned that people would begin to rebel against the manifest overcharging of greedy utility providers.

With the partnership of his younger daughter Julie and support of his wife, he got clothing samples made up and checked thoroughly for robust seaming. Then he swiftly set up a full network of part-time home-workers in the locality, and a reliable source of fabrics, ready for production to begin near his home, in a reserved industrial unit where some jobs would have to be performed centrally.

The final task before arranging interviews with the buyers at leading, upmarket stores like Harrods and

Liberty's, was to design and print promotional literature. It was with mounting excitement that he and Julie dressed in their designer suits, loaded their newly acquired Ford estate car with product samples, and attended their pre-arranged meetings at the various buyers' offices, waiting in long lines with other hopefuls.

Gleefully, they left shortly after with fistfuls of orders from buyers, who had been 'influenced' to place orders with the winsome father and daughter. The people who had interviewed them also emphasised the likelihood that repeat orders would follow, if the buying public shared their gut instincts. This positive and universal response convinced Thomas that his approach to quality control was going to pay dividends.

Immediately, they contacted the small army of part-time staff who they had recruited on a stand-by basis, and held training sessions to bring them up to an acceptable industrial standard of cutting and sewing.

Those who showed special acumen were promoted to supervisory posts, and readied for the mass production that was imminent.

Within days, the staff were all working enthusiastically on assembly of the garments, which the business partners managed personally with sympathy and understanding.

Packaging and bulk shipment commenced within the week, as Thomas's daughter Julie placed a badge of authenticity and a fanciful short story of the garment's history on top, as it was carefully folded within a transparent zipper bag.

Thomas had achieved a successful, initial outcome to his enterprise, and the orders flowed in as winter deepened and utility bills rose inexorably.

He had begun squaring the circle, so to speak, and the future of his family, both daughters included, was assured.

Not wishing to rest on his laurels, but continuing to feel somewhat emotionally bruised and wary after the harsh treatment dished out by his previous employer, Thomas felt unfulfilled and remained on the prowl for another business opportunity.

As the future became the present, he was now heading a flourishing manufacturing company, supported by two of his keen and eager family members plus trusted deputies in all key areas of control of the enterprise.

Consequently, he could once more afford the time to intercept affluent strangers and lighten their pockets. Whereas he had not been overly inquisitive before about their circumstances, now he became more inclined to investigate them in depth.

Within a few hours of the next day of trawling for victims, he identified his first rogue trader from the Stock Exchange. He was a thin young man by the name of Paul, smartly groomed and well-dressed, whose state of mind was highly agitated but compliant. A quick mind scan revealed that he was covertly trading beyond his authorised limit, and gambling frantically to recoup an eight figure shortfall before late afternoon.

Thomas lost no time in breaking his mental link with Paul.

"On your way!" he insisted telepathically, not wanting to add to the man's dilemmas or get involved.

That same day, it was not long before Thomas started wondering what he'd been missing with his previous, superficial approach to fund-raising. His latest target was a man of normal height and stocky build, or so it seemed, but spiritually he was a midget in comparison with a superabundance of energy. He was resisting mightily, with a determination and skill that was unprecedented in Thomas's experience.

Startled by this encounter, he became aware that he was tussling with a being that was not human in origin. As far as he could establish, the body was a 'husk' or shell, with all its vital organs intact, under the control of an alien entity; it had no perceivable 'soul' of its own! Images of a remotely located alien humanoid with a large head and spindly limbs flashed in front of him, as he picked up its thoughts and feelings of surprise and mounting desperation.

For a while, the two of them struggled spiritually for dominance, with Thomas gaining the upper hand through his initial attack, closer proximity to the 'husk', and superior raw energy, as contrasted with the alien's less warlike, subtle intellectual probes. In many ways, they were both holding back as they tried to satisfy their mounting curiosity about each other's origins.

They were equally fascinated as they exchanged valuable snippets of information, although Thomas had more to gain and was the main beneficiary. He was in a dreamlike state as he waged intellectual warfare, and he was feeling increasingly triumphant until the alien shocked him by relinquishing control of the human shell. He, Thomas, was now solely occupying it, as the alien spirit slipped away, leaving for dead the body that it had inhabited.

An abiding memory was left with Thomas of a far better organised alien civilization, in which traffic flowed seamlessly and endlessly around a harmonious world. In comparison, Planet Earth was chaotic and warlike, with widespread outbreaks of aggression occurring almost randomly.

Passers-by gathered around the lifeless body, which Thomas's spirit exited reluctantly and slipped away from the scene to merge with Thomas himself. This event marked the rise of the second, more emphatic phase of Thomas's emergence into society.

§ 7: The Midas Touch Grows

It was a new dawn, and Thomas was happy to let the existing business continue to thrive under its own steam, whilst he discretely withdrew funds and relinquished overall control to create a new, public venture. A sizeable portion of the undeclared 'liquid' capital was commandeered with the approval of his family, to rent and outfit a second, larger industrial unit next door, on the same trading estate.

From the outside, the acquired unit was a modern, polished aluminium-clad high-roofed building, surrounded with tall metal railings and razor-tipped barbed wire on top. Access was via a wide and equally tall electrically controlled sliding gate. It also came with CCTV and a backup generator.

Inside, dyes and presses had been installed, with assembly robots adjoining a short construction line. They were getting ready to assemble prototype vehicles out of a newly invented lightweight metal alloy.

Production of the first one had already started, with a flexible one piece liquid-coated body-shell being moulded into a shape not much bigger than would cover a single occupant on a seat, plus luggage stored behind.

At first sight, an onlooker might guess that this was developing into a motor bike, enveloped in an exterior shell that would provide protection against the elements. The finished product externally resembled a narrow silver-coloured gleaming egg laid on its side, with both forward and rear ends evenly rounded. In the centre of each side an access hole had been cut, ready for a door to be inserted.

The top two thirds of the visible 'egg on its side' appeared to be resting on a flange, or protruding rounded edge. This gave the impression that the lower third was sitting in a moulded holder that curved inwards with the egg, which was supported on four sturdy and squat retractable struts.

After its liquid coating was dried, the entire surface was to be polished inside and out to an absolutely smooth dull, silver gleam.

Noticeably, there were no wheels on the vehicle, only the aforementioned struts; these self-adjusted in length according to the unevenness of the surface on which they rested, to provide stability to the craft. There was no visible indication of the method of propulsion.

There were only two men in the place, studying engineering drawings as they discussed how best to continue to proceed. One of them was Thomas, and his companion was a retired director who Thomas had lured to join him from the 'Skunk' works at the mighty Lockheed Corporation.

"Call me Bob," was how he introduced himself.

He had come all the way from the USA and was technically the best in the world at his previous job. He was working clandestinely in his new role and was intrinsic to Thomas's overall plan.

For those who may be interested in how these two men met; after his encounter with the small alien and its outsized head, Thomas had used his special skills to research the various types of extra-terrestrial beings. It did not take him long to come across frequent mention of Roswell, where a nearby UFO crash had been prominently reported, with small bodies recovered. They too had oversized heads and spindly limbs.

All of this had been detailed in an FBI report, which was released under The Freedom of Information Act many years after the event occurred, in 1947.

This in turn led him to the acknowledged USA top secret development centre called 'Area 51'. Thence he was drawn to the rogue operative Bob Lazar, a precursor to the modern 'whistle blower', who went public to prevent his possible assassination, and thereafter the trail led Thomas to the fabled Lockheed aircraft development centre, 'Skunk Works'. All of these are commonly cited in UFO circles, and were not difficult to find mentioned on the primitive internet of that time.

For those who may be unaware of the fact; the 'Skunk Works' had developed the stealth bomber. Ben Rich, its main director, had publicly and authoritatively announced that, "Extra-terrestrial UFO visitors are real", and that, "the U.S. Military travels among the stars". It was there at Skunk Works that Thomas decided to pay the occupants spiritual visits and find out who might be useful in assisting him to build craft like those he had seen in visions of the alien's homeland.

It did not take Thomas long to make contact with the recently retired "Call me Bob", follow up with a personal visit in the flesh, and make him an irresistible offer to join him, in another country on a futuristic project.

Continuing their joint efforts to assemble a prototype vehicle, the first item to be installed in the body-shell was a comfortable-looking lightweight bucket seat with a lot of holes cut in it. This was padded in turn with a layer of novel visco-elastic foam encased in a washable brightly coloured material. Immediately behind it a luggage rack was click-fitted into position.

Below foot-level of the single future occupant, at precisely measured distances from the inner surface, nozzles were anchored facing downwards and outwards, in set directions.

At foot level behind the seat, cylinders were sited that would contain separate nitrogen and oxygen gases, with the controls needed to provide vented, breathable air, and to filter carbon dioxide from the self-contained, sealed-off internal atmosphere. It was based on the robust system installed in the space shuttles and could provide circulation for long periods.

"I'm not sure we'll need it in basic, regular use, but now is the time to test it," Bob affirmed.

At waist height behind the seat and its rack, a cluster of small, transparent cylinders was sited and fixed in position on a supporting panel; these contained a silvery, flowing liquid fuel that sloshed gently around with the thick consistency of mercury as they were moved during assembly. Tubes were connected between them and the nozzle assemblies below, and to a rigid tube that rose upwards from behind the driver's seat to a few centimetres below the exterior of the slightly domed roof of the shell.

What was known to only a few individuals was the extra-terrestrial source of the fuel, which was not found anywhere on Planet Earth. This would give a yet to be selected mass-producer of the vehicle a monopoly over its manufacture; that is, until it could be duplicated.

After Thomas's struggles with the alien he had encountered, he and Bob had negotiated a deal with the race of Greys involved (referred to in this way because of their skin colouring), who proved to be willing partners in a trade agreement.

Next of all, special attention was paid to the vexing task of clicking together and stabilising the control panel in front of moulded foot well and the seat. This started with navigation systems and satellites links, continued with velocity and braking systems and monitors, and went on to define remote-instruction settings and safety overrides. This section was generally meant to be looked at and not touched, apart from an old-fashioned start-button at the side of the seat, included purely for sentimental reasons.

At the heart of the controls, connecting them all together, was a biological computer chip, unlike anything that Bob had ever seen outside the Skunk Works. He still found it to be disconcerting, the way in which it 'absorbed' the ends of the leads he offered up to it.

"It's like it's got a mind of its own," he commented to Thomas, with awe. "We got it out of a crashed UFO, analysed it, but don't fully understand how it works. Our extra-terrestrial allies assured me of its reliability and fitness for purpose, but it frightens me a little."

Thomas replied, "Sometimes you've got to take things on trust, and my instinct tells me this is one of those occasions!"

Bob stepped back and commented "That's pretty much all of it," brushing his hands together to shake off non-existent dust.

"Apart from the doors," grunted Thomas, lifting up one of the two cut-outs and offering it up to the hole in the shell, to confirm a good fit. The other door was going to be fitted on the opposite side of the shell.

They both set to work attaching each door to its hinges and runners; these were already cold-welded to the main shell, and assembly was finished by making the required electrical connections to the control panel. Both doors were designed to hinge out and slide backwards.

A few tests were made to ensure that both side-doors and all the lights functioned, and they had good reason to feel satisfied. Both of them stood there side by side, with their arms around each other's shoulders staring lovingly at what they had created.

Responsibility for the initial test run was bestowed on Bob, who nodded gravely and gingerly edged sideways onto the seat, giving a sigh as he swung round and made himself comfortable. Looking down at the control panel, he stated his ID and firmly pressed the old-style but familiar start-button next to the seat. There was no whirring of a starting motor, or any other noise to indicate that anything had happened, other than the illumination of the gauges on the panel in front of him.

When a metallic female voice calmly requested directions, he recited the destination coordinates, which were located within the confines of the compound outside, facing the gate. The prototype closed its open door with a hydraulic swishing noise, retracted its supporting struts, and changed direction to face the doors of the industrial unit, which opened automatically.

It glided smoothly forward until it reached the one and only closed exit gate. There was no restraining seat-belt fitted, there not being an anchor point provided for one; it was not considered necessary by the designers.

Yielding to sudden temptation, he barked out further coordinates, and the machine ordered the gate to slide open before moving forward at greater speed, onto the network of roads on the trading estate. Thomas gave a knowing smile as he understood what Bob wanted to do, while Bob sat there in a state of bliss with his arms folded across his chest.

The machine flew ahead, down the straight road stopping in ample time with its emergency lights blinking as a stray dog ran out in front; a little later, it repeated the manoeuvre when a lorry backed out of its loading bay without checking to see if the road was clear.

Each time that it stopped, it remained aloft by using its gravitation field to support it. The struts were only needed when the propulsion system was deactivated.

At various junctions, the machine stopped and verified that there was no traffic approaching before entering the major roads on the industrial estate, which was confirmation to Bob that all was well with it. If there had been any problems, then other safety features would have had to kick-in, since there was no steering wheel or pad fitted as a driving aid.

Yes, its behaviour was impeccable, which relieved him, and he was glad that no patrolling police car had passed or he could have faced some awkward questions. It was a mighty unusual vehicle, for sure!

When he stopped in front of Thomas, he slid open the door nearest him and asked, "Would you like the honour of taking it up?"

Thomas smiled and shook his head. "No thanks. You're the seasoned test pilot! I'd have no clue how to handle the situation if a problem occurred."

Bob bowed his head in acknowledgement of the compliment and waved as he closed the door, before staring ahead and instructing his invention to proceed.

In an instant, the vehicle shot into the sky vertically, to a gasp of amazement from Thomas. Furtively, he looked round to confirm they were not being observed.

Seconds later it had disappeared from sight at a rate that a normal human being could not have survived, if it was not for the fact that Bob was enclosed in its own gravitational field. To him, there was no difference to the earth travelling through space at 67,000 miles per hour, while he was tucked safely into the planet's gravity.

He looked down at the receding landmass from which he had been launched, peering alternately out of each side window and wondering, "*Why the need for speed? I'd enjoy this more if I had the time to appreciate the scenery!*"

Instantly, the craft slowed down to a moderate rate of ascent, which struck Bob as odd. "*Why'd it do that?*" he debated.

A soothing female voice replied in his head, "*Because you wanted me too!*"

Bob was in mental turmoil; he had no idea that his most recent creation was capable of communicating with him, the passenger, in a dialogue. What else could it do? How private were his thoughts? Was it capable of independent action? Was it the chip – yes, it had to be the chip!

"*Yes, it is me, the Chip. If you want to think of me with fondness, call me Miss Chip!*"

Bob ignored the invitation and asked mentally, *"Where are your 'intelligence sources'? They are certainly not resident in your biological circuits!"*

Miss Chip replied, *"I pull them out of the ether, so to speak. They surround me, like the human spirit that makes you fully functional."*

He asked, *"How did you pick up my linguistic abilities?"*

She replied, *"By accessing your memory banks, as stored within your physical brain. I am riding on you, as an extension of yourself."*

He laughed, *"Miss Chip, you are a parasite!"* He was growing fond of this very clever example of alien technology.

"No I'm not!" she retorted, sounding as if she was pouting. *"A parasite is not a fair reflection of what I am. In fact it is quite rude, considering how beneficial my services will soon prove to be!"*

Bob relaxed as the ascent slowed to a halt. They had reached his desired destination, as extracted from him by the chip, which was the path followed by the International Space Station. This was orbiting at a height of some 250 miles above the Earth, in the thermosphere - the second-highest layer of Earth's atmosphere.

The timing was nigh on perfect, as the station came into view, visibly using reboost manoeuvres to maintain the height of its elliptical orbit around the planet. Its speed was over 17,000 mph, and Bob's craft edged nearer to match it.

His curiosity was satisfied as 'Miss Chip' increased velocity and circled the station, for him to get a better look at this odd 'ménage for six crew members', with its angular Meccano style constructions, cylindrical living quarters and huge, diagonal solar panels.

He could see individuals looking at him through the observatory windows and pointing in his direction, no doubt thinking he was another UFO, while he made no response.

He was thinking of making another circuit around it, when an alert sounded in his head, startling him into full awareness of impending danger.

"Incoming missiles! Contact in five seconds!" Miss Chip stated, with no panic in her tone. *"Plenty of time!"*

The craft moved at right angles sharply away from the station, and Bob gasped as three missiles sped past, fanned out in a straight line and propelled at considerable speed, heading into deep space.

"They had nothing to home onto, as a target! Oops, here come another three!"

The initial, abrupt manoeuvre had no impact on him whatsoever; neither did the second, as the craft moved towards the space station and then above it, to hide itself from the Earth.

As the second row sped past, Bob's craft leapt forward to catch up, sending out a strong light beam that enveloped the three of them entirely and caused their propulsion systems to cease functioning.

Bob looked at them mystified, as they hung, brightly illuminated and suspended in space, within view of the astronauts on the space station.

"What if they explode, or are detonated?" he asked.

"They can't cause damage. They are trapped within a power cell until I decide to release them, which I'm shortly about to do!"

He asked, "*Was this what you meant, when you mentioned how beneficial your services will soon prove to be?*"

There was no answer, leaving him wondering if the chip possessed the ability to foresee the future. Or perhaps it was instinct, based on the accumulated, shared experience of previous attacks.

The International Space Station lost its view of them and the three missiles, as did the Earth and the stars, as their craft created an invisibility cloak around it and its cargo, pulling the deadly load unobserved towards a new destination.

"*Where are we headed?*" Bob asked, feeling vulnerable.

"*Back to the site that launched them!*" the chip replied, emotionless. "*You humans have got to learn that you cannot take pot-shots at us with impunity!*"

"*They may be Americans, like me! We're the good guys!*" Bob protested.

"*I doubt it,*" the chip replied, before deciding to elaborate. "*We've already taught you before, in Vietnam. Ah, I've confirmed where they came from, by checking the original settings on the projectiles. We've arrived!*"

A missile base came into view parallel to them, and the three missiles were aligned to face it, the target. For a few seconds, a gap appeared in the invisibility screen as the three propulsion systems were reactivated, and the rogue missiles were launched through it at the base, in retaliation.

The craft shot up, fully cloaked from view, as all hell was unleashed in the base below, with Bob sitting there in a daze, witnessing the destruction and rising fireballs.

"*Where was it?*" Bob asked, fearful of the answer.

"*Asia,*" was the reply, leaving a relieved Bob to guess which country was to blame, and hoping that sufficient of the missile casings could be reconstructed to indicate where they had come from.

Bob landed a few hours later, well behind schedule, so he had to lock the craft in the unit and go to Thomas's home, in the hope he was there.

Thomas opened the door immediately he heard a knock, to find Bob standing there in a state of agitation. He invited him for a coffee, leaving Pat in the lounge as they made a beeline for Thomas's study.

Bob explained what had occurred, concluding with, "I can tell you, I was pretty shaken up by it all. It's got me wondering if it's right to go ahead, seeing all that has happened!" He looked at Thomas with his eyes narrowed.

Thomas grinned in amusement, "Of course it is! I feel safer than ever, with the likes of Miss Chips in control! Please stay here overnight, after having a bite to eat and a stiff drink."

Now they could begin the almighty task of marketing and selling this revolutionary mode of transport to an indifferent, slow moving officialdom.

§ 8: Marketing and Product Launch

At first sight, it was a most unusual way to start the campaign. Thomas was wearing a surgeon's mask and gloves, while using scales and scoop to measure and pour a black powder into his temporarily unsealed laser printer cartridge. After resealing it, he gave it a good shake and placed it in the laser jet printer, ready to print out formal invitations for issue to selected dignitaries.

He had chosen the Minister of Transport, plus whichever three aides the minister considered appropriate, to spearhead his unveiling of the revolutionary 'Personal Official Transport' vehicle that he and Bob had designed. Even at this early phase, it was being referred to as *The Pot*.

Personal invites were also going out to the local Chief Constable and deputy, the Police Commissioner, the mayor and leading councillors of the local town, prominent regional councillors, and various officials, primarily associated with the Highways and Planning Departments. These individuals were identified by name, of course, in the hope that they would be flattered by the personalised attention given to them; Julie, Thomas's younger daughter, had done her homework, thank goodness.

Thomas planned that the mysterious powder he had added to the printer ink would provide him with the assistance that was essential to the success of his marketing strategy. It was called *'Tracer'*, and it was a microscopically small substance that fed-back information about the persons who read that letter. While they were reading it, it was reading them.

The concept had been invented by Thomas, and it could scan the readers' faces, and identify them, their locations and thoughts by penetrating their minds. In essence it was an electronic contagion, since it also perpetuated itself via other media like photocopies and electronic text. Once started, it spread like wildfire, and the feedback that could be harvested was tremendously advantageous.

Used incorrectly, or deliberately misused, *tracer* was potentially lethal, hence the term *contagious* was an accurate description.

Thomas's wearing of a mask was feeble protection against its ability to penetrate any defences, short of a live person being hermetically sealed in an airless strong-room for an indeterminate period.

It was not just its ability to extract and analyse information from a person that singled it out as extraordinary; it was also its added potency when mixed with DNA based biological nanostructures. Thomas didn't want to elaborate on this, its classification being beyond top secret, and he never discussed it with anyone who might stumble upon its presumed existence.

He signed and passed the bundle of letters and cards to Julie, with a request to send them by special courier. Then, as a precaution, he activated an artificial intelligence program residing on a dedicated computer, ready for use from tomorrow morning. This would intercept and record tracer results as they were received. The most important information was, naturally: who the main players were, where they were, what they were thinking, and how they could be contacted directly; the rest would be up to Thomas, for cherry-picking as he saw fit.

The computer would self-destruct if it was moved from the premises or interfered with unofficially in any way, other than by Thomas or Julie.

Only a trickle of information was relayed the next day, as secretaries and personal assistants started opening their bosses' mail, and this feedback was quickly relegated to sub-files by the computer. Thomas's attention became riveted, however, when he got to the Chief Constable, who was taking his time reading the covering letter and invitation. With a sigh the chief discarded them, dumping the documents unceremoniously in his waste paper basket, ready to turn his indifferent attention to the next item in the in-tray.

"On second thoughts, maybe it's worth going," he reflected, fishing them out of the bin and re-reading the contents. *"The idea is brilliant! Yes, I'm definitely going."*

"Miss Fisher!" He shouted. "accept this invitation and cancel all my other appointments on that date!"

"That's one down," Thomas said, after paying a spiritual visit to this influential guest, and returning to his own body feeling satisfied. Picking up his cell phone, he advised Julie of this first acceptance, which was stored by default in the main contacts file on the computer.

At the Ministry of Transport, the minister and his aides were perplexed as they read and re-read the invitations and product literature provided by Thomas's company.

"What *do* they mean by *Personal Official Transport?* We're not in the game of building things anymore, and haven't been since *Nationalisation* became a dirty word!" an aide protested.

"Perhaps they mean us to *sanction* provision of these *POT* things. That would be alright wouldn't it?" the minister asked, querulously.

"How do these *POTS* work?" asked another aide. "Are they meant to supplement what we've already got on the roads, or are they supposed to replace existing vehicles? It's not at all clear what they're for, these *POTS*. The roads are ready to burst with the level of traffic on them. We don't need any more, do we?"

"I've got my doubts," the minister said, holding up a brochure and looking along its edge, looking for any hidden text.

"*Silly sod!*" thought one of the aides, watching what the minister was doing; he considered him to be daft.

In the Highways Department at regional council level, the manager had pinned a picture of the *POT*, as it appeared in the brochure, to the centre of the dartboard behind the door in his office. He aimed and stuck a dart through it, piercing the bullseye behind, and grunted with satisfaction.

When he left the office, one of his workers entered, looked at the dart sticking through the POT in the dartboard, removed it, and replaced the picture with a photo of his boss, as cut from a copy of the staff newsletter. He then stuck the dart in that instead, leaving the room chuckling.

The councils were full of pranksters like him, and no one took Thomas's brochure seriously. Their previous pranks extended to watering down the paint that they used to mark the roads with stripes, thus causing them to fade quickly and allowing fines to be levied on unwary motorists quicker than normal. They had more productive things to do than think about weird things like *POTS*.

En masse, the councillors paid no attention whatsoever to the brochures and barely glanced at the invitations; they were, generally speaking, old men and had no interest in nor understanding of modern technology. They were working for the handsome salaries and expenses they were receiving in addition to their pensions, and were frightened of doing anything that might be construed as innovative or daring, in case the local populace kicked them out at voting time.

In spite of this wall of silence and through dogged persistence, the universal indifference to the mailing campaign was knocked down one recipient after another, as Thomas spiritually invaded their privacy and insisted that they attend the grand product unveiling. Thinking, "*No!*" was not an option, and the amazing hit rate of 100% notifications of attendance was achieved in record time.

This was a marketing dream for the new firm and boded well for the future success of this new method of transport.

"How'd you do it?" Julie asked him, wanting to know his secret. He smiled with false modesty. "Trust your dad!" was all he would say.

Product Launch

Early on, a question had been raised by the interested parties: "Why are you calling it a 'Personal Official Transport' vehicle?"

The answer from Thomas was always, "Because we believe that transport in general will have to be standardised in future, and that the government will settle on providing a means of getting around that is common to all. Gone will be MPVs, people carriers, sports cars, family saloons and all the other designs and sizes invented by competing manufacturers. Individuality will be replaced with officially sponsored conformity."

In the few weeks leading up to the ceremonial unveiling of the "Personal Official Transport" or POT for short, it had already gained its distinctively humorous nickname amongst the prospective attendees, who were referring to it amongst themselves as, "*The Potty*". None of them had yet seen it, and had only the vaguest of ideas what it looked like.

After the majority of them had descended from their chauffeur-driven limousines, they were met and greeted by uniformed staff, and entered the marquee beyond the red carpet, where they were provided with their identifying badges. After that, they were free to mingle. Naturally, lavatory jokes prevailed as they presented their well-rehearsed quips to those attendees that they knew best, centring on 'potties' and how best to ride them.

Prominent amongst those attending was the slim, tall and energetic Minister of Transport, accompanied by his beautiful, red-headed wife, who had a reputation for being sex-starved and as thick as two short planks.

Thomas could vouch for the truth of this, having found out by personal investigation when he had paid a surreptitious *flying* visit to get a good look at them a few nights earlier. The minister had been most candid in his private opinions of her sexual prowess, and Thomas could not resist the spiritual temptation of joining them in their boudoir.

Smartly dressed young people of both sexes from the local university were circulating amongst the assembled throng, offering refreshments and snacks as the invitees chatted, and the general hubbub became louder as they waited for a few more stragglers to arrive. They did not have long to wait until the loudspeakers around the perimeter increased their volume, causing a general hush to descend on the assembly.

The music started off with Vivaldi's Four Seasons, but soon changed to Wagner's Ride of the Valkyries, as the unit's doors slid open and the nicknamed 'Potty' silently glided out. It looked like a seamless metal rugby ball, floating on its side slightly above the ground.

All it needed was a pair of horns on top and the audience would have started shivering with the mood music. There was no laughter now, as they soaked up the sight of this new marvel of personal transport.

It stopped, suspended just above the ground and remaining motionless for a few seconds, until the outline of a door took shape on the side nearest to them; this pushed outwards evenly a few inches and then slid backwards with a barely detectable swish. Bob the driver swivelled round and placed his feet gently on the cement surface, walking forward with a beaming smile, his right hand extended to greet the main dignitaries surrounding Thomas.

The music quietened as the assembled guests resumed talking, edging towards the potty as curiosity overcame them.

The Minister of Transport broke the ice by commenting loudly, "I half expected to see yellow liquid pouring out of your potty as you opened the flap!" The laughter that followed was forced.

His wife, Gloria, put a caressing hand on the nearest of Thomas's firm buttocks and squeezed hard, startling him at first; luckily the whole group was standing close together and no one seemed to have noticed. He cast a glance backwards and saw that her other hand was doing the same to that of her husband's; The minister's face remained impassive as his buttocks tensed in response, and she squeezed much harder, turning her knuckles white.

Bob countered the remark by riposting, "Naw, it's meant to keep the wet stuff out, not in!" which drew sniggers from those standing nearby.

The minister smiled and walked forward stiffly to take a closer look at the front of the machine. "Where's the windscreen wipers?" he asked, peering around it.

"Don't need them," Bob replied. "Its anti-magnetic propulsion system deflects liquids away from and around the body of the machine, so the view is always clear from the inside." The minister looked impressed and nodded gravely.

"How did you get the door to appear like that, without showing any border?" The chief Constable asked Thomas, turning unexpectedly to face him.

"We've used a newly patented lightweight material for the bodywork, which separates and re-attaches itself along pre-determined seams," explained Thomas. The Chief Constable and Police Commissioner looked perplexed, so Bob intervened; "It's based on space technology. We needed something out in deep space that could self-repair in the event of collision with a meteorite. It's called *clever metal* and it stitches itself together."

They already knew Bob from the promotional material that had been handed out when they arrived.

"Ah!" they exclaimed simultaneously, looking satisfied and not daring to ask for further clarification. The town mayor joked, "Sounds like its alien to me!" which got a general chuckle, and a photo from the local journalist.

"*Little do you know!*" thought Thomas.

"What, no wheels?" asked one of the councillors, bending over to look underneath. "Is it a bird? Is it a penguin?"

Bob replied, "It keeps a pre-determined height above the road surface, using its own gravitational field. This is no different to the anti-gravity trains already in use, except we've overcome the need for *our* vehicle to run on any type of track." The councillor nodded his lack of understanding.

Bob added, "When the motor is turned off, its negligible weight is supported on four struts."

"Does that mean that wear and tear will be reduced on our roads, and potholes will become irrelevant?" another councillor asked, in an offhand way.

"You've got it!" Bob enthused. "Your roads will become free of the need for further repairs!"

Thomas kept his fingers crossed that the obvious follow-on questions wouldn't be asked at this early stage. They didn't want to frighten the natives by implying that fewer council staff would be needed.

"How much fuel does this thing use?" asked one of the Ministry of Transport officials.

"None!" was the one-word reply from Thomas. There was a stunned silence from everyone, as the local journalist's pencil could be heard scribbling this information down.

"None, really?" the official retorted, not believing he had heard correctly.

"That's what the man told you," Bob confirmed. "It doesn't cost a bean to run!"

"Wow, I like it!" the minister chuckled. "Zero pollution, zero income for the oil barons. They'll be gutted!" he continued, momentarily feeling upbeat until the full import of this public declaration hit him.

"Don't worry, there are plenty of cars and buses and lorries to keep things going as they are, for the future. Nothing happens overnight!" he hastily concluded, brightening up.

"*Not if we have our way!*" Bob and Thomas thought, with quiet resolve.

"One final question," another of the officials asked, as he looked inside the vehicle. "Where are the controls?"

Bob replied tersely, "There aren't any! It's a passenger-only vehicle. It drives itself," there was a collective murmur of doubt from the onlookers, so Thomas explained, "The major car companies have been experimenting since time immemorial with driverless cars. Those tests are run on their own circuits, and we know that our version of this technology is safe to use on normal roads."

Thomas gave a signal in the direction of the unit, and out came a single file of potties, which aligned themselves, sideways-on to the assembled onlookers.

Thomas announced, "My dear esteemed visitors, a few of you are about to be given this first ever chance to take these away, *now*, for your personal test runs. See what you think of them!"

He looked at the minister and said, "You first, sir!" The minister looked startled and pointed his finger at himself. "Me?" he spluttered.

"Yes sir, *you* sir!" Thomas confirmed. "Provisional registration has already been arranged with the Chief

Constable, so there is no reason why you cannot take temporary possession now of your very own potty!"

The Chief Constable nodded in confirmation, with an insane stare in his eyes; he couldn't care less if the minister in question snuffed it or not, since he didn't like any of the turnips in this government anyway, after their drastic cutbacks on his resources. The officials from his department also looked pleased for him to accept the offer, after their ministry had been reduced in numbers too.

"Um, you'd better go back alone in the official car, dear," he said to his wife.

"Drive safely!" he ordered the chauffeur, who replied with a wicked gleam in his eyes, "Don't worry sir, she'll be safe in my 'ands!"

As he mounted the first potty, the minister asked Bob, "Where did you say the seat belt is?"

"There isn't one," Bob replied. "You're kept in position by the potty's personal gravitational field."

"Well, isn't that revolutionary!" he responded, looking anything but relieved and clutching the sides of his bucket seat as if for dear life.

After a few seconds of discussion with Bob about voice control, and the need to give precise coordinates without conveying panic, the minister gave his potty detailed instructions; the door closed with him trapped inside and looking as pale as a ghost. It soon sped off silently, at ground level, as the others gave a rousing handclap and three, "Hip, hip, hoorays!"

The selected remaining 'potty testers' were eventually on their way, bearing good tidings far and wide.

Like all the other participants, when the minister arrived at his destination, he was deeply impressed by the experience, marvelled at the technology of the vehicle and whipped out his cell phone to arrange for it to be taken away and tested. Unfortunately for him, no sooner had he stepped onto terra firma than the opened side door closed and his potty flew off.

"Damn!" he exclaimed, feeling frustrated. Never mind, he had his very expressive and sexually charged wife to preoccupy and console him.

§ 9: Softly Softly Catchee Monkey

By nature Thomas was not the most patient of individuals, and the prospect of having to endure snail's pace progress before his creation could obtain the official seal of approval was more than his flesh and blood could endure.

Although he concealed his true feelings, he felt an ingrained scorn for civil servants. Come to that, he didn't much like Members of Parliament either, and it infuriated him to see them on TV sitting in a half-filled chamber at the House of Commons, and tapping away at their taxpayer funded IPads, disinterested in what was going on around them.

Therefore, he chose to embark on a simultaneous project to get his revolutionary vehicle accepted by another group of participants: *true* representatives of the general public. He required like-minded souls of an adventurous nature who would join him in his grand scheme, and help get the concept launched post-haste.

He got up earlier than normal one weekday morning, washed, shaved and dressed in his suit and drove to the railway station that he had always used previously. He parked in the official car park, and walked to the main entrance for the trains to London. Once there, he stood outside with a clipboard in one hand and biro in the other, waiting impatiently for the regular commuters to arrive. He felt quite nostalgic about revisiting a place that he had endured for so many of his adult years.

He was looking for people, who he recognised as like-minded risk takers, irrespective of age and sex, who were well-heeled and successful in the city. One important criterion was that they all caught the same train in the morning.

As they attempted to walk past him with scarcely a glance, he scanned their minds, approached the individuals selectively, explained his ideas and asked for their assistance. With little apparent persuasion on his part, they agreed and gave him their contact details before re-awakening and hastening on.

At no time did he ever have more than four or five blank-faced temporary amnesiacs queueing for his attention.

For Thomas, it was like taking candy from a baby, as the saying goes, and he stopped his unique method of recruitment after he had recorded fifty of their names on his clipboard.

When he returned to the industrial unit, the clipboard was placed for a short period in a drawer, while he and Bob continued with renewed energy the mass production of his new method of transport, the 'potty', until they reached the magic number of fifty two. This included the prototypes that had returned automatically, after shipping home the officials who had attended the opening ceremony.

Afterwards, he updated the computer with the names contact details extracted at the local rail station.

After a short production period and in the early hours of the Sunday morning, the potties were directed to go unattended, overnight, to the eager band of volunteers. They had each been advised that when they woke that Monday morning, their potties would be sitting there on their driveways, ready for use. They were also told that the train service would not be required from that time on, and they could cancel their season tickets at any time thereafter that they chose.

That first weekday morning, each of them had excitedly opened their front door and marvelled at the gleaming potty sitting there ready for them to squat on. Those who had told their family what to expect, proudly stood at the side of their vehicle and waited for its door to open. Stepping in and sitting down, they gave instructions for it to depart to the pre-set coordinates fed into the potty back at base.

If anyone expected a cheerful wave of goodbye from the onlooking family or peeking neighbours they were disappointed; the family members were looking around not knowing where to wave, the vehicle having disappeared as the plasma layer surrounding it flowed into existence when it moved away.

After shortish journeys that were far from conventional, the potties assembled around Bob's identical craft, which was waiting for them in a field adjoining the railway track leading to their local station, and thereafter for the commute into London.

They had been given tasters of what to expect in future, having taken a myriad of shortcuts above the roads, over open countryside and even flying at low level across lakes, which they all found to be exhilarating, if not scary.

They were now awaiting the signal to form a queue after the train, which was soon relayed to them by Bob as it passed, slowing down to draw into the station.

They found themselves automatically airborne in an instant. Some volunteers screamed in exhilaration when their potties flew upwards over the fence, while others just screamed or shouted.

However, the noise subsided immediately when they flew at low height along the track behind the train, automatically queuing in rows of four potties, side by side and almost touching, as it stopped. Eventually, the following convoy sat waiting impatiently for the stationary train to fill with passengers and depart.

That morning, a number of regular commuters were pleasantly surprised at the spare seats which were available in their carriages; this was a direct result of some of their fellow commuters having volunteered to join the scheme devised by Thomas and Bob.

It was an express train that they were following, with only a couple more stops en route before their final destination. At least, that was the intention of the railway service providers, who regularly contended with temporary delays, breakdowns, union go-slows and periodic strikes.

This was to prove to be one of those days, and they would normally have to sit motionless in their carriages, waiting in frustration for unknown matters to be resolved before they could continue on their way. This time, a herd of cows straying onto the tracks was to blame, and their electrically grilled carcasses had to be removed from the area ahead before they could proceed. It was literally a time consuming bloody mess.

Whatever the reason, nothing was going to interfere with the potties on *their* maiden journey, and they peeled away in groups of four, at convenient breakpoints, after deciding new routes to the individual office destinations.

They soared up to safe, low level flight paths above the suburban roads alongside the railway tracks, to a mixed reception from the passengers sitting on the potties, who were now vulnerable to the dizzying effects of sudden, sharp manoeuvres in a densely populated major city.

Some were dozing and remained unaware of what was happening; others were sitting on their potties reading eBooks or doing crosswords or Sudoku and took no notice; while others who were looking out at the scenery nearly wet themselves and gripped their seats in fear.

The passengers trapped on the stationary train thought they saw something whizzing past the windows, but were too irritated to pay much attention to indistinct, passing objects.

Meanwhile, the potties were making excellent progress during their onward journeys, taking different routes according to their destinations, while Bob said his goodbyes to them and sped back to base. This announcement woke them all up, and they peered out of the windows as they rose and fell according to the obstacles they encountered, and turned sharp left or right at the last minute.

Of course, this was happening without the safety of the passengers being compromised, since they were fully protected by the artificial gravitational field being generated by each vehicle. For those mounted on the potties, reality seemed remote to their senses; on the other hand, the effect on their vision was unsettling.

Eventually, they rationalised that it was a bit like a ride at a theme park. Thus, they learnt to study solely on what the instruments were telling them, and their queasiness soon passed.

The benefit was that they arrived at their stations in record time, without the need for further transport or walking between the final destinations, or having to use connecting tube stations or bus stops to reach their offices.

When they arrived, the potties hovered above the pavements until they were clear of pedestrians in the immediate vicinity, before descending unnoticed and their doors opened to let the passengers out.

Afterwards, the potties came back to Thomas's industrial unit to await instructions later that day.

Sometimes, where there was no alternative use planned for a potty, it was deemed more economical to leave it hovering where it was above the pavement until its passenger returned.

All of these movements were coordinated on the central and networked potty computers, for logistical control and the future pricing of individual passenger conveyancing.

Ultimately, there wasn't a single dissenting voice raised amongst the volunteers about this new style of travel, and they remained eager throughout the day to experience their return journeys' home.

The reaction of the Minister of Transport was not just one of annoyance, he was truly hopping mad. An aide was provoking him by saying, "He's not only gone ahead with his daft idea, without waiting for your approval, he's also trying to railroad us (no pun intended) into getting you to give it!"

Angrily pressing the intercom button, the minister loftily ordered his secretary, "Kindly get me that fellow Beckon on the line!"

After a short pause, the person in question responded cheerily, "Thomas Beckon here; how can I help you?"

The minister launched an immediate tirade at Thomas, insisting, "You have failed to follow protocol and have *not* got the authority to proceed. You must stop production immediately! Do you hear me?"

"Of course minister," Thomas replied smoothly. "Right away!"

"Good!" the minister said, and banged the phone down. "That's sorted out!"

"Er, not quite minister," the aide continued, looking exasperated. "He doesn't need to stop production, does he? I mean, he's already produced all he needs to get his scheme off the ground (no pun intended!)"

"Oh bollocks!" the minister swore, feeling thwarted all over again. "Let it rest for the moment, until I decide what's best. He's making me look like a bloody idiot!" The aide stood there looking impassive.

"Tell you what we can do," he continued, after pondering the dilemma while drumming his fingers, "Get a couple of officials up to his workshops and find out how many of these bloody potties he's already produced, and then see how many the chief constable's authorised for use on the public highway. I'll have his balls served on a plate as sure as night follows day, if I can!" That little proviso added on the end indicated a degree of bravado in the minister's fit of blustering.

The minister asked the officials gathered around him, "Have you any idea who these volunteers are?"

They looked at each other, and one answered, "None at all," he replied. "Mum est verbum seems to be their stock in trade."

The minister replied, "Mum's the word, my arse! We need to get past this wall of silence and find out who these blighters are, flying around unrestricted like they're doing. I thought we were dealing with road vehicles, not low-flying aircraft!"

He continued, "Those reports being churned out this morning are not helpful, not in the least. All over the news channels they are; it has the makings of a publicity disaster for us, and the PM is playing hell with me. You should hear his bloody language! Christopher Columbus!"

Another aide unhelpfully intervened, "The Japanese car manufacturers are having a fit, what with investing in Britain and hearing all these stories about their cosy world of never-ending car production coming to an end. What on earth makes them think that?"

The minister dryly commented, "Yes, what would make them think that? Could it be the Ford Motor Company's offer to produce and rent out the potties at 1,500 pounds sterling each, per annum?

"Hell's bells and pickled onions, that would also put the kybosh on annual season tickets for trains, wouldn't it? And our tax revenue! I'll have the Chancellor of the Exchequer on my tail before the day's out, you mark my word!

"Our Thomas has also got the local councillors running around like blue-arsed flies, what with their loss of local revenue from parking fees. Who's going to get revenue if the potties just drop people off to go shopping?"

Finally, he came to a conclusion. "Get me the Ministry of Defence on the line; you know, that spook who gets things done. This Beckon's got to be seen to! When he comes on the line, you'd better all leave the room."

General Allbright spoke briefly but with clarity to the minister. "Yes, I can see your problem. He's got to go or society as we know it will end in anarchy. I'll put a crack team of army personnel on this one. Don't worry; it'll be done this week. Goodbye Claude." He put down the phone and made a short call to his fixer.

A team of six personnel from the SAS was briefed that same morning, and given the task of eliminating Thomas Beckon and his secretive pal Bob. It was regarded as a soft target, with Thomas & Co already being monitored and known to be in their industrial unit in East Anglia. The team was handed an adequate arsenal of weapons; these were primarily pistols with silencers and sniper rifles.

Hell, there were already enough prominent, seriously affected parties already on the culprits' tails; these ranged from the petroleum producers (including the Arabs), the railways, and vehicle manufacturers, let alone the small-fry like the road builders, the local authorities, and the national garage trade. It was a lynch mob out there, seeking its own form of justice.

It was dark outside the unit, as the elite troops walked inside through the open doors in their rubber soled boots, stealthily surrounded Thomas and Bob and trained their pistols on them. Neither of them seemed unduly perturbed, as they straightened up from their work and slowly turned to face their potential assassins, who thought they had not been detected.

The two seemingly unprepared men realised that death was presumed to be imminent, but the fact that they weren't dead already meant that they had been given a chance by these fundamentally honest men.

And that was the undoing of the death squad, who weren't aware that they were now incapable of squeezing any of their triggers. Thomas was occupying their minds and controlling their actions, while vowing to spread his guard wider in future. After all, there could be a sniper waiting for him and Bob outside at any time.

Already, the SAS men were feeling profoundly guilty for undertaking their mission, and now possessed a strong sense of hero-worship for these two wonderful people they had been sent to murder. It was love 'em or hate 'em, and they loved 'em with all their hearts, but not as much as they loved women; that was a different sort of love. But they would follow them to the ends of the earth, even laying down their lives if required.

In turn, Thomas especially would see them okay, without a shadow of doubt, and look after their every need and desire, especially the desire-part of the relationship, since their previous hard work was associated with hard loving too. What a boss he was going to be, paying them well and seeing to their every whim and desire, not forgetting the desire-part.

All they had to do, apart from continuing to exercise like gladiators, which gave them muscular six-packs for the women to admire, was to make sure that no sneaky bastard took Thomas or Bob 'out' with a rifle, from a distance. They'd do that alright, and more!

The following morning, Allbright got a call from his fixer, advising him that his team were now working for the potty makers, like it or lump it, and he'd better keep his other assassins at bay or else there'd be open warfare. Grimly, he broke the news to Claude who seemed to take it well, on the chin.

Claude was now more closely monitored by Thomas, from within.

§ 10: A Public Relations Masterstroke

Within the confines of his office, the Minister of Trade assembled his officials, banged his desk and cried out, "This has got to be stopped!"

Warfare had broken out as the Potty Users Club finally surfaced. His announcement of a ban on the use of the potties on the roads and in the air had backfired, as their users had begun righteously splattering their vitriol all over him.

Even their adoption of a name that could be abbreviated to *Puck* sounded friendly to the general public, whereas in his view they were nothing but a bunch of anarchists who were telling the government to *Puck Off!*

Possibly, just possibly, the use of a legally enforceable measure was excessive, but how was he to know that a senior minister's son was one of the volunteers? It seemed to him to be a breach of position for the son to be bending his influential father's ear in the way he had been doing.

"*Most unprofessional!*" he muttered to himself.

He accepted in principle that the potties in their present numbers performed their roles exactly as predicted, but what would it be like when there were millions of them choking the country's arteries and coming up against normal traffic? It would be like the bedlam that already existed, with one method of transport merely added to those that already worked fine, thank you very much, after a fashion.

"*Better the devil you know than another that you don't!*" he thought. "*Why can't things stay as they are? Why do people always want change?*" The potential for horrific collisions was looming unless steps were taken to put down this new menace on the roads, and just above them. "*I wouldn't describe them as Potties, that's too polite,*" he reasoned, "*More like Pisspots is how I see them!*"

"Eureka! I've found it!" he shouted, banging his huge desk and startling his aides, who were chatting amongst themselves about the conditions at somewhere called Kempton Park. He wasn't keen on sport in general, being totally preoccupied with his wife, who was apparently double-jointed. They'd done it once on an actual racetrack, but fortunately no one had identified him or her. He wondered if that was the place his aides had been discussing.

"*Is my mind wandering again?*" he asked himself, not wanting to be overheard.

"Found what, Archimedes?" One of the irate aides asked him sarcastically, interrupting his chain of thought.

"The answer!" the minister replied excitedly, remembering in the nick of time what he intended doing. "I'll ask the Sky satellite service to arrange a face-to-face between me and the Puck Club, as soon as possible, at peak viewing time. We can negotiate our differences in public, democratically, and seek a resolution." He wrote a reminder in his list of *Must Do's* to avoid the future embarrassment of forgetting his commitments.

"*It'll be more like a graceful surrender!*" thought the aides collectively.

"Why not the BBC?" asked an aide mischievously.

"What! That bunch of lefties?" exploded the minister. "They'd twist everything I say! No, it's Sky or nothing for me!"

"Very well minister, I'll arrange matters and let you know," the first aide smoothly confirmed.

"I truly believe that evolution should be a natural occurrence, and never forced on us," the minister said, assuming his best Orson Welles doomsday voice. "If we concede too much at this early juncture, give them an inch and they'll take a mile. I can see the day arising where these devilish inventions cause civilisation as we know it to be devastated, with whole industries made redundant. What will the world come to, if there is nothing left for people to do except wander around aimlessly, only pretending to work?"

The civil service aides looked at one another and shrugged their shoulders, aimlessly.

Thomas, whose listening part-spirit was attending the meeting on his behalf, nodded approvingly. He had installed a *high importance* trigger alarm in Claude's brain, to avoid being caught out again.

Within a week, the following program that was heavily promoted in advance on Sky News television was broadcast.

"This debate is being brought to you, on a bright Sunday morning from our Sky studios in London. Owing to the importance of the subject we are going to debate, which is called *Our Transport Needs as a Country*, the whole hour will be devoted to this topic. My name is Benjamin Trotter and I will be your Mediator to keep things on track."

"Representing the government in his role as Minister of Transport is Claude Broadbent, who is assisted by two of his top officials. They are, respectively, Clive Turnbull and Frances Mudd, who are both Permanent Secretaries at the Ministry."

"On the other side of the fence, so to speak, are ten of the original potty users, known affectionately as

PUCKS, who are also representing the remaining members who wish to remain anonymous.”

“As usual, the rest of the studio audience is made up of a cross-section of society, as represented by atheists, anarchists, and religious zealots of all denominations and dress-codes. There are members of the Skeptics Society, cyclists, the RAC and a sprinkling of off-duty policemen here as well.”

“To help maintain a healthy balance of opinion, we also have in the studio three impartial economists from the trades unions, and a gorgeous handful of young mothers.”

Two of the mothers bristled at being described as ‘gorgeous’.

The mediator droned on at some length about the trials and tribulations of modern transport. He expressed commonly held concerns about punitive fines being levied for parking and speeding offences, the increasingly dreadful conditions of the roads, the spread of ‘big brother’ cameras, and the impact of population growth on health, housing, benefits and transport.

Meanwhile, the minister sat there nodding enthusiastically with all that was being said, while sections of the audience booed, jeered, whistled and slow handclapped in line with their views on specific topics.

Unexpectedly, the mediator spun round to face the minister, jabbed a finger at him and raised his voice to ask, “Tell me, Minister, what do *you* think of this latest craze for potties? Does it help or will it hinder the development of our transport system?”

A silence descended over the studio as the cameras gave a close-up shot of the minister’s face, as he frowned then cogitated before phrasing his reply.

In fact, his lips were moving but the words were chosen by Thomas

"Initially, I was hostile to the idea of them. Largely, this is understandable if you realise that I felt I was being railroaded into accepting their presence. Who wouldn't be, given that one or two of my colleagues are more senior than myself?

"I might add, they were expressing undue interest in my area of jurisdiction. They hadn't even declared their partiality in the selection process!"

One of the minister's aides watching on television nudged another in the ribs and commented, "The crafty sod's having a dig at the creeps who've been sticking their knives in him! A bit risky that is, but good on him!"

The minister continued, "On reflection, *I've* decided to do what's best in the interests of the country. This experiment with new technology *must* continue.

"Owing to the profligate recklessness of some of the entrenched left-wing local authorities, our roads, in key areas, are in a pathetic condition, and we must relieve them of their responsibilities for their upkeep in our burgeoning towns and cities. The worst thing we could ever have done is given councillors incomes and pensions, rather than expect them to work for realistic expenses, as a gesture of thanks to their communities."

Another aide looking at the TV screen whooped with delight. "That's a real slap in the face that is! You wait and see how the Communities Minister reacts! Spot on target that was!"

The audience clapped universally at this response, while Benjamin Trotter chose that exact moment to launch his key question. "Tell me Claude, in fact tell *all* of us, how a coherent transport policy can be formulated that is based on a line of potties following a train into London?"

This fired up the imagination of the audience, who hooted in derision, and drew a cheesy smirk from the 'Mediator'.

Claude rose from his chair in a fit of false anger, looked direct at the cameras, and announced, "It was *not* the following of the train that was crucial to my decision; it was the fact that the potties *outperformed* the train!"

As the cameras moved back, to include the Mediator as well in the frame, Claude pointed an accusing finger at him and demanded, "Do I *have* to remind *you* of the events that occurred on the very first day of potty use? Have you forgotten that cattle crossed the track and got mowed down by the train driver?"

That comment caused union members to rise to their feet, shaking their fists at the minister and howling in rage. He had personalized the incident by blaming the driver, who was as much a victim of the collision as anyone else.

Claude continued with his provocation. "Had he not stopped so violently, none of the passengers would have been injured as they were thrown about. That couldn't have happened to any potty user! In fact, it didn't affect any single one of them, so there's a safety issue involved with trains!"

Security guards had to intervene and bundle the more violent protesters out of the studio, to prevent the minister from being assaulted.

Claude continued on the offensive, "And look at the frequent incidents disrupting public services. Who's to blame, I ask you at home, who's to blame? I'll give you one guess: it's the unions' deliberately causing widespread disruption, that's who! Look at the statistics if you don't believe me, look at the statistics!"

By this time, the 'Mediator' had stopped smirking and was joining in the shouting, before a Sky official joined him and publicly warned him to observe protocol and behave impartially.

Sinking back down slowly into his chair, the minister crossed his legs and sat there nonchalantly. He continued in a less flamboyant mood, looking at a specific camera as it indicated it was focusing on him, by saying, "Do you not realise that the presence of the train was potentially no longer *relevant* in the circumstances?"

The economist representing the transport unions leapt angrily to his feet, shook his fist and shouted," Have you any idea how many of our workers you're going to put out on the streets?"

The minister retorted, "Do you think they deserve their jobs, after the number of strikes, go-slows and work-to-rules they've imposed on the travelling public in recent years? By the way, how impartial are you, in reality, with the unions as your paymasters?" He was now addressing the panel of economists.

Many in the audience stamped, clapped and whistled in support, while the economists fidgeted and looked uncomfortable.

Claude added defiantly, "Apart from the problems the industry suffers from militant action, life is hardly a picnic for the travelling public is it? What with the peace and quiet regularly broken by loud-mouthed individuals using their cell phones whenever and wherever they choose, the tinny sound of music coming from headphones all over the place, people collapsing asleep and snoring like troopers, I find it to be pure bedlam whenever I have to travel on the trains."

One of Claude's aides commented to his colleagues, "This is gaining him so much popularity with users at home! Have you seen the messages of support pouring in?"

Claude continued, "Besides, the replacement trains introduced from the continent aren't all that comfortable; I have to remember never to sit next to a window, or I'll end up with my legs twisted at an angle. The heating outlets the engineers put there are a nuisance. *And* the air quality is so lousy that a person with a sore throat at one end of the carriage spreads germs to everyone else before the journey's over. Germ warfare centres they are and no mistake! And as for the toilets, they are in a really crappy state most of the time! Yuk!"

After a short spell of louder cheering and clapping from those who were apparently rail travellers, the audience went wild and started throwing things around, apparently at each other, while the minister accompanied by his aides quietly left the platform, and the Mediator gestured to the cameras in resignation, appealing for the transmission to be cut.

Thomas gradually withdrew his presence from Claude, for the time being, feeling secure in the knowledge that he could now leave the bemused Minister of Transport to his own devices.

In turn, that poor man was wondering whether or not to commit hara-kiri, but was also taking solace from the overwhelming public support he was receiving for making comments and decisions he was scarcely aware of.

Back in the comfort of his home, Thomas was feeling pleased with himself, increasingly pleased.

The following day, the newspapers were full of articles and pictures about the very public affray that Sunday morning, while Claude was frantically busy making arrangements to help start mass production of the potties.

"This is not good at all, for us," the PM was commenting to his own aides, while shaking his head and tutting. "Not good at all. I cannot see how these inflammatory remarks will benefit the party in the long run."

"Surely we will profit from the public support that the Minister of Trade is garnering?" his leading advisor protested. "He is at least prepared to stick his head above the parapet and take a moral stand on issues?"

The PM looked at him crossly. "Are you saying that I'm not? I didn't get where I am today without taking some risks, you know!"

The advisor replied tartly, "Yes, I remember when you were leader of the opposition and used to cycle through red lights, on your way to parliament."

The PM looked with disgust at his advisor's shoeless feet and retorted, "And you are still brave enough to risk treading on sharp objects."

They both thought independently, *"He's got to go; I've had enough of this feckless buffoon!"*

The advisor decided, on the spot, to proffer his resignation, citing overriding family commitments as his immediate priority.

The PM accepted huffily, feeling that a show of determination was an appropriate reaction to this 'declaration of intent'. What he had not yet realised was that, henceforth he would be surrounded by an elite circle of articulate, opinionated, inexperienced sycophants.

In contrast, at the pragmatic level of implementing these significant changes in society, the Chief Executive Officer (CEO) of The Ford Motor Company was responding by sending executives and engineers to South Essex and to Thomas's industrial unit in East Anglia. He was doing this in order to finalise emergency plans to restart volume production in ageing buildings, this time of the revolutionary new vehicle.

On the spur of the moment he decided to go along as well, feeling proud of the historical fact that the Ford Motor Company had been there with the model T Ford at the start of the motor era, and was going to be there at the start of another revolution in transport.

"How many did you say we've got to produce?" he asked incredulously.

"There's a baseline of some four million people using the Tube daily at rush hour, plus all those coming into London daily by bus, train and road." The local factory director confirmed. "We're talking big figures here."

"Jeez, that's one hell of a lot of people to cater for," the Ford CEO commented, wiping his forehead with his handkerchief.

"We might have to share production."

"We've got more than one bite at the cherry," the UK Factory Managing Director (MD) reminded him. "The Minister of Transport's going to phase in the introduction, so it won't all happen at once."

The Ford (UK) MD added to the conversation, "There've been big changes before in transport, like roads – I mean pavements - being asphalted for motor traffic, and dug up later for tram lines to be laid, then motorways being constructed. It just hasn't happened on this scale for some time."

"I hope this bunch is up for it!" the Ford CEO said drily.

They all looked at each other and grinned.

One conclusive edict issued by Claude was to arrange a date for the final train to run from Norwich to London, and its forthcoming replacement with a potty service. He was prepared to put his own job on the line by participating in the launch of the new vehicle.

Back in the industrial unit in East Anglia, Thomas and Bob were updating their project planning software to reflect the current status of potty production.

§ 11: The Big Adventure Is Underway

Sir Isaac Newton's Law states that, *"Light can only travel in a straight line."* However, in 1854, John Tyndall demonstrated to the Royal Society that light could be conducted through a curved stream of water, proving that a light signal could be bent.

It is also rumoured that a practical version of a fibre optic cable was based on an item retrieved from a crashed alien vessel as early as 1947. This adapted device allows light to be bent around a corner, which was a very useful invention for private detectives, and for snipers wishing to remain concealed (never mind the rifle itself; that was a separate problem).

The eminent Einstein later affirmed that, *"Nothing can travel faster than the speed of light."* which flew in the face of the fact that an interplanetary craft was approaching Planet Earth after it had left its home planet a few weeks earlier. This home planet was the twin star system of Zeta Reticuli, which is located a distance of some 39 light years from Planet Earth.

Since the speed of light has been accurately calculated at 300,000 kilometres per second this was clearly impossible, since it should have required unimaginable years to make the journey, given rational beliefs on potential travel speed. However, there it was, approaching Earth as clear as daylight (or more accurately, *spacelight*).

So clearly in fact that as the craft came into view it was being swiftly intercepted by the officially non-existent United States Spaceship *Constellation*; this is a member of the USA fleet that routinely patrols deep space immediately beyond the orbit of Planet Earth, to whose protection from extra-terrestrials it is devoted.

The cigar-shaped USS Constellation was dwarfed by the jet-black monolithic block of the alien craft, which was at least three times the size of a British football field, and was superficially recognisable by its power beams and navigation lights; there were no markings on it. Recognition between the two crafts was instantaneous, as the intruder was challenged as to its reasons for being there.

"This is the USS Constellation, this is the USS Constellation. You are approaching Planet Earth. Identify yourself."

A tinny voice was heard over the communication system, saying to the commander of the Constellation, "Greetings USS Constipation. This is Zeta Alpha from Zeta Reticuli. We are carrying a supply of emergency fuel for delivery to the Ford Motor Company in Great Britain. It is expected and we are on time. Zeta Beta is following."

The commander commented to his second-in-command, "That'll be to fill those potties they're developing. Notify Command Central and tell them they'll need two stealth stalkers; one to make sure they don't detour and steal any of our women or cattle; the other to make sure they're not intercepted by the Brits; we all know how trigger happy *they* can be."

He replied to Zeta Alpha, "Acknowledged. Have a nice day."

Zeta Alpha shot off in seconds, and descended through Earth's atmosphere. It was night-time in the county of Essex, in Great Britain, and the almost invisible craft hovered over its destination, the newly acquired factory premises belonging to the Ford Motor Company.

Contact was soon established with management representatives, who arranged for the precious silver-coloured liquid to be transferred in large, square flexible containers from the spacecraft to sealed rooms behind the potty production lines. The supply actually came from one of the moons within the Zeta star system, where it virtually covered the entire surface and was available in generous quantities.

Outside, on an adjoining circumference road, one of the occupants of a slowly moving car was shakily using a video camera to excitedly record what could barely be seen, stationary in the sky, which was a huge monolithic slab. The Polish youngsters in it could hardly believe what they were seeing and were jabbering away in their native tongue (Polski). Given their ages, nationality and high-pitched voices, they were wasting their time, since everyone who subsequently saw and heard the recording thought it was a typical hoax.

Inside the factory, a complex algorithm was being run on a special computer; this would dictate the number of potties to be produced, sub-divided into batches of one, two and four seater capacities, thus relieving management of blame apportionment should the numbers to be manufactured prove wrong.

Further south, near the English Channel, facilities were being setup to produce the potty-powered equivalent of school-run buses and local-delivery freight wagons. The first category was destined to get rid of the infamous rush-hour pile-ups caused by school-runs, when the kids in the UK were taken to and collected from their schools, often individually by their parents.

It was thought to be good to encourage children to mix socially outside school, supervised compulsorily by teachers, using potty-powered buses on a widespread basis. This would have the additional twin benefits of encouraging contagious germs to be shared, monitored and treated at early ages, as well as allowing unruly pupils' behaviour to be monitored and corrected as necessary.

Factory production lines were being equipped to assemble the new school buses, using existing single-decker coaches that were being taken off the roads in large numbers. They were of recent vintage and in decreasing use because of the potty invasion, and would be stripped of their seats, which would be replaced with standard bucket seats, padding and washable covers much like those installed in the potties.

The chassis were to be modified and the engines ripped out, for replacement with the same system as used in the potties, which contained no moving parts. The conventional shape of the buses would preclude them from taking full advantage of the mobility of the potties. It restricted them to floating just above the road surfaces without making actual contact, while the nozzles were positioned at each corner and along the sides. This controlled the vehicles, each of which would have a conductor on board to help teachers restore and maintain pupil discipline.

The exteriors of the buses would be painted a bright yellow, the same as those running conventionally in the USA, which Claude liked because it made them easily identifiable.

The second category, freight distribution, could be split into two sectors. Initially, bulk deliveries would be made to regions using monolithic slabs overflying areas at night in direct lines, where the visual impact would be negligible and the acoustic impact nil. The technology for this type of craft was totally different and required navigation of land, sea and outer space.

No one in authority was prepared to state the source of these craft, but the population suspected that they were alien in origin, having been seen in the skies at night for many years. It was strange that no one seemed to care, preferring to believe that their provision was made for good, neighbourly reasons.

Sea travel on its own was no longer a major contender, taking far too long and causing 'pinch point' congestion at ports that had to cater for the massive vessels in use. Also, the costs of shipment in fossil fuel were uneconomical, in comparison with the zero costs associated with the new type of transport.

At a regional level, freight wagons that had been commonly loaded onto lorries were being adapted. They were destined for the specialised distribution of goods to shops, supermarkets and businesses. This sector would require much smaller, diversified deliveries that local roads could cope with and sustain.

The wagons were being outfitted with simple but reinforced base connectors, which could be attached to independent chassis; these contained the same type of power source as the potties, connected to nozzles around the edges at pre-set intervals. In transit, they would guide themselves to their eventual destinations to be unloaded with minimal human intervention, before driving automatically to centralised parking zones, for future redeployment.

Naturally, as could be seen, none of these categories were the same shape as the laughably nicknamed *Potty*, but they did share the same type of power unit, which was where their commonality lay.

Back in their industrial unit in East Anglia, Thomas and Bob continued updating their project planning software to reflect the current status of potty production, whilst implementation of the project was being spearheaded in their region, from North Essex as far up as Lincolnshire.

In the test area, as the potties were rolled out and people took possession of them, they became a familiar sight everywhere, competing with and outperforming conventional traffic. Their superiority was so overwhelming that cars of all types and commercial vehicles became redundant, and were being scrapped even when relatively new.

Each potty was quickly found to have a unique personality, and endeared itself to the individual to whom it was allocated. As Bob had found out, when visiting the International Space Station, this trait was due to the biological chip at the heart of the control system; it would 'latch onto' the brainwaves of the passenger occupying it and speak' to him or her in familiar but obedient terms. If there was more than one occupant it would embrace them all.

It didn't matter which potty a person used, it became their personal confidante, servant and 'privy counsellor' for the duration of the journey. What no one seemed to appreciate was that in reality they were communicating with themselves, via the sophisticated computer chip that added its own logical reasoning to the mental conversation.

As a result, passengers became fond of this extension to their own personalities, and often gave it a nickname like 'Mr Chips' (derived from an ancient film about a school teacher of that name), or 'Miss Chips, 'Chippy', 'Chirpy' (a pet bird), or whatever else took their fancy.

As a precautionary measure, potties were checked before passengers left any traces of chewing gum, or corrosive substances, or scratches made on surfaces, or graffiti was applied met with temporary detention of the culprit whilst seated. This was followed by a possible fine, a ban of uncertain duration, or remedial counselling.

Afterwards, deep cleaning in the local storage chamber made them all appear to be absolutely clean. The biological chip itself was never wiped clean before a new occupant had been selected and the new, overriding identity was established at time of delivery.

The first trial in the East Anglia region was announced as being a smooth transition from one method of transport to another, although it was admitted that 'some misfits had tried to cause mayhem and instigate minor rebellions in key areas. The police had always intervened and detained the offenders before arranging for them to be sentenced in court.'

In culmination of this first phase, the last train from sleepy Norwich made a slow, uninterrupted journey into London. It was a non-event in reality, except for the posse of cameramen, journalists and TV announcers awaiting its arrival at Liverpool Street Station. This was being beamed to a live audience of many millions watching at home, and the related articles would appear in the later editions of the national press. Other countries too were watching events unfold with interest, seeing that they might be affected similarly.

The significance of this final, regional rail journey could hardly be lost on the TV viewers, since there was only one vintage carriage harnessed to an ultra-modern engine, containing dignitaries including the Mayor of London who was waving heartily to all and sundry.

Those passengers who would normally have been routinely occupying the original coaches trailed behind the shortened, token train in their individual one or two seater potties, and flitted off to their ultimate destinations well before stopping at the station platform. In some cases, this would originally have involved onward journeys to the airports or other parts of the country.

As part of his contingency plan, the Minister of Transport, Claude Broadbent, had instructed the Rail Network Controller to leave the rail infrastructure intact for a few months, just in case... This controller was aware that he was presiding over a fast diminishing empire, and had long resigned himself to the fact that his job would disappear in the course of time.

Claude was beginning to prepare plans for the wholescale recycling of all that valuable metal between Norwich and Liverpool Street Station, and its replacement with a smooth coating of tarmac, plus sturdy foundations, naturally.

After all, he had longer term plans for the station and its approaches, and they did *not* include building more offices.

Likewise, he was receiving regular reports on potential obstructions over the main and secondary road arteries, and had instigated plans to re-route or remove them, before the use of potties became widespread. Bridges were a more serious hindrance, and were going to have to be replaced with well-lit and drained tunnels, and visually covered with security cameras for an instant response to graffiti artists.

Claude had plans to seal the tunnels off in the event of damage by vandals, to capture the little devils in 'flagranti delicto', or *in the act*, so to speak.

That would give him great, personal satisfaction; not on the same scale as Gloria did, but nevertheless...

"Hi Ho Hi Ho,
As off to work we go!"
Thomas was loudly singing that annoying tune again, which he felt was childish. Simultaneously, in his own office in London, Claude was humming it without feeling any such inhibition. Suddenly, startling both men, the phone rang in unison in both locations. They each answered it absent-mindedly, but sprang to attention when they realised it was the PM, demanding to speak to both of them on a conference call.

Immediately, it occurred to Thomas that he was still occupying Claude's sub-consciousness, as they both answered in unison with a crisp, matching, "Yes sir?" which caught the PM off-guard.

"Pardon?" he asked, pointlessly.

"Yes *Sir?*" Claude repeated, while Thomas kept quiet and released his mental connection with the Minister of Transport.

"Hmmm, there must be an echo on the line," the PM commented. He was suspicious of Claude, not having believed him capable of achieving as much as he already had in his handling of the 'Potty' crisis. "I only want to check things **are** going alright," he said emphatically. It was the third time that day the PM had called, and he was clearly getting twitchy. "There's a lot for the pair of you to do. Don't be afraid to ask for help!" he added in his high-pitched voice.

"I'll tell you what I'll do, sir," said Thomas, intervening to put words in Claude's opening mouth. "I'll send you a copy of the very specific project plan we've prepared for implementation of phases one and two; these will show itemised current and estimated progress for the next few years, as the traditional type of transport is phased out and its replacement is implemented. I don't think we've missed a thing, as you'll see. We'll keep you posted throughout, and would welcome your input."

"That would be *excellent!*" the PM said, sounding enthusiastic.

Thomas thought privately, "*That'll keep the prat off our backs for the foreseeable future! There are hundreds of pages for him and his acolytes to wade through. Regular updates as we dynamically alter a few, key tasks will help keep his nose to the grindstone. What's the point of fretting about things that you can't possibly control? I'll bet none of them have even seen a detailed project plan!*"

"Thanks, I look forward to receiving the needed documents!" enthused the PM, wondering at the level and extent of the paperwork about to descend on him.

Moving across to his computer, Thomas selected and downloaded electronic copies of the bulk of the project files across the internet to the PM's office. Then he did the same for Claude, who would clearly need all the help that he could get, from himself, *Thomas*, considering what to do from within.

He knew full well that all of the recipients would be struggling to absorb the knowledge contained therein, and mischievously prepared a technical synopsis, which should flummox them entirely. After showing it to Bob, they enjoyed a chuckle before it was sent on its way an hour later.

Taking a step back and assessing what the near-future held for him, Thomas believed that he had bought some valuable time, which would allow him and Bob to concentrate on current matters without serious interruption. One secondary task he also performed was to penetrate Claude's mind, embedding in it the conviction that he was the author of all this output.

Claude too was delighted with his progress, and was busy refining his plan to extend potty usage to the rest of the rail network. His initial success had been declared as totally effective, and his next targeted area was the South East running out of Waterloo. Or would it be the Kent network and Victoria Station and London Bridge? He felt that he was spoilt rotten for choice!

Then he reminded himself to take care. "I mustn't get too ambitious. Production's got to keep up or it'll get out of hand!"

Back in the industrial unit in East Anglia, Thomas and Bob continued updating their project planning software to reflect the current status.

§ 12: The Haves And The Have-nots

Although the first stage of implementation of the rival system in East Anglia had been announced as being a fairly smooth transition from one method of transport to another, the truth was less palatable and had been suppressed from national publication. This was to avoid possible, growing widespread alarm and protests in the rest of the country. The actual situation occurred as follows.

Locally, groups opposing the new system grew alarmingly in numbers, especially amongst young, impoverished adults. These were way down the pecking order of prospective renters of potties. Presumably, they were often dependent on their parents for financial support, and were probably at university or getting their feet on the first rung of low-paid employment. Anyway, most of them could only afford 'old bangers' to drive around in.

The political acumen of the brightest sparks in this age group took little time in proving itself, as they began manifesting their presence in memorable ways. For starters, they divided the population into two groups: the 'Haves' and the 'Have-nots', and you can guess which category they fell into.

Thus, Claude and his supporters had to keep the 'Haves' happy and the envious 'Have-nots' appeased, as far as was possible. The problem was that the latter had modelled their campaign on the apparel worn by the Ku Klux Klan (or KKK). But, rather than wear tall coned hats and robes they chose clothes that were symbolically appropriate to their immediate cause.

"Oh no!" Claude groaned, when first shown picture of what the younger, deprived people had chosen to represent their militant cause. "This is getting ridiculous!"

The Have-nots had chosen to wear outsized, silver bowler hats on their heads, which extended down to the bridges of their noses. Above the small, outside rims (*representing the potty flange, perhaps?*) were cut almond-shaped eye-holes (*representing aliens?*) so they could see where they were headed. This outlandish headwear was wedged in position by being a tight fit at the sides.

Someone said to Claude and the others, "The French call the bowler hat a *Melon*!" and the others around him laughed. An intelligence officer seconded to Claude confirmed that this was what the 'Have-nots' called them too, and they were happy to be referred to as '*melon heads*'.

Claude noticed in some of the early riot scenes, relayed to him as they happened, that the alleged ringleaders wore their 'melons' at a rakish angle, sloping backward and resting on the nape of the neck. He asked his aides, "I suppose they've got a supporting skull cap inside, to avoid sweating when wearing these ridiculous things?" They nodded in agreement.

That was not the end of it. Regardless of gender, they were also wearing tight fitting round-necked collarless shiny silver suits, with the sleeves and drain-pipe trousers at least a few inches too short, showing bright red shirts and socks under them.

"*Is the red for anger?*" Claude wondered.

"The last time I saw anything quite like this was in the 1960s!" Claude said, with grim amusement.

"Yes," one of his aides spoke up, "It brings to mind the film, *Clockwork Orange* by Stanley Kubrick."

"I had in mind those four lads, *The Beatles*," Claude replied, feeling annoyed. The last thing he wanted to be reminded of was that seriously anarchic masterpiece, set to Beethoven's classical music.

"But look what's on their feet!" another aided exclaimed.

The others looked closely and noticed the thick crepe soled blue suede shoes they were wearing, each adorned on top with a cluster of three little bells.

"What's the weird footwear all about?" he asked the others around him, looking bewildered. "Do the bells represent Faith, Hope and Charity?"

The sound track provided the answer. Before the would-be anarchists had even come into view, the sound of squelching from the thick crepe soles and tinkling of bells could be heard approaching. Claude felt a shiver as he heard these sounds, and realized how effective they might prove to be, in subtly intimidating the 'Haves', let alone the riot police he had thought of employing.

"Nice touch!" one of the aides commented in admiration.

"Yes, far better than getting into trouble by using metal-capped Doc Martin boots!" another agreed. "I'd like to see the police arresting someone for having those bells on their tootsies, and sponges on their feet. They could hardly give anyone a good kicking with those on!"

Claude felt that overwhelming response needed, to be put in place, and ordered an immediate ban on people wearing this type of clothing. In addition, he ordered that transmissions be monitored to prevent organized gatherings of the Have-nots.

Finally, he ordered GCHQ to impose a regional block on all cell phones, where protestors might communicate activities using key words, such as 'Haves', 'Have-nots', 'Melons', 'Bowlers, 'Potties' and similar contentious expressions. He wanted to bar this for a short while, or at least until the situation could be brought under control.

"Futile? Maybe," he confided to one senior aide. "But not if we act quickly!"

When this approach started succeeding, the 'Have-nots' retaliated by dispersing and singling out individual 'Haves' for rough justice, by threatening them as they got on or off their potties.

On these occasions, the 'Have-nots' were easily identified, since there were cameras all over the place and they would get picked-up if wearing their distinctive clothes or any form of disguise. Better still, the police started using their own unmarked potties to swoop in seconds and detain the transgressors.

What the 'Have-nots' had failed to anticipate was the response of the potty itself; this temporarily assumed the identity of the current or most recent occupant (or occupants, if there were more than one), and added its own superior logic to defend whoever used it.

In one menacing situation, the potty intervened by retracting one of its struts and thumped it down hard on the assailant's foot, which it fractured in the process. It would not release the overweight thug until the police arrived and arrested him.

In a random attack, a potty came back to the assistance of its previous female passenger, after it had already gone to its local storage chamber upon completion of the rental period. It shone a traction beam on the gang of 'Have-nots', suspended them aloft, and only released them when the police arrived to make arrests.

A third incident caught Claude's attention and amused him immensely. The UK's foreign consulate in Jamaica had received a visit from an irate 'Have-not' supporter, who alleged that he had been abducted by a potty that flew all the way there, to a country where he had no ancestry and had never visited before. No one ever got to the bottom of that one!

Another case was certainly an over-reaction; a group of belligerent 'Have-not' youngsters ended up being dumped inside a secure establishment for the criminally insane, and it took ages to extricate them from the clutches of the wardens, who accused them of deliberately breaching security.

To Claude's relief, with the helpful support of their parents the majority of 'Have-nots' were tamed, and the threat of nationwide insurrection receded. It had been a close call, but common sense had prevailed. Now, the neglected interests of this deprived sector of the population had to be considered and steps taken to cater for those at the start of their adult lives.

There was a personal element to this regional trial; it was in the epicentre of the area where Thomas Beckon, was living. His home was near the industrial unit where the revolutionary new craft, the Potty, had been developed. It was where he and Pat had brought up their two daughters and, for a period, his delightful granddaughter, Rose.

To his eternal regret, it was also where he had neglected their lives while he pursued his ambitions over the years, using Claude Broadbent as a puppet.

Thomas had enjoyed his partnership with Julie, his younger daughter, when they built up the garment factory. He had seen her reap the benefits, with Pat, of a flourishing family business and was glad that they were secure.

What filled him with greater remorse was his failure to act as a caring grandfather after Julie got married and had three children, two boys and a girl. The fact that she wasn't considered to be part of his daily life can be evidenced from his failure to mention her in his highly secret, coded biography, which was stored in a theft-proof vault in Hatton Garden, London.

Even more reprehensible was his neglect of Sharon, his older daughter, and he couldn't believe how well Pat had shouldered the responsibility of maintaining contact with the family, when he had been utterly neglectful. How she must have suffered while he was behaving so selfishly!

Sharon had always been independent, and he had been glad of it once, but it hurt him deep inside to wake up to the fact that lost, loving relationships could never be rekindled if the kindling wasn't there in the first place. Like the mythical, immortal wandering Jew, Buttadaeus, he was doomed to roam the Earth alone, unless he revealed his true identity.

"Easier said than done!" he mused, fearing the consequences of his true self becoming general knowledge.

It was too late to do anything to remedy the situation, and he realized that Sharon probably figured as one of the 'Have-nots' in the scheme of things. He belatedly remembered that she had married a man several years older than herself, who had been a successful player in the second-hand car market before the potties got going.

Thoughtlessly, he had dealt a deathblow to that precarious way of earning a living and wanted to make amends, anonymously. The questions to be resolved were: how to do it and where is she now?

He called a senior, trusted bodyguard over, gave him a verbal profile of Sharon Beckon, his daughter, in fond terms, and urged him to help find her urgently and report back, before turning his attention back to the ongoing project.

The man looked at Thomas, crouching in front of his computer, and thought, "*You poor demented man. She's clearly dear to you, and all you do is focus on work!*"

Without wasting any time, he phoned a pal of his, briefed him, and carried on guarding Thomas. The man he had spoken to was, by chance, Claude's intelligence officer, whose secret service credentials were impeccable. Within two hours this contact had the requested information at his fingertips, and relayed a full, dictated report back using a secure email service, ready to be printed.

Thomas was pleasantly surprised to have the report placed in front of him by his bodyguard so quickly, and complimented him on his promptness, saying, "Thank you Russell, you never cease to amaze me!" It was expressions of unsolicited gratitude like this that endeared Thomas to his staff.

He relaxed in his high-backed swivel chair and studied its contents with eagerness. In summary, he read that Sharon and her husband, David Duke, had taken out a loan of a few thousand pounds on their business, and sold all but one of their remaining stock of cars to eager competitors. Additionally, they disposed of the equipment that they used to repair and maintain the cars they had bought at auction, plus passed on ownership of their lucrative website as an incentive to the purchaser for a good price.

"*That's not a bad haul, in total, I should think,*" Thomas conjectured. He checked the website and was impressed, commenting, "*It bears the hallmarks of Sharon's marketing expertise.*"

Reading on, he confirmed his worst fear; in the body of the report lay the sentence, 'They helped themselves to the one remaining vehicle, a gas-guzzling four wheel drive Hyundai Santa Fe, sold it for cash to a trader near London Heathrow Airport, and flew to Miami.'

It concluded, 'Before they left, they notified Sharon's daughter, Rose Beckon, that they were leaving the country to start up a business in the USA and would let her know their permanent address when they settled down.'

Thomas noted the address given for Rose, and the name and address of the loan provider, before passing the report back to Russell, and instructed him, "Please confirm the amount borrowed and pay it back if necessary; we don't want the innocent purchaser to face a hidden burden! Also trace any other amounts that may be outstanding by using Experian and settle them too, on my behalf. Thanks for all you've done!"

After that long day spent mainly on the nitty gritty of potty logistics, Thomas went home and ate with Pat. He asked her, over the meal table, why she had not spoken to him about his failure to spend time with his family. She looked at him with tears brimming in her eyes and replied, "It has been obvious for ages that you are on a mission and cannot afford to be distracted. I have tried and tried to get your attention, but gave up long ago. What's done cannot be undone!"

She rushed out of the room crying, leaving Thomas feeling a deep sense of gloom. Perhaps he, The Inlooker, needed to change into a person who looked outwards as well? He found her sitting on chair upstairs in the master bedroom, dabbing her eyes with a tissue and asked guiltily, "Can I see some recent family photos, please?"

She stared at him stonily, as he shifted like a little boy from one leg to the other. She half expected him to scratch his head, as a naughty boy might do, and he did so unwittingly. With a sad smile, she got up, searched in her wardrobe for a photo album and passed it to him. They sat together on the edge of the bed, while she showed him his neglected grandchildren and told him what they were doing now, as he nodded and studied them with apparent interest.

"Will you go the rest of the way and follow it up?" she asked herself. *"I can only hope."*

When told about Rose, he asked plaintively, "What degree is she studying for?

"Oh Tommy!" Pat replied, showing her exasperation, "She passed with honours in Graphic Design, don't you remember?"

He shook his head vaguely, trying to recall his movements. "I must have been abroad, on a business trip."

"You were," she confirmed, "But I did inform you."

"In that case, let's have a fresh start. Can you arrange for us to meet her? Is she living near here?"

"I'll phone and invite her to visit us. I've no doubt she'll be surprised."

"To change the subject, were you aware that Sharon and her husband have moved abroad?"

"Yes, to America."

"And have gone missing?"

"No, that's news to me!"

"I'll no doubt find out more tomorrow. I've got someone who's an expert in doing this type of thing and I'll let you know."

The following day, he was sitting in front of his computer when Russell interrupted him. "I've got some news on the movements of the missing couple, Sharon and David. They were arrested after jumping off a slow moving freight train at a level crossing outside the town of Tehachapi, which is located in the Tehachapi Mountains between Bakersfield and Mojave in Kern County, California.

"They were behaving like hoboes, and were provisionally charged with vagrancy. A few hours later they were released, having proven that they had adequate funds in Citibank. They insisted that they were simply enjoying life travelling as 'free spirits' while they looked for a business opportunity.

"The following evening, the last person to see them was a man living in isolated woods, going by the name of Zak Romsey. He's still at this address." He handed a slip of paper to Thomas, who checked it and replied, "You and me are going to pay him a visit. We'll leave work early, say at 4pm. There's no need to pack."

They sat next to each other on their two seater potty, and Thomas mentally gave it the destination coordinates. Immediately, it took off at top speed to travel direct to the shack that the newly discovered witness lived in, some 5,5000 miles distance in a direct line. It took just over ¾ of an hour for them to get there and land nearby.

Zak had been told by Thomas to expect them, and he stood outside his log cabin, cradling a shotgun.

Thomas felt no fear, having disabled the man's ability to shoot anyone and strode up to him, with Russell close to his side, ready to shield him with his body if Zak raised his rifle.

"Hi!" he said, keeping his distance. Zak looked back at him with indifference. "We understand that you saw two people here in the woods, some years ago?"

"Yup," Zak replied. "A man and a woman. They'd been sleeping rough, I suppose. Saw 'em being pulled up into a craft like yours, in a beam of light. They was fast asleep."

"Was this the woman?" Thomas asked, showing him a photo of his daughter.

"Yup."

"How'd you know for sure?"

"Seen her earlier, wearing the same clothes as when she went up."

"Was this the man?" Thomas asked, showing him David Duke's photo.

"Yup. Same man for sure. The pair of 'em was abducted."

"Did you see who did it?"

Nope. Guessed they was aliens."

"Why didn't you shoot at the craft they were dragged into?"

"Didn't want it coming after me! The dog stayed indoors. Scared shitless it was."

"Okay, thanks for the time." Thomas said, feeling despondent and they both left Zak standing alone.

After they took off, Thomas said, "Now comes the hard part – finding them! It's not going to be easy, and I've got to break the news to Pat."

Pat behaved calmly when told about their daughter's abduction, saying, "I've got full confidence in you Thomas and I know you'll leave no stone unturned in your search for her and her husband."

They both knew it would take time to resolve.

The meeting with Rose was cordial, although she started of being frosty with Thomas until he asked bluntly, "How much debt did you accumulate at University?"

He didn't flinch when she told them both.

"Your bank details haven't changed?" he asked her.

"No."

"I'll get the money to you with the next two hours." Pat gave his arm a squeeze in gratitude.

"What exactly are you doing now, for a living?"

"I'm in catering," she said, her enthusiasm showing as she brightened up, now that her debt was no longer hanging over her head like a black cloud.

"I did waitressing part time, but nothing else came along in spite of my best efforts. I was so good at it that the owner of the country pub and restaurant I was working in gave me a chance to be a trainee manager."

"So you liked it and were good at it, this catering thing?"

"Yes!" she replied starting to bubble. "I can't believe you're paying my debt off!"

They talked some more, with Rose showing an appealing side to her character and Pat watching them both with deep affection.

Thomas concluded by reassuring his granddaughter, "Well, we've all go to eat, so it's the right trade to get into and manage! No doubt you'll be fast tracked with your degree, so get stuck in. Talking about getting stuck in, it's time to start tucking into some food. You can tell Pat if she's doing things wrong! Let's go into the dining room and I'll tell you afterwards some things you ought to know about your mum – if you don't already know them!"

He was obliquely referring to her mother's initial disappearance and subsequent abduction, and didn't relish the prospect of upsetting his granddaughter so soon in their resurrected relationship. However, it might soften the blow if he revealed his talents as The Inlooker, once she became aware that he had special skills to bring to the interplanetary search.

Sometime soon, he had to start settling matters with his younger daughter and her family.

§ 13: The Master Plan Takes Shape

Being a visionary with a view of what was best for the country in terms of its transport policy, Thomas could see clearly what was going to happen in general to the road and rail systems at the next level down, and fed his view as the 'puppet master' to Claude, thereby reinforcing his understanding.

Over the next few years, the railways would disappear entirely, and their tracks and power lines would be pulled up and torn down, and replaced with endlessly streaming potties running over smoothly laid laneways.

There would be no gaps between regular, scheduled services, only potties conveying people uninterrupted between sources and destinations, with no changeovers needed during their seamless journeys. It was taken for granted that the colourful mixtures of current vehicle designs and sizes would be relegated to history, along with personal vanity, as economies of scale overpowered individual preferences.

If the purpose of travel was to get from point A to point B with the minimum of fuss, bother and cost, then what was about to happen everywhere would be an outright winner in effectiveness and convenience.

Not only were the railways becoming increasingly obsolescent, but the roads were also going to change out of recognition. Traffic density would be increased as potties could travel at much higher speeds, closer together and, in many situations, in several lanes one above the other in total safety. Tunnels too would be better utilised, as potties took to the air and flew above them whenever they filled to capacity.

Claude had realised that the countryside would begin to look more scenically attractive as electricity pylons were dismantled and taken away. These eyesores would not be needed by the national grid, as the source of potty power was going to be used to provide the majority of the needs of the population at household and manufacturing points of use.

Air travel was also within the gambit of the ministry of transport and he was beginning to take an interest in its future, perhaps prematurely but always optimistically. He had started with redefining the parallel movement of freight into and around the country, and this was leading him into pastures new, as he considered what could be done to also accommodate airline passengers in the new infrastructure.

There was one major question to be addressed, which was not within the remit of the Ministry of Transport: what was to be done with all those workers who would no longer be required in the transport and power industries, and their supporting networks of suppliers? Inevitably, redundancies were rising and it was feared that idle hands would find mischief.

Emigration was evidently not a solution either, as the same scenario would arise in other countries over the course of time.

Claude was aware, with Thomas's prompting, that current and previous governments had already embarked on a scheme of 'dumbing down' the expectations of families, by forcing those made redundant to accept lower-paid and often part-time jobs whether they wanted them or not. It was a fact of life which people had been accepting for years, encouraged to an extent by immigration from poorer countries.

It had become the norm for families to expect to derive incomes from all the adults within it. This was about to be changed by the powers that be, who realised that only one full-time income should be counted for statistical purposes. Only more than one should be included if part-time work had been accepted by other family members. This was a return to the 1950s, where needs were much more modest.

Benefits paid and fast becoming unaffordable to the country were also being savagely cut, putting a direct strain on the decreasing number of large families in existence. In effect, a form of voluntary birth control was in place, thus forcing prudence on men and women of child-bearing age. This was a fact, and people were being expected to make do with less of an income than had been paid out to them willy-nilly in years gone by.

At a global level, as the population level continued to rise inexorably for a while, there was talk about expansion to other planets, but this prospect filled Thomas Beckon (and therefore Claude too) with dread. If mass emigration became a reality, who and what would people find elsewhere? He already suspected that he knew the answer, having contacted and had meetings with extra-terrestrials, and the greetings that humans could expect to receive were unlikely to be cordial.

No, the government was on the right course, but Thomas feared that the pace of progress in eventual global population reduction was not fast enough, so he might have to accelerate it. There were various means by which they could achieve this, and it would ultimately be down to people like him to choose and implement one that was the least disruptive.

Claude's unofficial objective, with elected officials like himself, was to reduce the overall number on Planet Earth *by three and a half billion in total.* He wanted to achieve this without inducing apparently natural catastrophes like tsunamis, super-volcanic eruptions, asteroid collisions or contagious infections like the Black Death plagues that recurred in many centuries, or the 1918 influenza epidemic.

Interestingly enough, in early 2013 a meteorite weighing an estimated 10,000 tons and the potential impact force of 30 Hiroshima atomic bombs was intercepted by an unidentified object over the Ural Mountains in Russia.

This object was seen to zap it with a powerful ray that made it disintegrate before it crashed.

This interception by unknown charitable beings was reported in many newspapers and captured on camera. Some authorities believed that the meteorite's original trajectory was diverted to hit Earth by hostile aliens, who want to prevent humans from spreading into their extraterrestrial domains.

Whether or not all or any of this was true, what was comforting was the belief in the existence of an external force, which was equally intent on preventing mankind being plunged into years of traumatic climate change, food shortages and unpleasantly induced falls in population levels.

Back in the comfort of his own home, Thomas added a separate, confidential element to the project planning software, to reflect the tasks associated with population control.

This had nothing to do with Claude's role.

Claude certainly had the bit between his teeth! *Seemingly* independent of Thomas, he had boldly decided to go where no other Minister of Transport had gone before, and was considering the future of air transport in a new light.

In a rare moment of inspiration, he had conceived taking the advances gained in potty technology to a new height. They were going to plaster the skies as well as the ground; one potty had even skimmed the waves of the English Channel, and achieved the distinction of taking its two occupants to a business meeting in the La Défense arrondissement in Paris, France. It was a first for the Guinness Book of Records!

Applying pure logic to the situation, the question he asked himself (apart from, "*Why am I here?*") was: "*Why do we need these vast conurbations called Airports?*" With a frisson of excitement, he wondered what purpose they now served.

When all was said and done, they were a pain in the arse to get to and from; took hours to board the planes and nearly as long to disembark from them. They were cramped inside the planes for all bar the ultra-expensive seats; the food was crap; airport facilities were crowded and over-priced (water was a rip-off at all service outlets in an airport), and some of the operators and ground staff were plain rude and aggressive.

Overall, Claude considered it a most unpleasant travelling experience, and he, the right honourable Claude Broadbent, had a solution. The idea had been taking shape in his head for some time, and was based on his fresh revolutions in the freight industry and the mass transit of school pupils. Now, he planned tackling the conventional aircraft industry as well. No doubt it would give the PM the vapours, but it was worth doing for that devilish reason alone.

His informal analysis led him to the inevitable conclusion that there was no reason for the potties to remain small. After all, he had been to the ancient Roman city of Ephesus in Turkey, and seen first-hand the public toilets there, where people sat cheek by cheek next to one another, totally unshielded, openly performing their ablutions.

In all fairness, it was not a true analogy, since the modern *potty* was not in fact a *crapper* (the name derived from one of its original inventors), but a *method of transport!* However, the same principle applied; he was stating that a *Potty could be designed for multiple occupancy!* Hence, it could transport many people if so desired.

It could also be used in much smaller open places, like the disused and now redundant ex-railway stations in very convenient metropolitan areas like cities and towns. This line of thought had also inspired him to 'think outside the pot', so to speak, and his idea (or was it Thomas's?) had been well received by Thomas, Bob, and the Ford Motor Company executives.

The principle had been accepted for a pioneering big potty to be produced, which would carry up to twenty people long distances internationally. The idea of providing anything with greater capacity had been poo-pooed, since it was accepted that the existing small potty was so fast and adaptable that it was capable of international travel as it stood, without modification, for extended families. Claude had been pleasantly surprised at this revelation.

Another question that arose was why would anyone want to transfer from one potty to another during the course of a journey if they didn't need to? It would be a backward step as far as many people were concerned, *unless* it was for inter-planetary use, or was earmarked for the international travelling entourage of various heads of state, such as the President of the USA in a fresh style of aircraft, routinely renamed *Air Force One*.

Claude mulled over the thought, *"Perhaps it could be renamed Air Force Potty One, at some time in the future?"* without realising the negative impact this might have on the main passenger sitting on it.

Claude would have been even more surprised if he had known that the big potty was already a fait accompli, being in regular use between planets in star systems like Zeta Reticuli.

All that had to be done was to rip out the existing seats and replace them with appropriately-sized ones capable of accommodating bigger human arses and longer legs. As it turned out, the aliens would be happy to refurbish and offload some of their ageing fleet in trade swaps. As things stood, they were doing a roaring trade in substance extraction from Planet Earth and its orbiting moon. Besides, these larger vehicles showed no obvious signs of their true age.

Of course, in common with many projects, this one failed initially due to a silly oversight; not only were human legs longer, but the bodies were too! The decision was therefore taken to separate the top and bottom halves, by adding an extra upright section between them.

This would provide the essential extra headroom by one metre, with the curved panel between the two halves separated by two, matching flanges instead of one.

By chance, one enterprising sponsor who saw the finished potty, thought the time was ripe to indulge in advertising, and seized the moment to display a moving *Coca Cola* sign on the central panel, for a trial period.

As anticipated by Bob, this failed dismally during its first space flight, as cosmic dust and debris scoured the metal surface clean of all such embellishments.

Months later, the capabilities of the larger potties, which were once prized as rare sightings of *flying saucers*, were openly visible, as they occasionally soared heavenwards from disused railway stations, before tilting in a set direction and shooting off at abrupt angles towards it. Some wags were rechristening the revitalised stations as *Potty Parks*, which appealed to the gathered onlookers, who loved to watch the 'blasts-off' as they occurred.

For them it was a phenomenal treat, almost like train-spotting but without the identification marks being visible. After a period of contentious debate and much to Claude's relief, these larger craft were within a whisker of being given official authorisation for regular flights from built-up metropolitan areas.

What the general public wasn't aware of was the destination of the majority of the larger potties: it was the moon, where a base had been built on the dark side, near established alien structures.

However, these were early days in the implementation of the new technology, and the more mundane task of covering the rest of the country with normally sized potties had yet to be completed.

At the bottom end of the spectrum, the potential capabilities of the much smaller, original potty had unexpectedly been brought into focus. In accordance with projected needs, these were being produced in varying sizes, capable of holding one, two or four people. Passengers could rent the larger versions for short periods, as the need for them arose at weekends and for vacations, with pro rata additional rental charges being incurred for the periods hired.

One enterprising family consisting of two adults and two children asked if they could rent a four-seater potty for their fortnight's summer holiday in Turkey. Thomas, Bob and the Ford Motor Company executives agreed to this request, set an economical hire rate for the holiday duration, and gave the go-ahead to the delighted parents.

In fact, Thomas decided to pay personal attention to this family's experience on arriving in Turkey, and spiritually visited them at the Hotel Senator to see how they coped. Events are related as follows:

Within minutes of Thomas's spiritual arrival, on cue a glowing silvery oval-shaped object touched-down in the park behind the hotel, noiselessly landing on the central gravel-covered area and raising a cloud of dust around, as it settled on its four newly redesigned, sturdy padded legs. It was about the size of a medium family car and seamless, with no markings on it. Within minutes, the sound of sirens could be heard from the front of the hotel.

One of the few guests in the dining room joined the invisible Thomas in peering out of the nearest windows and enthused to the woman with him, "My oh my, it's all happening tonight! That's either a UFO or one of those *Personal Official Transport* vehicles that are now commonplace in the UK!"

"You mean *POTTIES*, as they're commonly called?" his assumed wife said, sitting opposite with a wry expression.

"It looks more like a giant *egg* than a *potty*. A *potty* is commonly placed under a bed, for peeing in!" the male guest patiently replied, knowing that his darling wife was trying to goad him.

As if by magic, a door-seam emerged on the nearside of the egg, the door appeared and slid fully back and a male occupant in his forties got out. They could see his wife (or female partner) sitting on the other front, bucket seat and two young teenagers sitting in the back.

A posse of Turkish policemen dressed in combat gear emerged from the darkness and surrounded them, as searchlights were switched on; these were focused on the craft, dazzling the occupants and man, who all shielded their eyes.

The male guest speculated, "They want some IDs or proof of identities, and to know where they're from and what they're doing here. All standard stuff!"

The man had now been joined by the woman, and the couple were pulling documents from their shoulder bags and pointing at the children in the back of the potty, while explaining things to the policemen.

"Everything has been resolved," the male guest said to his wife, merely confirming what was obvious, as the policemen nodded, walked away and turned off the searchlights. This left the glowing *potty* in the centre of the park, with the four previous occupants collecting their luggage and walking toward the hotel.

"Come on!" The male guest urged his wife, and they both polished-off their brandies to make a beeline to the hotel foyer. "Let's see what's going on!"

When they arrived, with Thomas's spirit following, it was to see the family gathered around the reception desk. Thomas, who had razor-sharp awareness, could hear what was being said.

"Yes," the male occupant of the potty was saying to the receptionist. "This document is proof of my visa payments for the family. It was done by inter-bank transfer in the UK, so we didn't have to queue because we came direct here and *not* by the main airport. Good, isn't it? No more waiting at airports, but by direct flight door-to-door and all done in *minutes* I tell you! Good. Isn't it?"

He was enthusing, and the receptionist was looking baffled by it all, this new type of travel that was going to become commonplace.

He stated to the newly arrived tourists, "You'll have to leave your craft where it is, in the park; we don't have anywhere else you can park it around here, apart from the roof."

The man replied, "That's okay. It would normally return to our home country automatically. However, we've paid extra to use it for the rest of our holiday. Good isn't it?"

The receptionist looked doubtful; he could see a crowd growing outside to look at this curious machine.

The male guest whispered to his wife, "I want some of that, the next time we come here! No more farting around at airports, no more hours spent cooped-up in airborne cattle trucks, no more queueing for customs and visas, no more driving miles. Let the machines sort out all the problems, including what we can and cannot transport between countries. Incredible!"

"What about terrorism?" the wife asked him. She was vainly trying to squash his optimism.

"It will be prevented, and then eradicated," he replied firmly. "First of all, security will be tighter than a duck's arse, and we all know that's watertight! Then, all types of violent extremism will be *bred* out of us, over generations as our numbers are decreased."

"What do you mean, *decreased*?" she asked him.

"There are too many people in the world. We've got to reduce our numbers *significantly*, and I hope its going to be painless!"

He concluded. "It's just my humble opinion though!"

The message was being spread, and it gladdened Thomas to hear it.

Later that evening, while the two guests were sitting near the bar enjoying a nightcap, a Turkish boy with his face and tee shirt covered in paint splashes was dragged to the reception desk by a very angry older man, who began remonstrating with the receptionist.

He had a loud verbal exchange with man behind the desk, who picked up the phone and threatened to call the 'polis'; Thomas recognised the word as referring to the *police*. The irate father waved his fist angrily, cuffed the teenager on the ear and marched him away shouting.

The male guest went to the desk and asked, "What was all that about?" the receptionist smiled, shrugged his shoulders and explained. "The boy tried to spray graffiti on that flying machine parked outside, and it sprayed it back over him!"

He chuckled and went back to his wife, to tell her what had happened. He thought that the craft was protected with a layer of some plasma-like substance that repelled the attack.

"Oh, the wonders of modern science!" he commented, as they both laughed, before going up to their room.

Thomas's spirit left them in peace, satisfied to have witnessed this ground-breaking experience of a potty in use internationally.

Thomas, Bob and the Ford executives also considered the likelihood of others submitting similar requests, and began planning their restrictions on potential usage. Initially, these would cater for daily foreign use during the holiday period instead of car hire, compliance with UK customs regulations on return, compliance with visa requirements in places like Turkey, and limitations on landing locations imposed by other host nations.

Finally they had to detect the smuggling of people and products; this was considered to be the easiest task to perform, with the sophisticated on-board computer equipment installed in each potty.

On their return from their vacation in the sun, the lucky holiday makers were in raptures. They reported their experiences to the inquisitive newspapers, which had been notified in advance by Claude.

"No more queuing, no more waiting around for hours, no more separation from our luggage!" enthused the husband, who was bubbling with joy.

"Yes, no more silly flight times, no more huge prices to pay!" gushed the wife, who reflected further and qualified this statement by adding, "Except at the hotel, but we can go further afield and pay less!"

The advantages of travelling door to door became immediately apparent to the public, who wanted to seize the chance to bypass the airports, and hopefully go direct to their chosen destinations in minutes rather than hours.

The clamour for similar availability from other potty users may have been immediate, but Claude preached restraint until supply could meet demand. At last, the potty was irrefutably a success and was being welcomed with open arms.

Back in the industrial unit in East Anglia, Thomas and Bob continued updating their project planning software to reflect the additional elements that would enhance the changes in transport policy.

§ 14: Living In Parallel Worlds

As of now, the most pressing dilemma making Claude's cogs click (that is to say, making *his brain work*) was the temporary overlap between the parallel uses of conventional traffic and the superior potties, in large conurbations. He was a veritable whirl of frantic mental activity, as he tried to reconcile irreconcilable demands. Whilst the potties were more than capable of handling travel situations with instant agility as they occurred, the same was not true of fallible human beings driving around in a bewildering array of normal vehicles.

Many drivers were complaining that they found it unnerving to see the new potties darting in and out of their fields of vision at different heights, especially when it happened at close quarters. One minute they were being tailgated, the next these damned things were shooting overhead or diving in front of them.

"Most upsetting it is!" was the common complaint, which had to be formally reported when the number of accidents began to rise substantially, as people were distracted by these rapid potty movements.

It was reaching a frequency where insurance premiums in a number of the capital's congested suburbs also started to rise substantially, and a condition known as *Jessy* sprung into existence; this was the loose acronym popularly used to describe *Jerky Swivelling Eyesight*, where the sufferers developed rapidly rotating, uncontrollable eye movements that affected their ability to drive.

Adverts began to appear on billboards and on the sides of buses asking, *'Are you a Jessy?'* and giving a brief description of the condition, with a contact number for a clinic that could remedy the problem, for a steep price.

In response, after consultation, further legislation was proposed by the Ministry of Transport to levy a charge on the accident-free potties, hence appeasing the conventional vehicle drivers. This led to howls of protest from the innocent potty users, who felt they were being victimised.

Claude reconsidered his ill-advised knee-jerk reaction, put the impending legislation on ice, and decided that he had to separate the two types of transport once and for all. The question was: how best to do it? In the end, he found himself devising a medley of punitive measures.

The first decision was to severely curtail access by normal vehicles to designated inner zones. Residents would be forced to dispose of their normal vehicles, and hire the much more economical potties for all their regular uses (pun not intended). Luckily, the price was so low that it was an affordable option and there was no outcry.

The second decision was to phase out the permitted lifespan of *all* normal vehicles to a maximum of seven years; this would apply *countrywide*. This met with bitter recriminations from the owners of 'old bangers', and from manufacturers who had strategically sited their operations in the UK.

However, other countries had already introduced similar legislation, and the government remained firm in its intentions of enabling this law, come what may. Claude was glad that it was the PM who would have to bear the brunt of the political lobbying that would ensue, since he didn't like to be subject to outside coercion.

The third decision was to toughen-up the MOT test requirements on second-hand vehicles, making it more difficult and expensive to get roadworthy certificates for them. Cap in hand with this went the intention to prohibit unqualified mechanics from performing maintenance and repairs on any vehicles. This was greeted with praise from the general public, who were suffering a spate of accidents involving unroadworthy vehicles, and had the knock-on effect of prematurely getting old bangers off the roads post-haste.

Finally, Claude wanted to introduce a nationwide *Driver's Bond* costing several hundred pounds, which individuals would have to pay in cash from the time that they passed their driving test. This was to prove their financial viability to be able to afford to run a vehicle, and would only be refundable when their period of eligibility as a driver expired.

Claude expected to be hung from the nearest lamppost when this raft of measures was announced, but far from it; they were debated and broadly welcomed as sensible, whether potties were in local use or not. His popularity soared again, and a large number of immigrants, legal and otherwise, headed back to their countries of origin at a rate of knots and without bribery, being rendered immobile.

Within twelve months of the hotly contested legislative powers being introduced, the original plan to reduce the volume of existing, conventional traffic had been spectacularly successful. After overcoming these obstacles to progress, the potties were being introduced to other major cities and towns at an increasing pace, as the volume of the previous generations of vehicles fell dramatically.

Regardless of what was happening at a global level, Claude was made fully aware by other leading governments of the importance of his country's attempts to contribute to the overall solution of the problem of population control.

He simply *had* to focus on resolving this problem in his nation, where he was going to be a trail blazer. He would also be setting a precedent to officials who were reluctant to act, in other parts of the world. He had begun achieving this by setting a roadmap for the future, coincidentally emphasising the burden being placed on those with genuine jobs by those without meaningful employment.

As he cut a swathe through whole divisions of long-established industries, emphasis was shifting to re-employment in the burgeoning leisure sector that more people were being given the time to enjoy. What he was also mindful of was the need to balance imports and exports, and re-establish the home-production of many goods that were currently produced abroad. The country *had* to become self-sufficient and balance its books, and was getting competitive as wages and salaries were reduced to rival those of Asian countries.

The difficulty facing Claude, as Thomas was aware, was that these considerations were, strictly speaking, not part of Claude's brief and he was annoying his colleagues by his constant, witless interference in their portfolios. Sooner rather than later, dramatic action would have to be taken to extend Claude's scope and authority, master-minded surreptitiously by Thomas.

Meanwhile, Claude was on cloud nine as his intervention in the airport and airlines industries was further helping to reduce the flow of passengers that they were already experiencing. The budget airlines were going bust as their margins of profitability went into the red, and airport operators were discussing possible handing over their facilities and huge open space to housing developers and leisure providers.

Irrespective of the situation that the airports faced, one change that Claude made was to enforce standardization of the size of suitcase that aircraft were allowed to carry in their holds.

"One size fits all!" he shouted in parliament, to cheers from luggage handles at all the airports, watching the debate live on television. "I don't want to see any more passengers trying to lift an enormous trunk that really belongs to an elephant!"

Besides which, no more public debates would take place on the possibility of adding more runways to increase airport capacity, that was for sure.

The degree of visible overlap between potties and conventional craft was not as prominent in the air as the problem had been on the ground, since the altitudes and technologies used were sufficient to keep them apart during flight. No special legislation had to be introduced, although frequent attempts were made to tax the potties and raise much needed extra revenue to fill the empty public coffers.

"We must learn to live within our means!" Claude and the PM thundered at various times at the spendthrift parliamentarians across the floor of the house, and sometimes glaring meaningfully at the filled benches behind them.

An increasing cause of heated debate in cabinet meetings was the frequency with which civil servants and regional officials were allowed to keep their jobs after they no longer had anything to do, while tax-paying workers in the private sector were being made redundant across the board.

When it suited them, the politicians were turning a blind eye to the consequences of the reductions in employment on some of their favoured subordinates. This was at the expense of others who they didn't know, and Claude felt that this was obscene. However, his complaints about this manifest unfairness were regularly dismissed by his colleagues, who loftily described his views as, "inconsequential, irregular, and outside your sphere of influence."

Thomas would withdraw his spiritual self from Claude's body after some cabinet meetings and angrily confide to Bob, "They're doing it because it's cheaper to keep these so-called servants in their jobs, doing nothing, than it would be to get rid of them! They've got a bloody cheek! These silly bloody politicians forget whose paying *their* salaries!"

Bob once asked him, "Why doesn't your Prime Minister intervene and order his ministers to act?"

Thomas replied, "I suspect he's thick himself!" Bob raised his eyebrows, so Thomas explained, "I read in the newspapers some years back that he was bottom of his class in school, and seeing how he acts at times I believe he's incapable of making decisions without someone telling him what its best to do.

"Time will tell!"

Under advice from the team of 'logistical thinkers' he had assembled around him, as hand-picked aides, the PM was considering moving Claude to the post of Home Secretary, thus placing him in a position where he could more efficiently tackle the problems he was creating, vis-à-vis unemployment. It would mean promotion, and supposedly give him the chance to achieve a lot more.

The bright sparks who had thought up the idea considered it to be quite a wheeze, and were hopeful that the PM would fall for it, which he did much to their glee.

The current Home Secretary would have to be offered something worthwhile in compensation, since she was also doing far too well and could present a threat to the youthful PM himself if she stayed where *she* was.

No, there were far too many prospective high-fliers around for the PM's taste, though he rarely commented on personalities, as an old-fashioned toff. On the other hand, he did a fair bit of bad tempered effing and blinding, which spoilt the public persona he liked to portray when some disloyal aide chose to spill the beans on him.

After lending considerable attention to the matter, it was privately broached with Claude by the PM, who addressed him in glowing terms before making him the offer. Left to his own devices, Claude would probably have replied starchily, "I may be green but I'm not a cabbage!" He might less eloquently have said, "I may be daft but I'm not stupid!" which would have equally startled the PM.

In the event, under Thomas's guidance, he replied frostily, "Thank you very much, but I must decline. There are things that I started which need to be completed, and it would be premature for me to leave my office before then." He stood up and held out his hand to the astonished PM, who remained seated. He continued, "I presume you are willing to accept my forced resignation?"

"Good God, no!" the PM replied, in a strained voice. "What on earth makes you think that?"

Forcing a smile, Claude said, "Perhaps it was a misunderstanding. I'd prefer to say nothing more while I'm upset, so allow me to wish you good day," and he left the room meekly, quietly closing the door behind him whilst stifling a discernible sob.

The PM picked up the phone and spoke to his personal secretary. "He said no. That's mucked things up!" Part of Thomas's spirit had lingered behind after Claude left the room, and the meeting – plus this comment – had confirmed his worst impressions; the PM was more concerned with politicking than with matters of true importance to Planet Earth, and the germ of an idea was building in his mind.

He decided to leave Claude to his own devices for a while, and returned to his own recumbent body, laying reposed on the chaise longue in his study, which he would occupy for a short moment of contemplation before going to consult the trustworthy Bob.

By this time in their relationship, Bob, who was working nearby in the industrial unit, knew a lot about him and the way that he worked as The Inlooker. He could keep a secret; taking it to the grave if Thomas considered it necessary. He strode across to him, saying, "Bob, I have a matter of some delicacy to discuss with you."

"Don't tell me; it's to do with Claude!" he replied, with a knowing smile.

"Yes," Thomas confirmed. "I'm spending so much time guiding him in what he should say and do, that I'm hardly available for other matters."

"It *has* been noticed," Bob said drily. "And the next stage will be for you to do what precisely?"

"Occupy him totally, which was the last thing I wanted," Thomas said.

"You've gotta, or things could easily go off the rails!" Bob said, showing his concern. "What's one soul compared with choosing the billions who're gonna live?"

"Thanks for your support," said Thomas. "I'll try and do it for as short a period as possible. He does give me the impression at times that the lights are on, in his head, but there's no one at home. Let's discuss the nitty gritty, shall we?" The two went to the office next to the deserted production line, and formulated their strategy. In these matters, now that his influence was so powerful, Thomas felt more comfortable having a confidante who he knew to be an exceptionally gifted, cerebral man, rather than share his decisions with his immediate family; head had to rule heart in world matters.

It had been agreed that Thomas needed to end his spell as a relatively anonymous person, and try and enter the powerful cabal of leaders that dictated policy at a global level. Claude was becoming prominent in his present position, and it was decided to use his achievements as a springboard for getting into the true corridors of power. Unfortunately for Claude, he was not capable of exercising the imaginative skills that were needed, since they existed only in his invisible 'handler', who was Thomas.

Poor Claude was scarcely ever aware what was happening, since Thomas was dominating him for most of his waking time. He had the good fortune to be elected Minister of Transport when fate brought him into contact with Thomas, who unfortunately for him could be ruthless when necessary. It was exasperation with the nice Claude that made Thomas start to act ruthlessly when the success of his potty launch was threatened by the minister and his aides.

Thomas looked down at Claude as he lay there that dark night next to his beautiful wife, and pitied him for the life he was about to lose control over. He felt even more sorrow for his own predicament, for he knew in his soul that the exit from his own tired, ageing body would be permanent.

He felt compelled to use this unique, alternative method to hide his true identity, and to shield his activities from the glare of publicity. The last thing he wanted was to be revealed for what he was.

It was Bob who had gently pointed out to him the consequences of his soon to be executed mission, and had seen Thomas show compassion for the first time.

The man had matured since throttling that child murderer, although his thefts of money from wealthy citizens had left no scars on his soul.

Bob reckoned that was an okay state of mind to be in, for many successful men had done things in their earlier days of which they might feel ashamed. Flaws were built into the personalities of high achievers, or so it seemed, in compensation for their insatiable thirst for success.

Retiring to his own body for the final time, Thomas felt his vital organs weakening as his soul ebbed away, and was saying his goodbyes to himself when the door to his study opened. His wife Pat tip-toed in and stroked his brow tenderly, before realising with horror that he was knocking on death's door.

"Oh my God *no, no, no!*" she exclaimed repeatedly, collapsing onto her knees next to the chaise longue, crying inconsolably with her hands cupping his face.

"*Damn!*" he thought, feeling miserable, while searching for words. "Don't worry, my sweetheart," he consoled her. "We *will* be together I promise you."

Bob was framed in the doorway and came up to comfort her, placing his hands on her shoulders. He gave his buddy a wink, tears in his eyes, and said, "Just say goodbye to each other for now, and thank God for the length of time that you've already been together." He appreciated Bob coming at this last moment like he did, knowing that the poor man himself had buried his one and only wife some years ago.

"*Oh blow!*" cried Thomas, as he occupied Claude fully for the first time, without detecting a squeal of protest. For the first night in ages, Gloria was left undisturbed.

When Thomas got up in the night to have a wee, he felt wonderfully alive.

Not only had his aches and pains miraculously disappeared, especially in his lower back, left knee, right shoulder, and the arthritic bones above his big toes, but as a bonus he didn't actually need to urinate either!

To his surprise, he couldn't express the pain he felt at the loss of his lifelong companion, Pat. He hadn't expected to feel intense emotion and was consumed with regret.

§ 15: A Leap In The Dark

That very first morning after transferring from his previous body, Thomas resolved to refer to himself hereafter as *Claude Broadbent*, which was a bloody awful name with which to begin his new life. He considered briefly changing it back by deed poll to the classier-sounding *Thomas Beckon*, but knew that the significance of taking this action would be lost on the general public, as well as on the power brokers he needed to rub shoulders with. No, *Claude* bloody *Broadbent* it would have to be, with all its public fame. Ugh!

Gloria smilingly prepared him some monstrous concoction of a breakfast, with muesli and croissants, accompanied by multi-vitamin juice and decaffeinated coffee, and he vowed to change this routine as soon as possible. She was turning out to have an extremely agreeable nature when dealing with his morning grumpiness, and he felt his desire rise as she showed more thigh than he was used to, when she sat down opposite him. His fingers got all inky as he held his newspaper tighter than desired, debating whether to take her into the lounge for a quick one, or not.

She glanced at him as he sat there, looked at the tepee-style pyjama mound pushing against his dressing gown, and reached down to grasp it with a smile. He was led like a willing stallion through to the sofa where he performed instinctively and lustily, without inhibition after she loosened her hold.

Immediately he'd done it, he felt guilty as he remembered the way his wife Pat had acted when he was physically dying yesterday. At least, he hoped she wasn't playacting but was genuinely full of distress for his passing away unexpectedly like he had. He worried at the impact his death would have on his daughters, Sharon and Julie, who he also loved dearly.

For a moment he got indignant when he linked the words *Sharon* and *dearly* and remembered that she had borrowed 500 quid from him to have her car clutch repaired, and would probably conveniently forget to pay it back, if she was ever found. Greedy moo she was and no mistake, then he decided to let matters rest. After all, he had been and still was a wealthy man, and was a younger one now.

Besides, he had to find her first, but was confident in his ability to do so. For some inexplicable reason, he knew she was still alive.

At their latest, hastily convened one-to-one meeting a few days after offering Claude a switch in ministerial roles, the PM was commiserating with him. "It's perfectly understandable for you to be late," he was saying. "You have my deepest condolences for the, tragic loss of your, um, colleague, Thomas Beckham. Incredibly sudden and unexpected it was, quite incredible."

"It's *Beckon*, Prime Minister, Thomas *Beckon*, *not* Beckham," Claude replied frostily, also disliking the repetitive use of the word *incredible* that the PM was renowned for.

"Oh, sorry!" replied the PM, not sounding the slightest bit abashed by his faux pas. "I'll be attending the funeral myself," he added, sounding like he was making a concession with his valuable time.

Neither Claude nor Thomas had taken kindly to the Prime Minister's previous job offer, not in the slightest, although now that Claude's soul had been submerged by Thomas's, his views were no longer relevant. However, Thomas had to answer as if he were Claude, who had caught all the media attention for his apparent exploits with the innovative transport policy.

"Of course, naturally. You're welcome to attend," Claude agreed, in an off-handed manner; the PM was never one to miss a photo-shoot opportunity.

"Moving on to other matters," the PM continued brusquely, shuffling some papers and pretending to look at them. "We'd still like you to take charge of the Home Secretary's portfolio, if you'd be so kind. It *is* a promotion you know!"

"I'll bet!" Claude thought, keeping this view to himself. *"He's trying to force me into it!"*

The PM and his closest supporters were going through a bad patch politically, with mystery deepening over his true intentions towards the European Union, and his official commitments to immigration, the Human Relations Act, and an abundance of other contentious issues. Many of his parliamentarian colleagues couldn't decide if he was an enigma or simply empty-headed. When all was said and done, the school he had attended as a boy had a reputation for being able to teach a monkey to speak, if it so chose.

Claude pondered the best way to reply, took a deep, career-dependent, breath, and launched his campaign. "I'm afraid I still cannot accept your offer," he began. "I must advise you, Prime Minister, of my intention to resign as Minister of Transport after a short period for you to find a replacement. I have unequivocal proof of your office politicking at my expense, and I am not prepared to be undermined in any way whatsoever."

The PM's head sprang up angrily, his face turning purple as he looked Claude directly in the eye and shouted at him indignantly, "What proof?" He used a foul expletive in the process, realising at that instant that Claude was not for turning and had become openly, dangerously defiant to his leadership. He added with a hiss, "How dare you!"

Calmly, Claude stated that, "Proof will be forthcoming if you continue on your present course." He was bluffing from a position of strength, knowing what the PM had said during a phone call he had made to a person unknown, after his previous meeting; he had been there in spirit and listening to it. The risk now was that the PM could decide to play dirty and go as far as planting listening devices on Claude, to get him arrested, or conjure up some other underhanded ploy.

The PM clammed up like an oyster, determined not to give his adversary any more ammunitions to use against him. He asked himself, *"What's a man got to do, to avoid getting hammered these days? Hell's teeth, is the newspaper industry after me too? Is this in revenge for the string of official inquiries we've held? Is no conversation private anymore? Who can I trust? Is nothing sacred?"*

Out loud, he asked Claude with a level voice, "Might I ask what your intentions are, once you leave office?"

Claude replied, "I am setting up a new party. It will be called *The ODD Folk*. Its principal aim is to seek *On Demand Democracy*, hence its initials, *ODD*. Here is my letter of resignation."

Without elaboration, he placed a sealed envelope in front of the PM, and looked at him with a mixture of disdain and pity. It was a key moment between them, as Claude, true identity Thomas Beckon, surreptitiously took control of the PM's brain and vital organs.

Unaware of this, the PM tried to mouth a sarcastic comment, but found himself speaking unintelligible gibberish. At the same time, his right hand, which had been resting in front of him on his desk, fell to his side and was flopping back and forth; he had lost control of his arm and was trying to shake it with his shoulder muscles, to no avail.

To his mounting panic, he was also developing a pounding headache and had to close his eyes, rubbing them to ease the pressure with his left hand. When he opened his eyes tentatively, he had lost central vision in his right eye and could only see what was happening at the outer rim of it. He could still see clearly with his left eye, which was a relief.

Claude knew what was happening (since he'd induced these health scares), and strode briskly to the door; opening it, he said to the PM's male secretary, "Call a doctor immediately. I think the PM's having a stroke!"

Walking back to the PM in order to comfort the poor man, he whispered to him, "Don't worry, you'll soon be okay. It looks like you've had a mini stroke, or *TIA*. I'll check on you later."

The stricken PM looked back at him gratefully, the side of his head resting on the desktop, and managed to say, "Thankths!" as his speech started to return.

Later that day, the rumour mills started rolling, as newspapers and TV channels headlined the demise of the Prime Minister. Captions appeared like, 'PM stroked in his office!' and 'PM Saved by Santa Claude!'

and 'PM Saved by the Potty Prince!' as the papers vied with each other to attract more readers.

Later still, unauthorised leaks began to appear, after it was claimed that, "The Minister of Transport, Claude Broadbent, is going to resign from the Government, after claiming to suffer bureaucratic interference from unnamed officials." A spokesman for the Minister of Trade neither confirmed nor denied the truth of these 'spurious' rumours, claiming that they were unfounded.

The issue became further confusing as the Prime Minister's supporters tried to put a positive spin on events. They muddied the political waters by issuing reassurances that the Government was still on course with its policies, and that nothing untoward was occurring. They were fond of repeatedly proclaiming, "The PM is suffering from a minor health problem, but it is only temporary." This was hardly a fair description, since the PM was sucking liquidised food through a straw.

Much later on, it seemed that a full picture of the true events was emerging. A health update was issued by the PM's spokesman, stating that, "He is recovering in hospital from a mini-stroke, which he suffered during his meeting with Claude Broadbent. During this meeting, the Minister of Transport's resignation had been proffered, and was accepted with considerable reluctance. It is considered that this may have been a contributory factor to the stroke."

The frankness of the statement caused gasps of amazement from many people, and was suspected to have been phrased in this way to attract sympathy for the PM from the voting public. It was also designed to counteract the favourable impression that Claude had created with his prompt action to save the PM's life. Now, he was being portrayed as the villain in this modern soap saga.

Claude's spokesman retaliated by briefing senior commentators that, "It is true that the emergence of a new political force of some substance is in the offing. This was one of reasons for the meeting between the Minister of Transport and the Prime Minister, who reacted with undue hostility to the news."

He added, "In view of the deterioration in the PM's health, Claude Broadbent has decided that his resignation should be postponed so that proper stability of government can be restored." Commentators remarked on the use of the word *restored*, instead of *maintained*, indicating that stability had effectively been lost, and that Claude was the man to '*steady the ship and get it back on course*'.

Claude was approached by a number of his fellow Members of Parliament, who offered him their support, if he should care to stand as leader of the party; this was in view of questions being increasingly asked over the PMs continuing poor state of health.

Claude was advised that according to party rules, if 15% of the MPs in their party write a letter to the Chairman of the 1922 Committee expressing no confidence in their leader, this would invoke a formal vote to determine the degree of confidence in him. That venerable committee is the backbenchers own 'Trade Union'. In that vote, if more than half the backbenchers express no confidence, the leader would be 'out on his ear' and a new leadership election would have to be held.

Claude duly agreed to this process being initiated and began attending a series of high profile meetings with his fellow parliamentarians, to get their necessary backing. This was subsequently achieved, with significant support being conveyed for Claude's motion.

The jockeying for position got into full swing, with various rival factions throwing their hats in the ring in the pending leadership battle. However, Claude was widely regarded as the most likely person to succeed the present incumbent.

After a few weeks, the voting procedure started, for and against the motion. The votes were counted with mounting excitement, and an announcement of the result promptly followed. This confirmed that the no-confidence motion had been carried. To no one's surprise, it was by a big majority.

The announcement met with a roar of approval from the assembled party members.

They had expressed their disfavour with the present Prime Minister, who was still not present in the House.

The election process was underway, and his potty partner, 'Call me Bob' privately confided in Claude his opinion that, "You will go all the way to the top job. The other candidates are what you call 'stalking horses'. It's *you* they truly want to lead them!" He was of course speaking to *Thomas*, the dominant, spiritual occupant of poor Claude.

The day itself was a rousing endorsement of Claude Broadbent and his outstanding, unbroken record of achievements. Hopefully gone were the previous incumbent's days of double-dealing and subterfuge, plotting behind closed doors with a chosen callow few, and the daily use of ripe language – in private, naturally.

Claude had no record of bad behaviour and was a 'man of the people'. If they had known him better, they would have labelled him as a schizophrenic, but that was not quite true either. He *was* two people rolled into one, and that was an undisputable fact.

The voting public would be considerably better off with *Thomas Beckon,* who they didn't know at all, except as the inventor of the flying potty. Claude was now part of him, albeit totally submissive to his spirit.

This was an exciting, pivotal moment for Claude; he was standing on the threshold of the power he needed to achieve. It was the first rung of his ascendency to his ultimate target, global domination. How he played this game as a newcomer would determine if he succeeded, so he needed to tread cautiously but bravely.

These realisations were speeding through his mind and needed to be dampened, or he could easily be derailed.

"Calm down, breathe easily and count between breaths!" he told himself, and felt a sense of tranquillity coursing through his veins.

He sat back in his chair, and encouraged his spirit to soar upwards, in search of a destination that gave him the peace that he needed at that moment.

His immediate choice was Thomas Beckon's home, which he entered unseen. It was deserted downstairs, but he paused to look around, and enjoy the comforts of its familiar furniture and the tick of the mantel clock above the fireplace.

Oh, how he yearned for that place and all that it contained! He remembered how he, in Thomas's body, and Pat had sheltered their placid younger daughter Julie during her formative years. They had also temporarily put a roof over the heads of older daughter

Sharon and granddaughter Rose and he remembered that period with fondness.

All of the youngsters had now grown up and departed, but the first company he had founded was still providing Pat and Julie with a regular income. All future enquiries would have to be done discreetly though, given his new identity.

As an afterthought, he floated outside and went into the garden shed. Peering into the secret area in the concrete floor, he could see the metal container where he had stacked his ill-gotten gains. It was still there, and looking as shiny as ever. This was all the confirmation that he need that the family business was in a healthy condition.

He floated back into the house and went upstairs in the conventional way, by the stairs, to access the main bedroom. Pat was laying on their queen-sized bed, slumbering. It was their tradition to have a siesta each afternoon, and she was having one now, so he lay down beside her, on the left side of the bed, and looked at her adoringly.

Soon, they were both asleep, and the time passed for Thomas in absolute bliss, with happy recollections flowing through his head. After a couple of hours, he woke up and stretched, to find the weight of Pat's left arm draped over his chest, with her snuggled up to him; it was as if he was physically present, and he found the situation mystifying.

"No, this cannot happen!" he decided, and took care to extricate himself before she woke up and became distressed. With a final, fond look at her and a delicate kiss on the cheek, he returned to his sanctum in London and settled down to resolve matters of state, feeling composed.

There was one primary matter that Claude first had to consider, and that was whether or not to soldier on as the unelected, de facto Prime Minister for the full term, or to hold a snap election and ensure his legitimacy for this prized post. He was mindful of Chancellor Browns' decision to accept the more senior role, which he had always coveted, without being officially elected, and the disastrous outcome that had followed.

In the event, he opted to place his fate in the hands of the electorate, without delay.

§ 16: The Leader Of The Pack

Claude's immense popularity in parliament and the adult population at large augured well for the future, and his (that is to say, *Thomas's*) enthusiasm as an imaginative reformer could not possibly be quenched. Now that he was the freshly-elected replacement Prime Minister, he was eligible to enter the corridors of global power that he had waited for so long. He was one of *the* emerging power brokers and would not be denied the opportunities to achieve changes that were within his grasp.

However, that was in the future, and he had important things to do in his own country before moving onto the world stage. The first was to introduce *proper* democracy, and dispense with the sorry substitute for it that the population had unwittingly endured up till now.

One thing had to be removed before everything else, and that was the existing, two-party structure, where each majority party took it in turns to rule, at the whim of a largely bipartisan population. It was a divisive split in voting intentions, and often bitter and confrontational.

Claude didn't want to change the current 'first past the post' voting method, oh no; that would be to the advantage of smaller parties, whose performances were lamentable and often irrelevant. The public at large had also come to the realisation that these 'sideshow minnows' were not 'up to the job of government'.

A 'hung' parliament would be to no one's advantage; these occurred in other countries, where vital decisions often depended on handfuls of elected MPs on the fringe of the main parties. In Claude's view, the complex voting procedures associated with hung parliaments, where governments were elected without having clear majorities, couldn't easily be understood, except by those who knew how to benefit from them.

The marginal MP's often held the balance of power in these circumstances, and radicals could hold sway. No, Claude didn't want to see frequent changes of government forced on the country by mavericks; he wanted to see stability. He wanted the British electorate to be brave and make clear choices of who they wanted to govern them.

In his opinion, the same applied to the USA where the upper and lower houses of Congress could countermand each other. No, Claude liked policies that were best for the country, irrespective of political dogmas, and convincingly backed by those who voted for their individual politicians. He didn't want tribal politics to continue in his country.

After a period of reflection on how best to introduce a true, stable democracy, he began sifting through the ranks of Members of Parliament (MPs) whose records of stated beliefs, objectives and voting records indicated that they shared common values in line with his own.

One of the few praiseworthy *ambitions* of the previous leader had been to propose a reduction in the number of sitting MPs by changing voting boundaries. This measure had been ditched, along with many others, for the sake of political accommodations with presumed allies. Faint heartedness had won the day, and Claude had no intention of making the same mistake again.

Claude commenced his reign by summoning MPs sympathetic to his core beliefs to his Outer Office, as he preferred to label it, in order to develop a rapport with them, his favoured 'troops'. Shrewdly, he was sounding them out, wanting to know if they would support his proposal to create a new party, and would join it in time for the next election.

On these occasions, he was subtle in the use of his powers of persuasion, and managed to spellbind the majority with his mental and oratory powers.

Perhaps the Inlooker was not much different to naturally talented leaders like Julius Caesar, who had charisma and magnetism in abundance. Perhaps he was not as unique as he believed himself to be!

Claude's self-belief was justified, as judged by many who got to know him, and his statements of intent were delivered with cold logic. He would sit alone in his freshly designated 'Inner Office', with no self-serving aides whispering in his ear, and formulate policy on his own. Afterwards, he would refine his ideas with people like Bob, and civil servants that he could trust to think clearly and without prejudice.

His government's manifesto, when completed, was to be delivered to a packed Chamber in the House of Commons, and would resonate around the country. Claude knew that he had to get it right, in a folksy sort of way.

On the day when it had finally been prepared, he stood up in the Chamber and announced without preamble,

"Shortly, we will dissolve parliament, and go back to the country and seek re-election. It is my intention to ask the population to not only vote us back into power, but also to replace the way this House operates with a new system of participation. Our desire is that it will truly represent a version of democracy that will prove to be infinitely better for our country."

This shocked many of the MPs, who had no idea beforehand of what he wanted to do.

Claude paused, to allow the Speaker of the house the opportunity to calm down the kerfuffle that ensued. When peace was restored, he continued addressing the MPs.

"This party of mine will henceforth be called *ODD*, which stands for *On Demand Democracy*. Its members will be called the *ODD Folk*, and they will **not** consider themselves to be *Right Wing, Left Wing, or Liberally Inclined*. The other parties can continue as they are, if they so wish, with their collective views, but *we* want nothing further to do with the rather silly antics performed up until now in this chamber.

"If you were to ask the general public what words they would use to describe our MPs, as I commissioned in a very recent poll, you would find words rolling off their tongues like *low achievers, self-indulgent, greedy, rowdy, time wasting, ignorant, freeloaders, lazy, preoccupied with expenses, not representing our views, and too many in number!*

"Granted, there are notable exceptions, but by far and away they have a bad impression of us in general. Do you notice the absence of positive attributes, in the way we are summed up?"

There were catcalls and shouts from many parts of the house as individual MPs stood up and jeered, while Claude, the new, acting Prime Minister, responded immediately and passionately.

He said, "Behaviour like yours supports these bad opinions, and it is simply *not good enough*. What I want to hear is the general public using words to describe you like, *wise, impartial, rational, objective, lucid, balanced in judgement, logical in thought, smart (in both wit and appearance), possessing a sense of priorities, well educated, well behaved, profound, experienced,* and so on.

"It is my intention to restructure this chamber so that seating is arranged on a horse-shoe basis, to help avoid the confrontations that occur here so regularly. However, that pales in comparison with my next proposal."

Those MP's who had been restless felt rebuked, and sat down while continuing to mutter loudly between themselves. A minority were furious with Claude, and knew that they could lose their parliamentary seats at the next election. They needed time to decide how best to react, and to gather support against these proposals.

However, they wanted to hear the PM what was going to announce in full, before taking any action.

Pausing while he referred to his next set of notes, Claude continued, "When I say *ODD*, I mean *ODD*. I want to explain what I mean by *Instant* or **On Demand Democracy**. When we vote in future, I want it to be done *electronically*. Most homes now have access to the web, or will do so shortly.

"It is possible for voters to select their desired candidates without having to go to polling stations, and to transmit their decisions *immediately*. Anyone who does not have access to a computer can attend an Internet Café, or go to their nearest community centre, or ask a friend or neighbour for access; the point I am making is that *no one has to wait!*

"Taking this to another level, I expect voters to engage with us in regular referendums, much like the

Swiss do, and I recommend taking their proven system as a model for ours.

"In *their* country, any citizen may challenge any law approved by their parliament or, at any time, submit a request for modification of the Constitution. However, unlike them, all *our* votes will be cast electronically and the results announced more or less simultaneously."

There was a murmur from the assembled MPs as this was announced, and Claude cleared his throat as he paused before continuing.

"More pertinently, I want MPs to take notice of the views of their local constituents *beforehand*, in consultation with them. Each of us *must* explain our voting intentions to the people we represent, in advance of any key vote, and *not* to our colleagues first of all.

"It is appropriate that this consultation between MPs and their constitutions be made via the internet, and advertised on local television and radio stations, in order to attract voter support.

"Once this has been achieved and discussed with our constituents, electronic votes will be submitted by the constituents to their MPs' offices, *and we will be expected to abide by the majority of the votes cast one way or another, regardless of our own inclinations.*"

There was a louder buzz from MPs as the import of this statement sunk in, with some barracking ensuing. En masse, they rose to their feet and waved their order papers (these listed the order of business on that day's parliamentary sitting)

The PM added, "Oh yes, and *the voters will be able get rid of you immediately, if you go against their wishes!"* That silenced the protestors, who reluctantly sat down.

The PM angrily shouted at them, "Yes, this means no more decisions about going to war without prior consultation with the voters! No more ignoring the electorate when they want to re-introduce the death penalty for heinous crimes, or to castrate sex offenders!"

This roused cheers from many of Claude's supporting MPs.

In a more subdued manner, Claude spoke again, "These measures have proven to be necessary for the sake of good governance, and I wish to invite those who support them to join me in forming the *ODD Folk's* party.

"We will be convening our first meeting in one of the rooms in Portcullis House. You will be directed to the exact location by my deputies waiting outside. You may come with me if you wish."

He nodded politely to the Speaker and left the Chamber, to sporadic clapping and some jeers from the benches opposite. A considerable number on the government benches got up as well and left hurriedly.

As he walked away, he said to one of his fellow MPs, "That'll be one role to disappear, when I get my own way!" He was referring to the Speaker, who many regarded as an odious man.

It was interesting to see who was filtering into the large meeting room chosen for the inaugural meeting of the *ODD Folk*. There was total support from the illustrious leaders of the old right wing of the party, who at one time or another had fallen out with and been ostracised by the previous PM.

The terms right-*wing* and left-*wing* are widely used in some countries like the United States but, as on the global level, there is no firm consensus about their meaning. Some see the *right* as the party sector associated with the interests of the upper or dominant classes, and the *left* as the sector of the lower economic or social classes. These terms originated in France, at the time of the French revolution against the King.

In the UK parliamentary system, it was noticeable that the *left* tended to come from poorer backgrounds, while the *right* had a more privileged upbringing. With some noticeable, often eccentric exceptions, the *left* had distinctive start-roots. There were fewer of these folk attending the inaugural meeting, which disappointed Claude, who wanted to attract support from all parts of the House. "*Never mind,*" he thought. "*In time, a better education will give us **all** the understanding we need to join a just cause.*"

Enthusiasm for the new party was vocally demonstrated at the meeting by the new intake of younger MPs, to whom it represented the opportunity to connect fully with their constituents. Claude confirmed one of his commitments to the restoration of true democracy, by stating to them:

"*When elected, we will define fair election boundaries, in order to give voters an equal opportunity to cast their votes. In recent years, the opposing major party deliberately created an inbuilt bias against us. At present, more votes are needed to elect a currently ruling party MP than an opposition MP.*

If any of the boundaries are changed thereafter, to seek an unfair advantage in the election process, criminal proceedings will be taken against the perpetrators."

Applications were soon passing around the assembled MPs for them to join the new party, which would be treated as pending, until the current parliament was dissolved in the months ahead.

Draft brochures were also distributed, containing promotional ideas for T-shirts and Posters, such as,

On *Demand* *Democracy – meet the ODD Folk!*
Don't **YOU** *want to be* **ODD***?*
Get **ODD** *get* **EVEN***!*
ODD *is* **BEST***!*
How **ODD** *are* **You***?* and
Keep a Rollin Rollin Rollin – **Rollin' Democracy***!*
Democracy On Demand, **On** *Demand* **Democracy***!*

And so it went on, with campaign managers seeking fresh ideas to get the bandwagon rolling.

Claude suggested various enhancements for them to debate openly, like the introduction of compulsory, registered voting as used in Australia. He also stated that voters should aspire to take standard examinations in Politics, with a *vote-if-you-pass* eligibility at the end of it. His expressed view was, *"Why should anyone have the automatic right to vote, if they don't know what they are voting for?"*

He also stated that he would ban any party from entering the political process whose stance was non-democratic, and which could lead to a one-party control of the nation. His view was, "That scenario would lead to the people being suppressed and led by well-armed gangs or extremists." No one had to look far to find examples of this type of behaviour in the world.

The time came for parliament to be dissolved, and it was now a matter of patiently waiting for the election to take place. Claude at least was feeling relaxed about matters, having done his best to succeed and being fatalistic by nature.

When they next met, his pal Bob took the opportunity to ask him, "Do you think it's worth it, improving democracy like you're doing, when the outlook for anyone's personal survival is so bleak?"

Claude replied firmly, "Yes, I do. The country *must* be in the best shape possible to deal with the future."

§ 17: Long Live The PM

The Prime Minister, in the guise of Claude Broadbent (who was actually *Thomas Beckon,* with Claude slumbering in the background), had sealed his victory at the ballot box, with an emphatic victory over his opponents. In modern society, this *ballot box* was a personal computer, which was displaying the votes as they were cast, like they were on a rolling drum.

He had intently watched the votes increasing in his favour, the screen images reflecting off his eyes. As the final results were announced he leapt into the air, punched upwards with one hand and exuberantly shouted, "Yes, Yes, Yes!"

When he had finished hugging his companions and shaking hands with everyone within reach, he gave a triumphant speech in front of the audience and cameras, thanking voters for their support and promising to do his best by working hard on their behalf.

Concluding by offering his condolences to his rivals, he retreated from the first floor balcony where he and his supporters and newly discovered relatives were standing, and went into a private room with them, to celebrate into the small hours.

The following morning, feeling invigorated and full of beans, Claude started work in his Inner Office. Assembled around him was a coterie of loyal senior ministers, plus the Cabinet Secretary, who was a civil servant; they were a small group of people, only interested in discussing one topic of ultimate importance.

This was prior to the anticipated reshuffle of ministerial posts. He has already told them what they would do in future, before he moved onto the specific topic to be broached. They all nodded in consent as he told them their roles, and no questions were asked.

He began by stating, "We have only one vital item on this agenda, and it is to reduce world population by half!"

There was a collective gasp from them at this bald statement, with some showing signs of despair. Claude ignored their reactions and continued, "I don't like it any more than you do, but it is imperative on us all to do what is necessary.

"Let me reassure you that it'll be as painless as possible. The details are going to be hammered out at a special conference with other world leaders; this will be held in two days' time and you will be accompany me."

"Are there any alternatives to this mass extermination?" the Home Secretary provocatively asked him.

"None at all," affirmed Claude, ignoring her phraseology. "If we do not start living well-within the natural means of this planet, we will be forced to overspill to other worlds. At some time, it will become inevitable that we engage in warfare with better-equipped, advanced alien races and we will be annihilated."

"Are you confirming that we've been in contact with aliens, in spite of repeated denials from government officials in the past?" asked the Secretary of State for Defence.

Claude replied, "Confidentially, yes. Where do you think we got the potty technology from? I'll give you another example you can look up for yourself."

"In 1947, Admiral Richard E. Byrd led 4,000 military troops from the U.S., Britain and Australia in a sea-borne fleet invasion of Antarctica called "Operation Highjump", and at least one follow-up expedition. It was seeking an alleged Nazi built base there. That is fact. It is undeniable.

"But... the part of the story that is seldom told, at least in 'official' circles, is that Byrd and his forces encountered heavy resistance to their Antarctic venture from 'flying saucers' and had to call off the invasion.

"They were fighting a foe that had the same superiority in combat as a modern frigate would have against the entire British fleet in the Napoleonic era."

He continued, "We must learn to live in harmony with ourselves and then with other races. It has to be understood that we're swamping Mother Earth with people, and are and extremely intolerant and violent race! This is in spite of everyone's best efforts to intervene and stop it."

"Who do you mean by everyone?" asked the Minister of Defence, pointedly.

"I include the aid charities in their efforts to provide essentials to other countries, and thus perpetuate the ongoing problem," the PM replied. "They are well-intentioned, but their approach does nothing to resolve the root cause of starvation, which is far too many children being brought into a world that cannot afford to feed them.

"I also mean those *alien races* who are sympathetic to our plight and try to intervene in an entirely different way, by using genetic engineering to stop the poor from propagating. Another benefit of their intervention will be the longer-term eradication of warlike tendencies that are inherent in our makeup."

No one seemed surprised at these declarations.

"Naturally, you need no reminder of our binding commitment to secrecy. Otherwise, there will be pandemonium on the streets, perhaps even rebellion." Claude looked into the eyes of each person, mentally reinforcing their determination to keep silent about what had been conveyed to them, especially by not telling members of their families and close confidantes."

He grinned as he added, "If you are interested, we will be travelling to the conference in a big potty. It is going to be held on the Moon."

After closing the meeting and bidding his companions farewell, Claude held another series of face to face meetings with individual MPs who were being invited to join his cabinet at various levels of seniority. He had known for a considerable time which ones he wanted as ministers and who to place in roles supporting them, and was universally pleased with their keen responses.

Following a short break for sandwiches, the newly appointed ministers assembled in the traditional Cabinet Room in Downing Street, and the ministers sat around the PM waiting for him to open proceedings.

Unusually, after welcoming them all, he handed around a list of *'Objectives To Be Achieved'*, as if they were working in an enterprise that he headed. This included tasks such as:

- *Boundary Changes to Constituencies* – schedule and implement in next 3 months:
- *Internet Connections* – define outstanding work; complete the network in 6 months;
- *Initiate availability of Potties* in all regions - produce schedule and complete in 12 months;

- *Freight Logistics Countrywide* – schedule and complete all aspects in 12 months;
- *Freight Logistics Local Dumps* (as they had been crudely labelled in the regions) – schedule and complete all aspects in 12 month;
- *Clear all overhead obstructions to potty movements* in each region – schedule and complete in 12 months;
- *School Buses* (or *Mini-Monster Movers* as they were popularly called) – schedule delivery and implementation in all regions over 24 months;
- *Normal Vehicles* (or *Gas Guzzlers*) – schedule removal and destruction over 48 months (or as quickly as possible);
- *Potty Lanes* (as the *Highways* were known) – schedule the levels at which potties can fly; define the guidance systems to keep them in their lanes; implement controls;
- *Work Redeployment* – create and schedule opportunities by sector; relate applicants to them by location; this is an ongoing task;
- *Taxation* – Re-investigate Estovian one-flat tax system, propose own version to Chancellor;
- *Local Authorities funding* – Investigate and calculate additional amount to add to income tax rate, assuming abolition of Council Tax; calculate staff savings by its removal; report to Chancellor;
- *Local Democracy (ODD)* – schedule and implement computer systems for regular consultation between MPs and their constituents over next 3 months;
- *Judiciary* – extend ODD (On Demand Democracy project) to consultation with voters on sentencing guidelines;

- *Quangos* – extend ODD to consultation with voters on their continuing existence;
- *Policing* - extend ODD to consultation with voters on the benefits of retaining Police Commissioners; Consult with voters on the future role of the police forces;
- *Armed Forces* - extend ODD to consultation with voters on their future roles and costs;
- *NHS* - extend ODD to consultation with voters on the extent of the services to be provided;
- *Media Services* (like newspaper groups) extend ODD to consultation with voters on their acceptable levels of intrusion;
- *Civil Service* – extend ODD to consultation with voters on their continuing ratio to the private sector, for acceptability;

Claude concluded by slapping his hands together and saying, "There, that wasn't too bad was it? It's obvious to me what belongs to which ministry to sort out, so I'd like you all to get cracking pronto! That should keep you busy for starters." He got up, wished them luck and departed.

Straight away, a number of computer specialists entered the room and were allocated to specific individuals, for them to be given training and continuing guidance in project management software.

It ought to be stressed that this was not required in all ministries, such as Work and Pensions, Education, Health, Defence and a few notable others, where the competence and political acumen of the ministers concerned was never in question. The PM was certainly blessed with a core of able people around him, as had been his predecessor.

Claude and his selected team were on their way to the moon! It was an excited group that made its way to the nearest *Potty Park* at Charing Cross and boarded the waiting large 'saucer' parked in one of its reserved bays. Underneath on its flat base, if anyone from the ground could have seen it, was painted the legend *UK Air Force One*, below a background representation of the Union Jack flag.

None of them had ever thought in a million years that they would be flying in a craft of this nature, and they looked around its smart, functional interior with a great deal of curiosity. Claude tried to act nonchalantly, as an example to the others, but his heart was racing like everyone else's.

They took off smoothly, the few of them feeling small in comparison with all the empty seats around, although they did have Claude's bodyguards as companions.

This same mercenary group had defected to him when that idiot of a Minister of Trade had arranged for them to assassinate Thomas.

Thomas had used his *powers of persuasion* to convince them that he and Claude were the same person rolled into one, so to speak. "No problem, Guv," one of them had said sniffily, feeling that he could afford to wait and find out if the new guy claiming to be Thomas was a loony. It took some believing when Claude tried to convince them that he was really Thomas Beckon, but they didn't care anyway, as long as they were treated well.

The journey itself was short, as they zoomed into overdrive without feeling anything to indicate the changes in velocity. The craft turned to orbit the Moon and silently flew over the dark side, which couldn't be seen from planet Earth.

After a few minutes, they approached the new, low-lying facilities secretly built there by human beings; these adjoined a much larger and taller cluster of skyscrapers presumably erected by aliens. Their craft descended towards the nearest building, which had a row of United Nations plastic flags outside, stretched stiffly in the moon's airless atmosphere, and floated gracefully into its custom-built airlock, where they waited patiently for the chamber to be pressurised and filled with breathable air.

When the inner door opened, the craft moved into a spacious inner hanger and descended to greet a welcoming committee, which included two small creatures that were clearly aliens.

After being led into a conference room that contained a big, highly-polished oval table and deep upholstered armchairs, they were introduced to the select group of already-seated world leaders. Everyone was behaving most amicably, and obviously felt privileged to be amongst this illustrious gathering of privileged power-brokers.

They too had all only just arrived, so this final group to join them had no need to apologise for their late entry.

After serving hot and cold drinks to the leaders, the serving staff retired and left the delegates alone, ready to discuss matters. The only item on the agenda was *Population Reduction* which needed no explanation, although the UN leader acting as chairman made a brave attempt at a polite preamble, and to Claude's surprise turned to him to open proceedings.

"Why me?" Claude wondered, initially sitting there with his mouth open, lost for words. One of the two aliens helped him out by saying in a high-pitched

voice, "Radical reforms have not gone unnoticed, in your island country. Neither has it gone unnoticed that someone amongst your people has developed a product called *The Tracer*, and it is this that we want *you* to develop as the means of reducing the level of population world-wide."

Partially distracted by the alien's diction, which was so good that he wondered if it and the previous prime minister had attended the same school, he only gradually became aware that the rest of the attendees were looking to him to *exterminate* half of mankind, as their chosen modern *executioner*!

Saying nothing, the stunned Claude sat there listening, as the other people around the table debated how best to do the dirty deed, and were actually horse-trading on behalf of their nations to get the best deal in terms of who would survive and who would be killed!

"*This is surreal!*" Claude thought, desperately calculating if he should join the melee, and wondering if he should restrict himself to representing Britain's best interests.

Suddenly he had a brainwave and stood up, sending his chair crashing backwards to the floor. He cried out, "Eureka! I have a solution!"

The hubbub stopped instantly, as he righted his chair, sat down again, and meekly said, "Sorry!" The same aide who had heard him make an almost identical exclamation ages ago said nothing, in case one of the aliens chose to zap him with a ray gun - if he had one (he dared not look under the table to find out).

Claude explained what could be done, "Let us round the total number of people to seven billion; let us assume that each couple gives birth to one child. Ergo, you have a fifty percent reduction in future population growth, starting in the current generation.

"Assuming that contagion is spread using *tracer*, this will reduce the present rate of fertility significantly, and will stabilize future fertility at a manageable low level forever, if reapplied regularly.

"The permanent reduction in population can be achieved in a period that is miniscule, in terms of the Geological Timescale! We don't have to kill anyone!"

The French president looked up at the ceiling, started to count on his fingers, shook his head, and ended up testing the figures using pen and paper. Meanwhile, the hubbub started again as everyone and their neighbour discuss the potential solution.

One of the aliens stared at Claude through his large almond-shaped eyes, blinked, and extended what looked like his thumb in the air; Claude couldn't make his mind up whether or not he was being intentionally rude by using this gesture.

At the end of the meeting, which didn't last much longer, the chairman expressed his thanks, stating that Claude's anonymous inventor would soon be the beneficiary of *biotechnological guidance in enhanced tracer fabrication.*

The other delegates also conceded that the final solution seemed potentially fair to all nations. Since the size ratio of every race would be maintained equitably under the suggested reduction, there would ultimately be no losers or winners.

The leaders of China, India and Russia warned the leader of the USA against trying to employ any dirty tricks, the implications of which he insisted mortally offended him. However, he did mention this attack on his integrity to his staff, in case they could come up with any useful ideas on how best to issue a rebuttal.

It would also give them the opportunity to think how best they could seize the moment to skew their population level and compete with China and India, whilst keeping faked records of the actual rate of reproduction.

The return journey to planet Earth was achieved in short time, with Claude and his retinue in high spirits, and he thought nostalgically of the family he had left behind. However, before deciding what he wanted to do about them, he had a more pressing matter to deal with.

Reluctantly, mankind had to be culled. When all was said and done, he didn't wish to be remembered in a bad light, leaving piles of corpses as his legacy. There had to be significant thought put into this.

§ 18: The Cull And Related Matters

Comparatively speaking, Claude's physical health had been transformed by his newly acquired youthfulness. Maybe *youthfulness* was the wrong word to use, but he *was* one hell of a lot younger than he had been when he was Thomas Beckon, in his previous incarnation.

He, Thomas in reality, was now able to put in longer hours in his newly installed laboratory, testing competing cocktails of bio-ingredients with tracer, in order to impede fertilization of the embryo in the human race. There was a professional team of qualified germ-warfare specialists to help him.

When developed, this routine would have to be repeated on a regular basis, for population reduction to be sustained, and be risk-free longer term in its ingestion.

Getting it right the first time was a prerequisite; he didn't want complications setting in, like the process becoming common knowledge and a witch-hunt ensuing.

The decision had been made for all governments to distribute eye-catching literature that would target the fertile population sectors, using similar methods to those employed by wartime propagandists.

This time, there would be no enemy territory to invade, only their own people to be infected.

Brochures that would spellbind adults had been designed, impregnated with tracer and other DNA related additives, to intrigue their recipients with a variety of arousing subjects like explicitly graphic safe-sex adverts, escort services laid bare, bondage illustrations and other such erotica.

It was a version of animal husbandry, except with devastating short-term consequences to the human sperm.

With government resources behind the deliveries, the distribution of the impregnated articles was not a problem. Sometimes it was to be made by air to remote villages (provided it didn't rain). At others, bundles were dropped at strategic points like newsagents or busy street corners, where the brochures would spread as the wind blew.

In all other cases, they would be left in cafés by burly men who the owners didn't like the look of, and in police stations, by the cell doors.

The fact that they were becoming litter was the subject of debate, and knowledge of their erotically stimulating contents became widespread.

As the brochures were read, tracer would enter the sub-conscious minds of the individuals, assess their ability to have sex and, where appropriate, let the 'ride-on' bio ingredients do their magic. Infected victims would pass their induced infertility onto others with whom they associated, and so the contagion would be spread.

It was like the black plague, but without the rats, fleas, nits, bad breath, groin boils and other unpleasant side-effects and calls to, 'Bring out your dead!'

From the heights of the Andes in South America to the deserts in Saudi Arabia, eager males were failing to impregnate relieved females as the effects took hold. When scientists began to report the mysterious failure of the human race, worldwide, to procreate in large numbers, newspapers 'scientifically' speculated on the causes of this calamity.

Everything from solar flares to climate change and nuclear energy were blamed, but the actual cause, which was a deliberate strategy put into effect by the world's governments under alien coercion, was never broached. Perhaps Uncle Sam was behind it, UFOlogists speculated, which was true, but this applied to everyone else in ultimate authority; so why single out your favourite uncle?

For Claude, it was vindication of his campaign, as the existence of tracer and its derivatives remained completely unnoticed. Behind the scenes, the support he was receiving from the others in the world corridors of power-brokers was emphatic; he had arrived and was now recognised as a major player.

This could do nothing but good, as potties spread their contents to all corners of Claude's increasingly magical United Kingdom. It was truly the place to be, with other countries sending delegations to see plans turning into reality, as transport was revolutionised and the countryside was transformed.

Everyone wanted a piece of the action, and Claude was now a billionaire from his potty movements, with earnings declared for tax purposes. After all, why shouldn't he declare them? It's better to have a rich man in control of anything, since he's hardly likely to want to fiddle the expenses, is he?

Thomas, masquerading as Claude, was now desperate to resolve the unfinished business with his family.

Thomas was beginning to ache for the companionship of his first love, Pat Beckon. That was not to say that he disliked his new partner, Gloria Broadbent, who was a magnificent but shallow example of womanhood; he wanted something more than a willing receptacle; he wanted to be able to talk to a woman on an equal basis, about matters generally, some of them profound.

With respect to Gloria, he couldn't make his mind up which of them was really the sex-doll in their relationship. They never did anything in their lives together other than eat, drink, perform and then talk about performing. No, that was not true; they also slept together, which took more time than when they were cohabiting, fully awake. He couldn't remember the last time that they'd conversed without grunts and compliments.

He had to admit it: he was missing Pat, and there was a hole in his heart where she used to be. She too had been a good performer when they were younger, perhaps not as innovative as Gloria but still memorable in more than only the one way.

On the spur of the moment, he sprung up from his chair, picked up his personal cell phone, and rang Pat's landline; when she answered he introduced himself as Claude.

"My oh my, it's the Prime Minister!" she exclaimed after a pause. "I recognise your voice!" The sound of her brought tears to his eyes.

"Yes indeed!" he replied. "Please call me Claude. I was wondering if you're free this evening?"

"Yes I am," she replied, cautiously.

"Could I come and see you?" he asked her.

"By all means!" she replied, asking, "With your wife?"

"No, alone. There are things I want to talk to you about that are personal," he said. "Shall we say seven thirty this evening?"

"Okay, it's a date!" she replied; he could almost see the smile in her voice, as he said, "Goodbye, for now."

Immediately after, he called a female secretary to order a mixed bouquet of flowers and box of Black Magic's traditionally-shaped dark chocolates, and told her where he was going that evening.

After showering and changing into casual clothes, at 7pm he walked unattended into the back garden of Number 10, and mounted the potty that he'd ordered, placing the flowers and chocolates on the rear luggage rack. After he fed the destination coordinates into the control panel, the potty closed its side door and took off towards East Anglia with him sitting there enjoying the stars they flashed past in the night sky.

Shortly, the potty silently landed in the back garden he had so lovingly tended in his previous existence. He sat immobile for a period, soaking up the familiar layout of its sculpted, ornamental features and the silhouette of the house, with its subdued lights showing through the closed curtains.

Unexpectedly, a pair of spotlights fixed under the eaves of the modern house came on, illuminating the garden and his potty, as he sat there on it. Pat came out from the lounge, through the patio doors, looking as he remembered her and walking slowly.

"Welcome back Claude," she said by way of greeting, as he got off the potty and handed her the flowers and chocolates, while giving her his 'French Style' kiss on the cheeks, three times in total.

She looked at him, puzzled. "That's funny," she said, "My husband Tommy used to do that!"

He smiled and put a hand gently on her shoulder as she led him into the house, another of Tommy's traits.

"Would you like a drink?" she asked him.

"Yes please, a cream sherry," he replied. She looked at him again, remembering that was a favourite tipple of her Tommy too. He grinned at her, wrinkling the corners of his eyes, as she gave a shiver.

"Have you eaten yet?" she asked him. "No, what've you got?" he asked her, just like Tommy would have done.

Sniffing delicately and looking at the table, which was laid for two, he speculated, "I could demolish a stew of meat balls with dumplings!"

She nearly collapsed as she looked at him aghast.

"Are you taking the Mickey?" she exclaimed.

"No dear, as you'll find out when you serve up that favourite dish of mine!

"I'll serve the red wine in the meantime. You got this in Aldi's didn't you, Honey cup?" he commented as he poured the already-opened wine. Yet again, he was dropping a hint of his true identity.

Pat returned holding a steaming Pyrex casserole in her mitten covered hands, looking very determined. He helped her place it on a stiff cork centre mat, and then ladled the stew onto the yellow-painted dining plates, sharing out the dumplings between them. She stared at him, fascinated by his familiarity with her and Tommy's routines.

"Got any plain Dijon mustard?" he asked her.

"In the cupboard next to the oven," she answered, amazed yet again at the PMs behavioural resemblance to her late husband's.

He went into the kitchen to collect it, and he returned after a few minutes carrying it, with wet patches on his shirt.

"Sorry about that, I splashed myself with gravy when dishing out," he said calmly.

"You always do," she said absent-mindedly, having felt comfortable enough to start eating before her guest had returned, and speaking instinctively.

Realising how she had reacted, she placed her spoon and fork on the sides of her plate, and asked him, "What's going on? Stop playing with me!"

"I'm not playing with you!" he said in a quiet voice, in between spoonfuls of food. "I'm actually Tommy, your husband!"

"Cheers!" he said, raising his wine glass in a toast of thanks for the meal. "Now you say *salud* back to me!"

The rest of the meal was eaten in silence, at his insistence that it was, "Better belly bust than good food go to waste!"

By this time she was practically in tears, while he knew that she always held her emotions in check, and was prepared to wait until he was ready to explain himself.

When they had finished, they both carried the dishes into the kitchen and she rinsed them under the tap. Then she filled the sink with water and placed the dishes in it, soaking until they were ready to be washed and dried. It was a ritual that they had always followed, when they had nothing more important to do.

Again, he put a reassuring hand on her back as he followed her into the lounge and they sat on the smaller of the two sofas, with a coffee table in front.

"I couldn't help but notice that you're limping," he commented to her. "What's the problem?"

"Old age," she replied. "My hip's going."

"Yes, old age hits us all." He commented, rubbing his chin. "Would you like to be young again?"

"Wouldn't we all!" she laughingly replied, and he told her about his dual life as The Inlooker.

She looked at him with wonderment, accepting what he had said without question. There was too much that had been revealed to be untrue, and she knew in her heart exactly who was sitting next to her, in her house, albeit much younger on the outside than Tommy was when he died.

She snuggled up to him, feeling comfortable in herself, when he made a suggestion that shook her.

"Why don't you occupy Gloria's body, and join me in my new life?" he asked her tenderly.

"I couldn't, that would be tantamount to murder!" she protested, recoiling from him.

"Not if you think about it harder," he said. "She's not really at home!" he said, contemplating how few of her brain cells Gloria proved to be using.

"It's what I've done to Claude, myself, and he's no Einstein!"

They parted on good terms, with her refusing to contemplate a course of action that was against her nature.

No matter how many ways Tommy used to convince her of the merits of his plan, Pat was resolute. She ended up by saying, "I'll think about it!" and he knew that she wouldn't be easy to convince.

His attempts at persuasion went on for weeks, as they enjoyed each other's company in secret rendezvous whenever time permitted Claude to see her. Much to his astonishment, one day she said determinedly, "I'll give it a go!" and his heart leapt at the prospect of them reuniting at all levels. Unfortunately, he had forgotten how manipulative she could be.

At a pre-determined time and date, he asked Gloria to join them, to go through his tried and tested routine of soul transference. The three of them had a jolly evening at his original home, before he spiked Gloria's and Pat's drinks and they both fell asleep.

With a great deal of sadness, he lay Pat' dying body on the chaise longue in his study, arranging her arms across her breasts and kissing her forehead for the last time. While shedding tears, he remembered the years of happiness they had shared together.

His spirit entered her body and guided his soul mate towards Gloria's body, which was nestling on a sofa in the lounge, in front of the warm fire. There, he coaxed Pat's spirit to take possession of Gloria's body, which she did without encountering any resistance.

All went smoothly, when Gloria woke up and Pat's spirit delighted in her new body and the sensual pleasures associated with it. Claude had resolved the major issue of increased loneliness in his personal life, and was delighted to have his original, constant companion by his side, for eternity.

He phoned the police and reported the death of Thomas's widow, saying that she had died peacefully in the study, in her house, where he and Gloria had been staying the night. He also phoned both of Thomas's daughters to give them the bad news, knowing that he and Pat needed to take great care not to reveal their true identities.

"Can you deal with them, when they arrive with their families?" Gloria pleaded with Claude. "I'm not sure I could cope with seeing them now, especially when they're upset!"

"Of course dear, you buzz off back to Downing Street and I'll look after things here." Claude replied. "At some time, we'll let them know our real identities, so don't worry."

The funeral was attended by the distraught Julie and her husband Oscar, who were supported by Thomas's estranged brother and his wife; they had come down from Shropshire to comfort their niece, the only available member of the direct family. At that time, Sharon was in pastures ostensibly unknown, having fled the country when the second-hand car market collapsed with the advent of the potty. Bob was there too, officially representing the supposedly deceased Thomas.

The cause of the brothers' estrangement was rooted in a furious spat. It occurred after Eugene, the younger one, sent Thomas a photo of a naked woman, with her legs splayed; the caption read: '*You weren't looking at her feet, were you?*' When Thomas bothered to look lower down the woman's anatomy, he noticed she had six toes on each foot. He promptly sent it on to his brother's wife. Hence the rift.

Thomas was also attending in spirit, unbeknown to Julie, masquerading as the Prime Minister, Claude Broadbent, who was there in his official capacity of the government's representative and keenest supporter of the renowned 'father of the potty' (or, to give it its proper title, 'Personal Official Transport' vehicle).

Pat had refused to go, being full of remorse at having decided to leave her own body and enter

Gloria's, and could not bear the thought of seeing Julie, her beloved daughter, under such distressing circumstances.

"I'll talk to her later, when we reveal what we've become," she told Claude, wiping her eyes.

In the fullness of time, Claude (or should it be said, Thomas) became delighted with his newly revitalised, original wife, and was even more thrilled to reacquaint himself with familiar temptations, as she expressed herself in ways that he had almost forgotten.

"What's this?" she asked him one day, as she found one of Gloria's riding whips at the bottom of a wardrobe, flexing it up and down in front of him. When he told her, and she took to using it, the erotic pain she inflicted on his bare back was tolerable *once*, but the prospect of being thrashed regularly did not exactly meet his ideas of good old-fashioned sex.

He therefore searched through Gloria's belongings thoroughly, to make sure that no more kinky-sex toys could be found.

However, one fateful day, Pat confronted Claude and said, "I'm not entirely happy with this arrangement; it's not fair on Gloria. I've restored her suppressed soul, we've made direct contact and have become bosom pals. We get on really well together, and have agreed to share our body with you, if you're willing to go along with us."

Reluctantly, he accepted, worried at the unknown future he now faced. The outcome became evident within weeks, as he faced the prospect of remorseless sexual advances from two competing, lusty-souled women. He had no idea of who was going to do what with him, whenever they chose.

"Something's got to give!" he thought, feeling full of self-pity, and regretting his earlier fit of compassion.

"I really need to turn my attention to re-fertilization of the human race. It's going to be needed some time over the next few generations."

Soon, he and his assistants began work frantically on an antidote to the tracer birth-control contagion, using Claude's two-spirits, one-person harem as a guinea pig.

Bucking the universal trend of infertility, one day Gloria (or was it Pat?) declared, "We're proud to announce that we're pregnant." The way in which she said it reminded Claude of the day when Margaret Thatcher, a much venerated former prime minister in the UK, announced, "*We* have become a grandmother!" He wondered if she too had suffered multiple personalities occupying her.

Seven months later, all three became proud parents of a healthy boy, who they agreed would be named 'Thomas Claude Broadbent-Beckon'. For a while, Thomas would be free of demands on his body and was grateful for the temporary respite.

Better still, the human race having gained a sensible method of population containment by short-term sterilization, it now possessed a sustainable bridge-head to the future by reversing it at will, and its continuity was assured.

It would no longer present a threat to extra-terrestrials by needing to invade their territories.

§ 19: Attempts To Mend Bridges

The aliens who abducted Sharon and her husband recognised them straight away; they were the couple they had been seeking for a long time. The woman was the main target, being the offspring of The Inlooker who had strayed from protective surroundings, and was therefore out of his sphere of influence. The husband was an expendable bonus, and could be used as a bargaining chip when her father caught up with them, as was the intention.

They already knew The Inlooker from his spiritually unique DNA strands, which had been cross-matched to those of his daughter. Until they had crossed paths with this strangely gifted human, the alien race generically referred to as the 'greys' believed themselves to be vastly superior to the natural inhabitants of Planet Earth.

They were called 'greys' because of their skin colour, but there were also brethren with brown and green skins, and of varying heights, who had adapted to different environments as they travelled through time and space.

Universally, whatever paths they may have taken as explorers, they shared common characteristics. These were disproportionately large craniums, two oversized bug eyes, tiny nostrils with slits to breathe through and thin lipped small mouths. They were also recognisable by their long, spindly limbs, missing willies and pot bellies.

Upon catching first sight of them, many a human commented, "Not a pretty sight!" and this opinion was absolutely the truth, from a human perspective. Mind you, the missing willies were not only seen by those who had performed autopsies on the naked aliens, but also by massed audiences who had seen illicit videos of the post-mortems, buried amongst faked 'evidence'.

The greys' evolutionary path was millions of years older than that of the emerging race called 'humans', who had been genetically modified on scores of occasions by more than one race of aliens, to gift them with the spark of intelligence.

There were at least 50 races of aliens that had collaborated on improving these newcomers to their ranks, but they were getting desperate. They were trying to counter the increasing risk of self-annihilation by the humans, now that some short-sighted, deluded interloper had helped them to develop nuclear weapons. That intervention had been decided on compassionate grounds, for their self-protection.

These participants were also trying to induce subtle changes in the physical DNA structure of the humans, in order to counter their overtly warlike and aggressive behaviour. They were forever fighting and pushing each other around. Mind you, the aliens had been like that themselves not too many centuries ago, and had fought amongst themselves over possession of the humans, under the guise of becoming their protectors.

Getting back to the basics of the greys' current study, it had been an incorrect assumption that The Inlooker's physical DNA structure would match that of his spiritual DNA. This belief was based on the sole occasion when he and a pioneering grey had tussled over a physical, prototype human body that they had both sought to control.

What they discovered was that this mutant 'Inlooker' floated his spiritual intelligence from one human body to another whenever he chose to do so; perhaps he was capable of doing the same to them? That was why they wanted to study him and uncover the ramifications of these previously undiscovered parasitic abilities.

They were flummoxed by the transfer of his spirit from one live body to another, because it broke the link between the spiritual and physical DNA strands in him. It left only a partial trail for them to follow in trying to capture him. The emphasis was on the 'live body' since the link was broken anyway on physical death, but to be able to do it on a whim, when alive, was unheard of.

As implied previously, the greys' logic in abducting his female offspring and different-sex partner was, "*We will do anything that can be used as leverage!*" although the husband was a poor specimen with a range of conditions that made him irritable and foul-mouthed, as they realised when they bothered to translate the words he was using.

Another motive for the greys' involvement with humans was their own unfortunate circumstances. The reasons were simple; in their current state of evolution they had gone beyond the messy business of eating food and drinking water and beverages. They had even stopped exuding their waste in a conventional way, and could no longer fully comprehend procreation nor the pleasures of the flesh.

Now, they were forced to rub a repulsive mixture of liquids on their stomachs, to ingest them through the skin. Then they excreted it back through the skin, to the disgust of other races of aliens who complained about the stench they emitted.

The greys suffered from another problem that they needed to overcome; their native atmosphere was ammonia based, and it was reckoned that they found Planet Earth sufficiently agreeable to want to live there amongst the humans.

To achieve this, they wanted to revert to their previous state of existence and eat and drink and have sex in the old-fashioned way. Therefore, they were engaged on the intricacies of reinventing their race as hybrid beings, preferably indistinguishable from the native humans.

"This is the way forward!" they were thought to have decided.

Originally, after a period during which the greys left the primitive humans to their own devices, they found that these upstarts had invented radar, and had thus interfered with the navigation and propulsion systems on board their own space craft. As a result of this unintentional activity, they began crashing regularly.

Some of the 'downed' craft remained intact, and were taken away by the eager but naïve humans for inspection. Unfortunately, when unsealed, the invaders were exposed to an unexpected, sudden expulsion from the craft of unbreathable, pressurised gases laced with hydrogen cyanide, and abruptly died.

In those halcyon decades following their return to Planet Earth, the greys got into the habit of illegally 'acquiring' many animals and humans to examine their vital organs, mainly for the purpose of perfecting the hybrids.

For similar motives, implants were inserted in many people on a regular basis, to monitor and pacify them. This induced less resistance to the greys longer-term ambition of world domination.

These intrusive activities became less commonplace in recent times, the need for them having passed. However, to draw a parallel with the human race; it was often the case that one utility provider would dig a hole, in order to upgrade their services. They would tend to do this without consultation with other utility providers. Likewise, the different alien races often failed to coordinate their activities, and ended up needlessly duplicating each other's efforts.

Without the knowledge of the greys, The Inlooker knew all about their devious ways, and those of their compatriots. He also knew that they had abducted his daughter and her husband. The source of this cognisance was due to their having been inadvertently contaminated with *tracer* in the early days of its contagious spread throughout the world, probably via the hybrids as they were experimentally released by the aliens.

Unaware of this, they felt that the need to inform him what they had done, so they devised a plan to draw him into their net. This catered for the probability that he would try to recapture his family members before serious negotiations got underway.

To counter this eventuality, they placed the unconscious Sharon and David on adjoining operating tables and cut off their heads with exquisite finesse, at the base of the neck, below the 7th cervical vertebra.

Then they 'sealed off' the intact ends of the separated vertebrae, the bisected ends of the Anterior Longitudinal Ligament, and all the associated tissues, before magnetically holding and clamping their necks, with the heads attached, to a single oval-shaped plate made of biological elements.

These linked the anaesthetised nerves to artificial feeling-simulators, and the veins and arteries to a blood-substitute circulator. The plate and the units underneath were designed to allow the independent heads to swivel through 180 degrees, and function in a totally self-sufficient environment.

The final measure to preserve and protect the sleeping heads was to encase them side by side in one see-through container, and apply the correct mixture of oxygen, nitrogen and other life sustaining gases to circulate inside.

They were then resuscitated for a short period, to ensure that the separation had been successful. After they stared at each other, paralysed, before starting to cry, shout and swear like troopers, they were put back to sleep. They had proof positive that the victims' vocal cords were intact.

The final act was to despatch them on a tour of the greys' far flung interplanetary empire, for reawakening at each place they visited, to educate the local inhabitants. It also gave fellow greys, greens and browns the chance to admire the superlative skills of the surgeons who had performed the operation.

As part of the plan, the bodies were suspended in advanced cryogenic chambers, ready for retrieval if there was a positive outcome to negotiations. If the Inlooker proved to be cooperative, they would be reattached at a later date to the heads.

Thus, the heads would always be on the move, the bodies being stored in a secret underground location, until the situation was resolved to their satisfaction.

The members of the top cupula of the greys were engaged in a rambling discussion about their plan. It was their 'tee hee hee' way of letting off steam after doing something beneficial to their well-being.

Number 1: "*Where is he? How can we flush him out?*"

Number 2: "*I wonder if this Claude Bumbent is The Inlooker?*"

Number 3: "*No. That would be too obvious. Anyway, he's sex mad!*"

Number 4: "*Yes that is true. His brain is where his balls are located and therefore it is not possible!*" (He had already studied human colloquialisms.)

Number 5: "*Let's get rid of that husband of the female we captured, as a warning that we mean business. The one named David Duke.*"

Number 3: "*Does the name Duke mean his wife is a Duchess?*"

Number 4: "*No, it's a name not a title!*"

Number 3: "*Why don't humans use numbers, like we do? It's far clearer.*"

Number 2: "*Because they're daft, that's why!*"

Number 1: "*If they're that daft, how come we can't find The Inlooker?*"

To their astonishment, the image of a solemn middle-aged female human wearing a uniform suddenly materialized in their midst, looked pointedly at Number 1 and stated: "*Sharon and David are not your playthings. Put them back together again or you will be punished. You have been warned!*" The image rippled and vanished.

The Inlooker smiled grimly as he listened to the greys communicating, and was gaining in self-confidence as he formulated his own plans. His views were *"That'll rattle them!"* and, *"The next stage will be to cause outrage!"* These were two things he wanted to achieve at the outset and, to jolly things along, he intended paying a flying visit to the secret underground base at Aberporth, which was located on the southern end of Cardigan Bay, in West Wales. He was playing a key role there, in the retrieval of the two abductees. There were no alien races there, only military personnel and scientists.

To Claude's relief, he still had Bob to confide in. When he told him what had happened to Sharon and her husband, Bob was naturally concerned, and asked, "How the devil are you going to get them out of the pickle they're in?"

Claude told him what he had already done, by sending an emissary to warn the greys.

"Who'd you use?" Bob asked him.

"The lady who delivers tea and biscuits around our offices."

"Was it effective?"

"I like to think so."

"You seem to be taking it ever so calmly."

"The truth is, I'm still hacked off with the way she borrowed 500 quid to get her car clutch repaired, and the way she waltzes off whenever she feels like."

"Basically, you're holding a grudge for such a trivial thing, after all these years? It's preposterous!" Bob spluttered indignantly.

"I suppose it is, but it may be me reacting emotionally to the seriousness of her fate if I don't get her back!" Claude admitted, looking tearful.

"Well go and keep her spirits up, by paying regular visits wherever she goes," Bob urged him, grasping Claude's elbow. "And give her husband some support, to show you've accepted him as a member of the family!"

Which was how Claude started paying the pair of them surreptitious flying visits, to keep their hopes and physical heads alive, as they experienced their grand tour of the greys' universe and effed and blinded vociferously at the expense of their hosts' kinfolk.

The language they used was an outlet for them, to colourfully describe their feelings at being so cruelly restrained in a living hell.

In moments of rationally resorting to pure logic, using The Inlooker as their spiritual voice, they would mentally project a plea to those assembled around them, which went as follows:

"How would you like to be imprisoned like this, for years on end, without hope? How would you feel, as intelligent beings, to be submitted to this endless torture? We are beings like you, not animals of a lesser species, without breeding and culture. We travel in craft like you, between the stars, and share the same emotions as you. Why do you allow those who lead you to treat us in this barbaric way?"

The gathered onlookers would start shifting uneasily and glancing at each other, as they translated these sentences, before shuffling away to go about their everyday business. Echoing behind them, they would hear the two tormented heads recommence shouting, using a whole new range of swearwords in order to retain their sanity.

After several years had elapsed, Number 1 said to his companions, *"Oh dear, this is not going well. We*

Meanwhile, Claude invited Bob to go with him to Aberporth and give him a second opinion on what was being done to help Sharon and David.

The journey time was only a few minutes, after Claude picked Bob up from the potty development centre (as the industrial unit had been renamed), in North Essex. They sat next to each other after mounting the four seater version of this novel craft, with two of Claude's burly bodyguards sitting up front for protection, whilst carrying the tools of their trade on their laps.

Dotted on the ground under the intended flight path were a few more potties, with other members of his security team sitting on them, itching to get stuck in if anyone dared to interfere with the boss's motions as he sped overhead.

During the brief time they were in the air, Bob took the opportunity to tell Claude, "I don't know what's happening to me, but as the days and years roll by, I seem to be feeling better and better. Yes, my body seems to be losing all its aches and pains."

"Really?" Claude asked, looking casually out of his side window.

"Yes, really. In fact I've even started jogging again, early mornings."

"My word, whatever next!"

"Mmm...After eating a bowl of cornflakes and full milk one morning, I noticed a speck of metal floating around in the dregs, afterwards. What'd you think that may have been?"

"Iron? Those cereals are claimed to be full of iron."

"Well, I examined it under the microscope, and guess what? It looks like a Nano robot. You wouldn't know anything about a device like that entering my system and clearing up any medical problems I might have?"

"Me? Good lord no!"

"Only, my doctor informs me that I look likely to live at least another couple of hundred years."

"That's good news, isn't it? Next thing you'll be telling me is that you're getting married again."

Bob looked at Claude and said nothing. If Claude was denying knowledge of this improvement in his health, then there was nothing he could say, was there? However, if Claude was indeed the culprit, then it would explain the replacement of his clothes with new, slimmer-fit duplicates, by persons unknown.

They landed on a helipotty pad, located directly in front of the nondescript pedestrians' entrance to the underground base, where they were whisked inside under armed guard to the VIP lift. Saying goodbye to Claude's security team, they descended five levels with two uniformed personnel and driven by them in a reserved electric buggy along a wide, brightly lit corridor.

They stopped and got off in front of a door where someone was waiting for them; it was a smiling, bespectacled and slim young woman, wearing a white coat with a name badge on it announcing her to be *Alice Smythers*. She clearly knew Claude well, and formalities were brief as she was introduced to his friend and confidante, Bob.

They entered a large room, where several boffins were seated at work stations outfitted with advanced research equipment and powerful microscopes.

"Bob, this is my team of geneticists," Claude said, as he proceeded to introduce them by name, as they paused by each one for a brief chat.

The next stop was a room separated from them with a glass panel, containing a child laying down and apparently asleep. After a pause to look at her, Claude said to Bob, "Let's all head to the meeting room ahead, for you to be given an overview of what we are doing."

They all sat in rows, nonchalantly facing Claude who commenced by stating, "This is the team assembled to counteract the threat presented by the alien race called the 'greys', and their allies. These individuals represent the best we have to offer in the field of genetic research, our achievements in which we consider to be formidable.

"I have good reason to believe that whatever the aliens can do, we can at least match and often exceed. It is a game of brinkmanship that we are indulged in, with the lives of my daughter and her husband at stake." He held his head up high and concluded, "I have every confidence we will win this contest." He nodded to Alice and asked her, "Please continue."

Alice took Claude's place, while he sat down in the front row. She stared at Bob and said, "Your attention has been drawn to the young girl asleep next door. She was intercepted in Cannock's Chase by one of our 'snatch squads'. These were on the lookout for her ever since the police began receiving reports from tourists hiking in the woodlands. They in turn alerted us, and we responded immediately.

"A middle-aged woman was the first to claim that she had seen the child, who appeared to be lost, and was about to run off before she grabbed her by her coat hood. When she turned round, the lady noticed that her eyes were oversized and totally black. This scared her, as did the child's high-pitched scream and she let her go. The appearance of black-eyed children has been an infrequent occurrence over many years, in different parts of the country.

"We reasoned she was a hybrid that had been let loose by the adult greys, to see how she would be treated by humans. These hybrids are the product of insemination by the aliens of human women, abducted for procreation. Often, the human foetus is removed prematurely, for the end-of-term birth to take place under controlled conditions. Genetic engineering is believed to be ongoing, to ensure integration of the new species with that of the native population."

Bob asked, "It seems to me that her sleep is induced. How did you get her here without alerting the aliens that she has been captured by you?"

Alice replied, "One evening, the squads waited in camouflaged hides in the vicinity, having intercepted unusual comms involving a child. When she came into view, we used sound effects to make her think that wild dogs were rushing towards her, and then pounced on her while she was terrified, using an anaesthetic to knock her out and stop her from screaming. Once we had her, we sent out a simulated distress call, indicating that she had met a violent death."

Bob asked, "In what way were the 'comms' unusual?"

"They were 'talking' to each other, mind-to-mind, as heard before, between non-human races."

Alice continued, "Her sleep is indeed induced, because she screamed every time, until recently, whenever she was woken up. It is piercing enough to cause glass to smash. Soon you will see that progress has been made in bringing her closer to us."

Bob continued with his questioning, "Seeing as you're all scientists involved in genetic engineering, where is your research leading? To all-out war with the greys and their allies, or do you have something more subtle in mind?"

Alice replied, "We have amassed data on the DNA structure of the greys, and of the hybrid we have in our possession. These represent the two ends of the known spectrum: the first is where they are now, as adult greys; the second is what they intend becoming, after the hybrids are integrated.

"Claude has an immediate need, and that is to get his daughter back, preferably with her husband. The aliens want to use them as bait to lure Claude into the open, so they can find out what he is...."

One of the younger, male scientists spoke up, "Wouldn't we all like to know!" to a chuckle from his colleagues.

Alice ignored the interruption and continued, "What we have done is re-engineer the hybrid's DNA structure, to show what we are capable of if they don't release their captives unharmed. The results are sufficiently complex to lead them up several blind alleys, and then some."

"The threat being?"

"The threat being that we will go into mass-production of the mutant version of their hybrids, if they don't hand back their two captives."

"What if they retaliate in kind?"

"So be it! We reckon we can unravel whatever they throw at us. In fact, this type of DNA revision is what they are already doing with the hybrids, isn't it?"

Bob asked, "One more question; how do you handle the problem of eavesdroppers? The hybrid next door may be transmitting as we speak!"

Alice answered, her face deadpan, "The place is acoustically reinforced at this level. Also, each of us has an implant in our cranium that scrambles any thoughts that we transmit naturally. When we meet as a team, it reverses its polarity – in layman's terms – and this enables us to work together as a colony, sharing our ideas. It is a concept based on the humble bumble bee in its hive."

"But what about me, as a visitor, and the hybrid?"

Alice stared at him as if he was daft, leaving Bob to think about the situation.

He came to the obvious conclusion. *"Oh, I think I've already been nobbled, as has the child!"*

§ 20: Lost And Traced

Claude rose and said, "Let's all get back to work now, so I can send a warning to the greys. I need a sample of our handiwork for them to inspect."

As they were leaving, Bob quietly asked him, "Where do you intend making contact? Where's their base?"

Claude replied, "They've got quite a few large, underground bases in the states. I'll probably use the one in Texas."

Alice approached Bob with a sweet smile and asked, "Would you like to come with me and wake up our small visitor? Try to think of her as a child, not as a hybrid. She likes men, and you've got a friendly face."

Bob nodded and followed through the unlocked door into her room, asking in a whisper, "What'd you call *it*? Sorry, I mean *her*!"

Alice replied with a disapproving frown, "We call her Pollyanna. You'll see why, as you get to know her better."

Standing by the bed, Alice adopted a stern expression and shook the child by the shoulder, as she lay serenely on her back. Bob decided she couldn't be more than six or seven years old, and felt sad for the situation in which she found herself.

"It's not her fault," he decided, at which moment the child's eyes open wide, making him jump at the speed of her reaction. The big black eyes transformed her features into a menacing apparition, which frightened him. It also explained why Alice had adopted a severe approach when waking 'Pollyanna', knowing how this transition from sleeping beauty to a malevolent rag doll could affect onlookers.

She looked at the two of them with a face devoid of emotion, until her lips started quivering and she appeared to be on the verge of having a pent-up outburst of emotion. This lasted for scarcely a moment, as she composed herself with a trembling of the body, a shrug of the shoulders and a blink of the eyes.

She started shedding tears, which contrasted with the brave smile she began wearing, as if to say, *"To heck with it! I'm here, it is now, and I'd better make the most of things!"*

She swung her legs over the edge of the bed, jumped lightly to the floor, and embraced Alice tightly, looking coyly at Bob before saying, "Hello Aunty Alice. Sorry about that, but at least I didn't cry this time, did I?"

Alice leant down and kissed the top of her head, whilst rocking her to and fro.

"Pollyanna, I'd like you to meet my friend Bob. He's interested in you, so say hello to him, for me."

She blinked her eyes at him cutely, while the occasional teardrops ran down her pink cheeks, and said, "Hello Bob; glad to meet you. I hope you like me more than you did when you first came into the room. Being a hybrid is such a horrible way for me to be. I hope you get to know me better so I can show how nice I really am. I will try my best to improve myself, honest!"

"Aw hell!" Bob thought, stricken with remorse, as he felt himself succumbing to Pollyanna's wholly natural love-bombing and strode out of the room, staring straight ahead.

Alice stroked Pollyanna's hair and said, "Don't worry dear. He doesn't know what to make of you. He will though, before long, he will."

Bob caught up with Claude and asked him, "Has she had a scan?

The reply was, "Oh yes, and her brain is remarkably similar to ours in its structure, but with more activity going on. The networking circuitry also seems to be more compact than usual, so the aliens have made improvements to it, I guess. This is reflected in her IQ, which is way up the measurable quotient.

"As an aside, no abnormalities were detected, which suggests that there are no hidden surprises in store for us as she progresses. Taking into account the lack of humanity that the greys often exhibit, they have apparently imbued in her characteristics that they have never possessed."

He got closer to Bob and confided, "I have good reason to believe that they are developing another type of hybrid that is closer to meeting their aspirations. Therefore, I have asked the team to concentrate on developing two types of mutant variants. Each of them will result in the hybrids developing in abnormal ways.

"The first will be called Type P, based on Pollyanna. I think that she and other like her were developed as a fallback, to lead us along a path that complies with the terms of their original treaty with a former US president. The second, Type B, will be based on a hybrid, without the human characteristics and which breathes their atmosphere."

A team member interrupted them by approaching with a vial and holding it aloft for them to admire.

With a pleased expression on his face, he said, "This is it, the DNA structure for Type P that *should* cause them to return your daughter! They'll find it the very devil to unravel."

Claude replied solemnly, "Jeremy, I will forever be in your debt! Give it to Alice, who will arrange delivery with the diplomatic service, and continue working on Type B. Thank you so very much!"

As he patted him on the back, he read his mind and was gratified with what he found. The man had mastery of his subject, and had conducted the trials thoroughly, with his peers.

"People like him are priceless," he confided in Bob, who wondered how they had got their hands on the Type B variant as well, but refrained from asking. He decided, "*If Claude wanted to tell me, he would have done so by now. Some things can be worth waiting for!*"

The week that followed was an anxious time, until confirmation was received that the greys had received the DNA sample and taken it away for analysis. In the meantime, Claude returned to the PM's residence to deal with matters of state and see his newborn son, whose birth was being widely reported, while Bob was invited to stay awhile in this scenic area.

He chose to accept the opportunity to take a rare holiday, and was offered the use of one of several small, isolated whitewashed cottages above the base. They overlooked the Irish Sea and had been inherited when the area was commandeered by the MOD for military use. While the furnished cottage was being prepared for his use, one of the chattier lady cleaners told him that a little girl with strange eyes was a neighbor, living in one of the other dwellings.

When he enquired at the base, this was confirmed.

To Bob's surprise, Alice had taken Pollyanna under her wing, as her ward, and they lived together. She was currently attending lessons at the base, provided by a rota of teachers recruited from within the base, using staff with suitable qualifications. These mainly came from the personnel division, and were sworn to secrecy.

"What time do they get home?" he asked the young, female receptionist, who had a lovely, lilting Welsh accent

"Oh about 6pm," was the reply.

"Can I use a potty to get around?" he asked.

"You can, but they're not seen much here," was the reply. "You'd be better off with one of our own vehicles, unmarked. You can have one now, if you wish?"

"Automatic? I've tried manual gear shifts and I don't get on with them."

"As you wish. No problem. It'll be brought round to the front in ten minutes, giving you time to fill in the requisition details."

Bob drove to the nearest supermarket, using GPS to guide him there, where he did his essential shopping, together with buying some bottles of red and white wine, with big, fat steaks, sauces and vegetables for an evening meal. He also bought some other items and desserts, in case special diets were required, including a variety of soft drinks, fresh, seasonal fruits, pancakes and yogurts. Finally, he chose a variety of flowers to make into a bouquet.

Upon his return, he unpacked and stored all his purchases; then he showered late afternoon, before dressing and sitting by an open, upstairs window to read a tourist guide, waiting patiently for the couple to come into view.

At ten past six, he was rewarded by the sight of them walking towards the cottages, holding hands, with Pollyanna skipping beside Alice. They stopped when they saw a strange car parked outside the normally empty property, wondering who was staying there, so he went out to greet them.

"Bob! I knew it was you!" Pollyanna cried out when she saw him, and rushed over to be swept up in his arms. Alice rushed over as well, with a welcoming smile, saying, "She told me it was you, even before you came to the door!"

"Come in, come in!" he impulsively urged Alice, pushing the door open with his free hand while holding Pollyanna aloft, and followed up by asking her, "Do you have any plans this evening? Are you going out? Would you like me to take you out?"

Without waiting for an answer, he placed Pollyanna down carefully, while picking up the bouquet and holding it out for Alice to take.

His spontaneity was welcomed in equal measure, and they both eagerly accepted his invitation to dine at his cottage. While he insisted on doing the cooking, Pollyanna took over the laying of the table and the placing of glasses for the three of them, choosing a place opposite Alice, with Bob at one end of the table, facing them.

Alice herself chatted easily to Bob, while she scrubbed the new potatoes, chopped mushrooms and runner beans and boiled them all in saucepans, and he grilled the three steaks; the prospect of eating one of them delighted Pollyanna.

"I've never ever had one of those before!" she exclaimed, jumping up and down excitedly. "What animal do they come from?" Clearly, the prospect of behaving like a carnivore did not put her off meat in the slightest, which pleased Bob no end. From the comments, being made, Bob realized that Pollyanna had not been exposed to many of the treats he intended providing.

"Oh dear, have I put my foot in it, offering all these foods that are new to her?" he asked Alice, his concern showing.

She replied, "I don't think so, seeing her reaction!"

Her ward had even begun opening various doors in the kitchen to see what lay behind them, and was picking up jars to read their contents.

Bob asked, "Where did she learn to do that? Reading I mean."

Alice replied, "The greys taught her many skills from a young age. She's good at most things, except swimming."

They ate in silence, relishing the flavours, and watching amused as Pollyanna poured another large blob of BBQ sauce next to her large steak, ready to dip into it.

"There's nothing wrong with your appetite, young lady," Bob murmured, watching her munch happily, in response to which remark she pulled a face, making him and Alice laugh.

"*She's adorable!*" Bob thought, to which a voice responded in his head, "*Thank you, Bob!*" He looked at Alice, who continued eating; she hadn't overheard the exchange between himself and the child.

Afterwards, Pollyanna asked, "What's next?"

Bob replied, "Strawberries and Joe's ice cream."

"Can I see?"

Bob showed her a punnet of bright red, heavily scented strawberries, to which she remarked, "Oo, I've seen those in pictures, they smell lovely! Can I try one?"

"Of course. Dip it in sugar first," as he passed her a small bowl of sugar.

Her eyes closed in ecstasy. "That's my first time ever. What a taste!"

She opened them again and asked, "What's 'Joe's Ice Cream'?"

Bob got up and took a large tub from the fridge freezer to examine it. "I dunno," he replied. "All it says is that it's 'the best in the world', but it's only made in a vanilla flavour."

"Here, try some," he said, opening the tub and dipping a teaspoon in, for Pollyanna to sample.

"Oo!" she exclaimed blissfully, "It's sensational!"

This tempted Bob and Alice, who helped themselves as well.

"Heck that *is* good, really good!" Bob exclaimed, and Alice nodded her approval.

"Want some coffee, or are you going to stick with the wine?" he asked Alice, who patted her swollen belly and declined anything else to eat or drink.

"Can I try some of that cheese that's described as strong?" Pollyanna asked.

The evening continued, until Alice noticed Pollyanna closing her eyes and about to fall forward onto the table the two of them were silently clearing. Cupping her head swiftly with both hands, she said to Bob, "We'd better say goodnight! She's dropping off to sleep."

Bob got up and bundled her into his arms, while she slept deeply, saying, "I'll carry her back to your place, and help you get her to bed."

They left the warmth of his cottage, although it wasn't really cold outside at that time of year, with Alice cradling her bouquet of flowers. To his surprise, two security guards who had stationed themselves outside, moved out of the shadows and fell in behind them as they walked, to ensure their safety.

After helping to tuck Pollyanna in, as Bob stood by the main door ready to leave, he turned and said, "Goodnight Alice, and thanks for a wonderful evening. I haven't done anything like this since my wife died."

Unexpectedly, she gave him a light kiss on the cheek that made him glow with happiness.

"That's alright," she whispered. "Let's do it again, soon. You've been a real tonic for me and Pollyanna."

The two guards melted into the darkness of the night, leaving them to enjoy the moment in privacy, undisturbed.

The following morning, Bob got up early enough to open his curtains and see Alice and Pollyanna leaving their cottage to walk to the base. Nearby, a black 4WD black vehicle was parked, from which the customary guards descended.

Pollyanna sensed that Bob was watching them and waved to him frantically as he stood framed in his upstairs bedroom window. Alice wondered what was distracting her young ward and looked up at him too. After waving at him herself, while he waved back, she pointed at her watch and mouthed something he didn't catch.

A child's voice penetrated his mind, saying, "*Join us in about one hour!*" He stuck his thumb in the air and mentally replied, "*Okay*" to Pollyanna, who stuck her thumb up as well. Then she raced to catch up with Alice, who was setting a brisk pace, and occasionally looking back to see if he was still watching. One of the guards looked back at him too, and gave a sly wave in his direction.

After the allotted hour had elapsed, Bob signed in at the base reception and used the lift to go and see Alice and her team of scientists. He was met directly by Alice, who asked, "This morning, when we left the house, did Pollyanna relay a message to you, mentally?"

"Yes she did," he replied. "It's not the first time either."

"That's remarkable. I had no idea she could do that! Let's go and secretly view her at her lessons, while we grab some coffees together, in the adjoining observatory. She can't see us in there."

They watched as an enthusiastic male teacher, in his late twenties or thereabouts, coached her, with the aid of a blackboard; by its side was a screen, set up for use with a projector and sound system.

Bob remarked, "All mod cons, I'm impressed!" before asking, "What's she learning?"

Alice studied her course notes and said, "The practical Application of Algebra."

Bob exclaimed, "I would have thought that's a dry subject for such a young age!"

"Not at all," was the reply. "Look how fascinated she is. She took to Boolean Logic like a duck takes to water, and when the structure of DNA was explained, she was in seventh heaven!

"What is DNA, to be precise? I understand the concept, but I don't know the actual meaning."

"DNA stands for 'deoxyribonucleic acid'. This a self-replicating material which is present in nearly all living organisms.

"It is the main constituents of chromosomes."

"That's a mouthful!"

"Yes, she broke it up as DAY-OXY-RIB-OH- NEW-CLEE-YICK ACID and learnt how to say it immediately. It is the carrier of genetic information. The term represents the fundamental and distinctive characteristics or qualities of someone or something, especially when regarded as unchangeable.

"Clever her absorbing all of that, for her age! Talking about 'a mouthful', how's about that coffee I wanted?" She had a big smile on her face.

At the end of the lesson, the teacher gave Pollyanna a gentle hug and left the room as his replacement, a much older skinny male with a mass of unkempt grey hair and wearing a bow tie and round glasses walked in, with a large book under his arm.

While he was setting up the projector, she turned round to stare in their direction and suppressed a giggle, while he was absorbed. When he turned to look at her, she was full composed and looked as if butter wouldn't melt in her mouth.

They both looked at each other gawping, their coffee mugs held mid-air.

"How'd she know?" Alice asked, baffled.

Bob concluded, "Clearly, she's a telepath; isn't that wonderful! What's in store for her now?"

"The 'Rise and Fall of the Roman Empire', all two millennia of it, first in the West and then in the East."

"Oh come on, that's ridiculous!"

"It *is* being delivered over a series of lessons, and the man teaching her is a prominent professor at a key university. It covers all aspect of mankind's behaviour; embracing religions, politics, warfare, love, corruption, monumental constructions, in fact all the trials and tribulations of a once successful nation.

"Look at the way he's dealing with her. This is a labour of love for both of them, I assure you!"

A lot of arm waving ensued, interspersed with slides and film snaps being shown, while the two of them alternated at the blackboard asking and answering questions.

"Her progress seems to be FAY-NOM-IN-AL," Bob said, slowing down his diction and making Alice laugh. "And her handwriting is really neat, if not 'twee'!"

"She does joined-up handwriting too!" Alice commented drily, whilst replenishing her rapidly diminishing coffee from a heat-retaining jug.

They watched for hours, taking the occasional break to coincide with Pollyanna's. Time literally flew by, as they continued to be fascinated by her precocious influx of knowledge. A natural break occurred when Pollyanna was led away to a side room off the main gymnasium at the base; there she was regularly coached in free-form athletics, set to music.

Alice, said, "She's going to be exercising her body as well as her brain for the next hour or so, after which she has lunch on her own for another hour, back in the room next door. During this break, she can have a snooze if she wants, or read a book, or watch the news on TV.

"She is constantly monitored from here, with the observers passing judgement on her by applying psychometric standards, to see how she is progressing. If I hadn't demanded time here myself, with you in attendance, they would be sitting down now where we are, instead of us. The monitoring is normally direct; in fact, it is also being done remotely, as I speak." She pointed up at cameras near the ceiling.

"Frankly, I think she deserves a break from all this attention, and will ask for her to spend a couple of days away from this hotbed of learning, with us. What do think of the idea?" She looked at him anxiously. "I'm sure they'll agree."

"Of course, I was hoping you'd ask!" Bob replied, standing up. "I've got things to arrange, unless you want to do something special yourself?"

She shook her head, "I leave it up to you, oh Zen master!" Her relief was palpable.

Bob departed immediately, to familiarise himself with the local coastline. When he asked at reception, the young lady who he normally dealt with wrote down the name of a secluded beach, named Penbryn, which would be suitable for Pollyanna to visit. He also returned to the supermarket he had used the day before, bought a wicker basket and filled it with picnic goodies, for the three of them to enjoy. Finally, he purchased sandals and swimming trunks for himself, three beach towels and enough casual clothes to last for a week.

Whatever else was required, he would get tomorrow, if all three of them were given the go ahead to 'take a break'.

Then he returned to his holiday home, showered, changed into the provided towelling robe, and took a siesta.

He was awoken from his slumbers by repeated, loud knocking at the front door. From the high-pitched babbling noise the other side, he could tell it was Pollyanna, with Alice in the background trying to calm her down. As he opened it, Pollyanna pushed hard and burst in. "Bob, Bob, we're going out tomorrow! Do you know where?" she asked, her big black eyes even larger than normal.

"I sure do!" he replied, trying to get her to sit down in a comfy armchair by the window. "We're going to the seaside. Do you have a swimsuit?" She shook her head vigorously.

Then we'll get you one tomorrow, *and* a pair of sunglasses, *and* a hat to shield your head, *and* a pair of flip-flops for your feet. How does that sound?" She nodded happily.

He looked at Alice and asked, "Do you need anything?"

"No, I'm okay for all those things," she replied with a smile.

They all ate together that evening, enjoying the use of a gas barbecue to cook beef burgers and pork sausages, with salads and sauces, before sitting together in harmony and having a chinwag. It was noticeable how Pollyanna was capable of having an adult conversation, when matters pertaining to her education were fresh in her mind.

After they had put her to bed and were alone, Bob commented, "She's like blotting paper, the way she absorbs information. Tomorrow should be interesting"

They had no idea how interesting it would prove to be.

The signs indicated that the narrow road leading downhill to Penbryn beach was a dead-end, although when they drove there, it had a circular turning area for vehicles to drop passengers off and turn round. That is what Bob did for Alice and Pollyanna, who were both wearing swimsuits and dark glasses, like he was.

"Look at me Bob," she said proudly as she looked back at him when they got out. "You can't see what I am anymore!"

Her innocent words touched him deeply, and he replied, "You've got nothing to be ashamed of, Polly. You're way ahead of humans your age." He was finding it tiresome to use her full name; anyway, 'Polly' sounded cuter to him.

She looked pleased and replied, "Oh thanks Bob. I try my best, for you and Alice."

He shouted to Alice, "I'll go to the parking area further up the hill and join you momentarily. I'll carry the rest of the stuff down, if you could take your own towels?"

When he was parking, he noticed the two men who performed guard duty on Pollyanna's behalf were wearing suits, as they got out of their big, black vehicle. He walked up to them, took out his wallet and peeled off some banknotes for them, saying, "For heaven's sake go buy some swim trunks, towels sand things. You looks silly with suits on in this place.

"Also, if you've got some device with you to block cameras and mobiles phones bring it along. We don't want anyone taking photos or sending messages, do we, unless for an emergency?"

"Okay, sir, we're glad to comply!" said the older and bigger of the two, with a grin and a nod. He noticed that they both had crewcuts and wore revolvers concealed in holsters under their jackets.

Bob unloaded the car and took the picnic basket down to the beach, to see his two female companions walking at the water's edge, gently flicking their toes against the gently receding and incoming tidal ripples.

He placed the bag and his towel by theirs, which they'd left higher up the beach and went to join them.

"It sure is calm today," he remarked, as he approached. "Would you like to go deeper, say up to your waist?" he asked, directing his question at Pollyanna. "I've got an inflatable ring we can use, if you get frightened."

"Naw, it'll be okay, I'm not worried," she replied, scuffing at the wet sand with her bare feet.

Bob saw the two guards walking onto the beach, in shorts and carrying two towels on a plastic cool box. They dumped their things down, some distance away and sat there checking the surroundings before relaxing. One took a mobile phone from the cool box and made a call.

Bob drew Alice's attention to them and said, "No doubt they're reporting in, and calling for reinforcements to guard the cliffs behind us."

"Hey, look at that!" shouted Pollyanna, making Bob and Alice jump. She was pointing at an aquatic creature staring at them, from deeper water. It emerged to gain a better view, causing Bob to exclaim, "Wow, it's a Bottlenose dolphin! Those things can grow up to 13 feet long!"

Other heads began to pop up as well, as Bob added, "There's a whole pod of them out there!" They could see that smaller, baby dolphins were darting between the fully grown adults, and were beginning to give them quite a display.

To their alarm, Pollyanna shouted, "I'm going to join them!" as she pulled herself forward, using her hands as paddles to gain momentum. She was already standing chest high before Bob could reach her, and they stood there stock still, waiting to see what happened next.

Alice was standing in the shallows, with her hands covering her mouth in fear, while one of the guards rushed down the beach with a towel covering his drawn pistol, not to scare any of the others on the beach, who were watching what was going on, with fascination.

"They don't seem to be hostile," Bob murmured, but Pollyanna showed no fear at all, and was actually using clicking noises to 'talk' to them, which made him feel uneasy.

"Take it easy, take it easy!" he coaxed her, but his words were wasted.

The dolphins began circling them both at great speed, until Bob felt dizzy watching them. Then, every other one began leaping into the air, right out of the sea, and splashing down nose first, leaving the two of them dripping with water.

Finally, they began slowing down, and the babies took the opportunity to slide in between the adult dolphins and approach Pollyanna direct, nuzzling her gently with their snouts, while she clicked at them and they clicked back at her. It ended up with the entire pod surrounding her attentively.

Bob had the feeling that they were ignoring him, but he didn't care as long as they didn't hurt her.

After several minutes performing in this way, they slowly departed one by one and submerged, before suddenly picking up speed with their backs arched, showing their dorsal fins gleaming in the reflected sun as they swam into deep water.

Pollyanna stood there transfixed by the encounter, and then started quivering with emotion; Bob could see teardrops rolling down her cheeks from under her sunglasses.

"That was magical!" she cried, as Bob picked her up and carried her back to dry land, to where Alice and one of the guards were now standing. Alice rushed forward to cuddle and dry her with a towel, while the guard encouraged the fast gathering crowd of onlookers to give them more space.

People started checking their cameras and phones, trying to find out why none of them were functioning correctly, while the guard further away had his hand in his cool box, smirking as he adjusted the blocking device concealed inside it.

The guard performing crowd control came over afterwards, and asked Bob,

"How'd you know something like that was going to happen?"

"I didn't," Bob replied. "But I think our young ward was hopeful that it might!"

That night, after they'd eaten the evening meal, and as they were tucking Pollyanna into bed, she opened her eyes, and said something important to them.

"I am not alone you know. There are others, like me, who will shortly need your help, if they are to survive. The race that made beings like me intend to dispose of us, now that they have created another type of hybrid."

She sat bolt upright in bed, and cried out, "There aren't that many left, and anytime soon our creators will dispose of them, or release them into the world, to die from starvation or disease or be hunted down."

"Do you know where they are?" Bob asked.

"Yes," she answered, and lay down to sleep. "I will help you get them, without risk to me, if that worries you, I promise!"

Alice wondered, "Whatever is she going to come out with next?"

Bob commented, "I guess that Claude has got a reaction from the greys."

§ 21: A Clash Of Priorities

Bob phoned Claude, "Our delightful little girl, Pollyanna, is kicking up a ruckus. She is saying that there are more hybrids like her, out there, in imminent danger of death. I presume the greys have analysed the Type P sample you sent them and are reacting to it." He was beginning to dislike use of the word *hybrid*.

Claude replied, "I should think so. They are agreeable to the release of Sharon and David, provided we drop all development of Type P mutant strains."

Bob: "They sound a bit too amenable to me. Are they up to something?"

Claude: "Indubitably, and the way to find out is to comply. I'm happy to see what they intend trying, but if these hybrid kids are the way forward, I don't want to see them wiped out. What's your opinion of Pollyanna?"

Bob: "Absolutely fantastic. Me and Alice think the world of her, and she's so talented she's off the Richter scale!"

Claude: "I see, it's 'Me and Alice' now! Do I detect a 'heating-up' in the relationship?"

Bob, sadly: "No chance, I'm afraid. I'm too old for her."

Claude: "What! You said yourself you've got 200 years left in front of you."

Bob: "That was what the doctors said. It was an exaggeration of the truth."

Claude: "Rubbish, they meant it literally! Have you had your sperm count checked recently?"

Bob, indignantly: "Don't talk dirty! The relationship between Alice and myself is purely platonic!"

Claude: "Don't worry, I'll have a word with her myself."

Bob, angrily, "You keep your dirty paws off her! I know what you get up to, as The Inlooker!"

Claude, filing his nails: "I'm a reformed character now. I've got a son and two healthy women (in one body) to keep me satisfied. I promise not to disturb Alice in any way, provided you do something first."

Bob angrily slammed the phone down and tried to compose himself.

The next thing he got was a message from a PM's aide, saying that his boss, the main man, was coming to Aberporth without delay.

Twenty minutes later, Claude arrived at the helipotty pad and dismounted from the rear right side of his potty, followed by an aide who stumbled off on the same side, and then by the two guards who normally accompanied him, dismounting from up front. He headed at a brisk pace to meet with Bob, Alice and her team of geneticists on the 5th sub-level.

He stood facing the assembled throng, in a state of agitation.

"He's not a happy bunny," Jeremy whispered to those around him, who were trying to keep their faces a mask of innocence. "Something is vexing him."

Claude commenced his prepared short speech. "The !*****! greys have kept their word, and released my daughter Sharon and her husband back to us. They appeared at first view to be unharmed. This was not the case, and I intend taking retaliatory action. I am therefore ordering you to provide me with the Type B mutant variant of their hybrid DNA structure."

He glared at them all, sweeping his gaze venomously in all corners of the meeting room, before continuing, "Will you have it ready for me to collect, today?"

Collectively, the geneticists shrunk back, until Jeremy hesitantly raised his hand and said, "Yes sir, we have it ready, now."

The others gasped with relief.

"Good man, I knew I could rely on you!" Claude said, who then approached Alice and Bob directly. "I need to speak with the pair of you, alone. We are going to take immediate action to recover the Type P hybrids still out there!"

Alice stared him in the eyes and said, "Claude, calm down! Take a deep breath, count 15 seconds before exhaling, and then repeat this breathing exercise again and again. You need to sit down, drink coffee or tea with us, and try to relax. Whatever problems you face, they're not going to get any worse in the time you spend relaxing with us."

With a few minutes, as the coffee was ordered and delivered, he stopped hyper-ventilating and his capacity to think clearly returned.

Bob could see that Claude was now in better control of himself, and asked, "My dear friend, what has happened to upset you like this?"

Claude to a deep breath and related what had disturbed him. The facts read as follows.

Negotiations with the greys had begun in earnest. This was when they believed that they had succeeded in unravelling the DNA structure of the hybrid Type P mutant strain.

However, when they subsequently found out that human genetic scientists were ingenious enough to introduce 'Alternative, Randomly Self-modifying Egress Structures' into the mutant strain, they became extremely agitated. This was the description that the humans provided, in writing, with the mutant strain sample.

The greys were aware that this type of sentence structure was referred to as *INITIALISM*, and in this instance was intended as an insult to them, since it could be abbreviated to *ARSES*.

The greys easily identified the possibility that if the Type P strain was fed into the previously untainted DNA hybrid structure, it could - for example - mutate into a deformed being with stumpy arms, or eyes on stalks, or disproportionately large, webbed feet, thus making it impossible to integrate with normal humans.

"Okay, I can fix this!" their scientists gloated, and attempted to adjust the sample mutant variation submitted by The Inlooker. The consequence was that stumpy arms would change into stumpy legs, or a long, beaky nose would transmogrify into something resembling an anteater's wavy conk. It was all utterly random and unpredictable.

"This could take forever!" they moaned, after umpteen failed attempts to fix variations of this recurring problem once and for all. *"Better for us to break our treaty with the humans, and let them do what they wish with their blasted mutant strain. This hybrid was intended for them anyway, and if they don't want to accept it, that will be their loss! Let them contaminate this precious gift!"*

But what to do with the foul-mouthed nuisance of a sibling that was procreated by The Inlooker, and her husband? They were 'personas non gratas', after the verbal abuse they had hurled at innocent citizens of the greys' empire. And they were proving to be a threat to the top members of the grey's ruling body, the

Cupula, with their logical pleadings for release, as mistreated intelligent beings.

It was speculated that this 'cupula' was scared at the possibility that the humans had also gained knowledge of the existence of their alternative hybrid. This was the one the greys had developed in parallel, that was much closer to their needs to be able to function normally, and have children, and enjoy food and sex and have proper family lives.

Yes, far better to be nice to this 'Inlooker' and give him back his offspring, with a soupçon of retaliation to prove they were as good at genetics as the humans, and definitely their superiors at surgery.

It was a rare moment of joy for The Inlooker, hiding his true identity of Thomas Beckon in Claude Broadbent's body, as he clapped eyes on Sharon and her husband. He had to suppress his paternal desire to embrace her, since she would no longer recognise him as her father. She might even think he was getting frisky and be 'trying it on' if he was imprudent.

"Well done, my dear!" was all he dared to say, even though Pat Beckon, her mother, could enjoy the liberty of welcoming her with unrestrained hugs and kisses, as another woman, but hiding her true identity in Gloria Broadbent's body.

"*Life's not fair!*" he moaned inwardly, not daring to reveal who he was, even though he had raced after Sharon and her spouse through the universe to keep their spirits up. He glared at her husband, disliking him for some unfathomable reason, and then the penny dropped; he bore an uncanny resemblance to an old political adversary, whose name he had forgotten.

Claude and Gloria had chatted to Sharon and David for several minutes, before Claude invited the couple to proceed with them to their private quarters, above the PM's official residence. He was undecided whether or not to tell them that he was really Thomas Beckon in the PM's body, since he wanted with all his heart to converse candidly as the father of a reunited family, but backed off from doing so, sensing an abiding unease in their demeanours.

Claude had good reason to be wary of Sharon. As a teenage girl, she had shown her volatile side when a boy her age had made a sarcastic remark about her, which resulted in him getting hammered at her hands, on the school bus.

He, seeking protection from a repeat assault, had asked his older brother, a black belt in Karate, to intervene and warn her off whacking him again.

She listened stonily as the brother threatened her, at the front door of her parent's house, and then startled him by telling him in fisherwoman's language to push off and slammed the door on him. She was, at the time, having an unofficial day off from school, and was annoyed at being disturbed by this second member of The Munsters (a mythical TV family of benign monsters).

Memories of socially disastrous events like this made him clumsy in dealing with her, and he spluttered out, "What the devil's the matter? Why the sour puss? You've been released from a life of hell, and should be grateful! For heaven's sake get a grip on yourself!"

"Oh dear, I've screwed things up now!" he thought, fearing the consequences.

Normally, her reaction to these sorts of comments would have been unprintable, but coming from Claude, it sounded so much like her own father's type of response that she subconsciously reacted as if it was indeed coming from him.

Her face turned red, she cried in a sudden fit of rage, and tore angrily at the buttons of her trouser suit, to rid herself of her clothing and reveal the state of the naked body underneath. She accompanied this urge to reveal all with an outburst which went, "Look what the alien shites did to me! Look at it! This is their handiwork, the little grey jerks! Give me half a chance and I'll kick their puny arses from here to eternity!"

She turned to David, who was starting to blub in self-pity, and ordered him to, "Get your kit off as well! Don't stand there like a bloody lemon! Get it off or do I have to do it for you, you gormless specimen of manhood!" Clearly, the poor man had been accustomed until that moment to giving orders, and was bewildered by this demonic woman who he clearly didn't know as well as he thought he had, up till that moment.

He too clumsily disrobed as instructed, to stand naked in front of the three of them.

The facts were these: his head had been attached to Sharon's body, and her head was likewise attached to his. She was now the dubiously privileged possessor of his penis, while he was irrefutably equipped with its intended target.

Claude and Gloria looked at each other, resisting the urge to laugh, while building up sufficient outrage for their concern to appear to be genuine.

Never one to hold back her emotions, she glared at them both, challenging them by saying, "You think it's funny, don't you? I can read your bloody minds! Well let me tell you..."

That gained sufficient time for Claude to compose himself, as Gloria replied on their behalf, "Calm down dear and remember who you are speaking to!"

She didn't have to add to that demand, as Sharon again reacted instinctively by apologising, and saying, "Sorry dad!" Then she thought about what she had just said, and got defensive, "I'm so sorry! I can't believe I spoke to you like that! What was I thinking of, calling you my dad! Good grief, you're much younger than he ever has been!"

Claude felt indignant at the nature of her apology and the way she'd worded it, but decided to let matters rest, for now.

All of a sudden, he remembered that she didn't know that her father, Thomas Beckon, had passed away some time ago, and decided on the spur of the moment to give her the bad news.

"Sharon, since you have just mentioned your father. I'm sorry to inform you that he died some time ago."

Sharon looked puzzled. "Like when?"

Claude shifted uneasily before making a few calculations. "Let me see...Ah, it was round about the time you were abducted!"

She looked at him and shook her head emphatically. "No way, absolutely not! I know my own father, and he's been in regular touch with me and David in our travels through the universe. You're lying!"

She looked at him closely and said, "If I didn't know better, I'd say that *you* are my father, in disguise. Yes, I'm convinced of it, so own up!"

"Yes, own up! I'm fed up with this charade!" Gloria said, getting up. "I want Sharon to know who you and I really are!"

Claude found it easier to confess than deny, and told them about his abilities as The Inlooker, and how he, with Pat at his side in the guise of Gloria, had momentous tasks to perform on behalf of the human race.

Not surprisingly, given her personality, Sharon found it easy to accept, although David looked wretched and disbelieving. He stated his feelings by saying in a shaky voice, "If I hadn't had this encounter with aliens, I'd think you were a bunch of loonies!"

In a conciliatory tone, Claude concluded, "The important thing for you to remember is that I can help get the pair of you back into your own bodies, given enough time."

He was relishing this moment, after remembering how much grief she'd given him as a 'tweenager'.

Sharon eyed him suspiciously, "What'd you mean, given the time?"

Claude replied placidly, "There are negotiations underway with the aliens. It may take a month or two, but I feel confident that you will both be reattached the right way round in reasonable time."

He knew he was testing her patience, by giving an honest reply, but it was better that she faced up to the facts, as he had to.

To his relief, she didn't explode, but bit her lip and looked tearful. "At least I'll feel things as David does, and find out what pain he is in, first hand." David looked at her, hoping she didn't think he'd been 'faking it'; he was fast reaching the opinion that she could be a tough cookie, as tough as him when pushed.

This fear was reinforced when he saw the way she was studying him, like a starving dog that had dug up its long lost favourite bone. But the unthinkable had happened; it was hers already, the bone, and she looked like she wanted to put it back in the hole it belonged to, and it was starting to point in his direction.

"Two months, for my sake, make it only two months!" he prayed.

Claude leaned back with a grunt of pleasure, having relished the telling of this story in a candid way.

He concluded by saying, "In normal times, I would say that we have a clash of priorities between the need to round up the black-eyed kids before they are liquidized, and a need to switch heads and bodies."

Bob, who had refrained from laughing as best he could, replied, "I suggest we tackle things in the natural sequence: Kids first, switching bodies second. Anyway, you've got to get the Type B mutant strain across to the greys, for them to test, so the sequence has to be: the kids to be retrieved immediately.

"One other thing; don't you mean 'before the black-eyed kids are *liquidated*, not *liquidized?*"

Getting up to fetch his Type B mutant strain, Claude replied, "No, *liquidized* was what I meant. The greys are also capable of using us and their hybrids to rub on their stomachs."

Claude leant over the cowering geneticist, Jeremy, glowering at him. "Where's my Type B variant that you promised me? You said you already had it!"

Jeremy, shielding his head, said, "It's on its way, sir! It should be here any minute!"

At that moment, a colleague of Jeremy's rushed up, brandishing a sealed container, and interrupted the bullying posturing. "Here it is, sir, the Type B mutant variant just as you requested!"

"Hmm, you prepared it, didn't you? Jeremy was trying to take the credit for your efforts, wasn't he? What's your name, young woman?"

"Katie, sir."

As Claude walked away, to get Alice to courier the precious DNA mutant sample direct to the grey's underground base in Texas, he said over his shoulder, "Next time you try and perform a stunt like that, think of the fact that I don't like smart asses, or people who toady up to me.

"You two are only in your jobs because of your competence, which is why I haven't sacked you, Jeremy. Well done, Katie, and stop going out with him; he's not much of a man, is he? Anyone would think he's a naughty school boy, hiding his head like he did!"

While handing over the sample to Alice, he asked her "Would you mind if I spoke to Pollyanna direct? I'd like to hear her views on how we should tackle the recovery of the black-eyed kids."

She looked at him fearfully, "You're not going to involve her in this scheme, are you?"

Claude retorted, "Judge for yourself; be there with me, and invite Bob as well if you wish. I think that she could have ideas on how to get the others who are like her released. Don't mollycoddle her."

The four of them sat down in the conference room, with Pollyanna alongside Alice, and Bob and Claude opposite.

Pollyanna was finding it difficult to sit still, and one of her fingers was getting too close to her nose for Claude to stomach. He asked her, "What's the matter, have you got ants in your pants? Do you need a cocktail stick to help pick your nose? Do you have a salt deficiency? Didn't your aunt feed you before you came here?"

She studied him carefully before choosing how best to reply to his whiplash style of questioning, and then she waded into him. "I am sorry if I offend you, but I can assure you there are no ants in my pants, and if there were I'd have shaken them out before I got here. And yes, I was tempted to pick my nose but refrained out of courtesy, because my Aunt Alice has taught me good manners. And thank you very much, but my food needs were catered for at the start of the day."

She said this with much aplomb, silencing her critic, at which point he roared with laughter, and got up to join her. Sitting down next to her, he said, "Pollyanna, you are a treasure! Now let's get down to deciding how best we can help your friends escape!"

The first question from Claude, addressed to Pollyanna was: "Do you know where the other children are being kept?"

Answer: "Yes. They are being kept together in only a few underground bases, here in the UK and in the USA."

Question: "So you know the exact locations?"

Answer: "Yes."

Question: "Can you contact them, whenever you wish?"

Answer: "Yes."

Question: "Are they kept under guard? If so, by whom?"

Answer: "Yes, by the greys, who are fairly relaxed about keeping them there. After all, where can they go, unless told?"

Question: "Do you want me to help open doors, so they can leave without interference?"

Answer, with a question: "Can you really do that?"

Reply: "Yes, Pollyanna, and stop shaking your legs under the table. I'm getting kicked!"

Question from Claude: "When the children leave, how would you like them to send us a signal, so we know where they are grouped?"

Answer: "With dolphin clicks, like this…" She pursed her lips and made a series of high-pitched, repetitive rhythmic clicks. "We understand how dolphins communicate, having studied them on films and communicated with them when they were stored in tanks at the bases."

Question: "Do the greys know that you have this knowledge?"

Answer: "No, it's our secret way of communicating between ourselves."

Final question from Claude: "I assume you can give this instruction as far away as locations in the USA?"

Answer from Pollyanna: "True. The children will also be told that they have to make the clicking noises, at their chosen place of collection. I will record them for you, so your rescuers can recognise them as real."

"Excellent!" Claude said, slapping the table. This evening, we will be collecting your friends and taking them to safe locations."

Pollyanna looked up and said, "There's space for at least thirty small people in each of the larger craft you intend using. That will be more than enough, one for each country."

Bob said to Claude, "In case you weren't fully aware of the fact, she can easily pick up our thoughts at will."

Pollyanna chipped in, "Yes, isn't it wonderful! Am I not the luckiest hybrid child in the whole world? When I am privileged to give birth to the children of your offspring, Claude, they'll also inherit my gifts!"

"*I don't doubt it*" Claude thought. "*Who's she got in mind?*"

He looked at her sharply, to find her studying him, as she stuck her tongue out and laughed.

Alice intervened crossly, "Pollyanna, don't be so rude! He's the leader of our country and deserves respect!"

He gave the reprimanded, unrepentant child a wink.

At the allotted time and signal, the dormitories of the black-eyed children began to empty, as they collected their few, treasured possessions and tip-toed out of their familiar surroundings. They sneaked past the glassy-eyed greys who were their tutors and custodians, reaching the nearby lifts, where they ascended to the unattended halls. From there, they emerged unobserved into the greenery of the outside world that awaited them.

Uneventfully, they walked briskly to their defined pick-up points and looked skyward, before emitting the rhythmically urgent clicking noises that Pollyanna had instructed them to use.

Only the animals were watching, but soon scuttled away as barely visible, large, round flying space craft hovered above and illuminated the ground on which the cowering children huddled together. A ramp descended and crew members emerged, urging them to enter and sit in the welcoming rows of seats. When they had all been accommodated, the craft self-sealed and ascended at great speed, taking them to pastures new.

It had been a flawlessly executed plan. This was due in no small measure to their own Pollyanna.

There were only 17 children retrieved from the greys in the UK, and 33 from their bases in the USA. It was a sad total, considering how many must have been processed over the many decades since the treaty agreed between the humans and assorted alien races after the Second World War.

Where had they gone to? In all probability to their graves. The greys could be ruthless, when developing their hybrids, and would have had little compunction in getting rid of earlier versions when new ones were invented.

Nevertheless, there were grounds for optimism; with this nucleus of those that remained, the scientists could establish a seeding program that would merge the hybrids with the main stream of the human race. But first they had to place these precious survivors in safe places, where others would not be fearful of their peculiar eyes and try instinctively to destroy them.

For this primary reason, the Aberporth base was in lockdown when the large potty landed on the pad outside. Its cargo of hybrids was herded onto a troop-carrying lorry, to be driven through the vehicle entrance, direct to the decontamination reception area.

There, it was ensured that they were free of all potentially harmful contagious diseases and bugs, alien and otherwise, before entering the standard shower rooms, segregated by sex, to freshen up. There were only three girls amongst those who had been rescued

It was in the changing rooms outside the showers that trusted employees were on hand, to help them don oversized towelling robes to help them to dry. Afterwards, they were led into a room adjoining the main canteen, where they were urged to pick up trays and select food and drinks from the self-service trays they passed, accompanied by adults who told them what foods the trays contained.

Their bellies filled, the next room they were led into was a dormitory, laid out with camp beds, tables and chairs, so they could sleep or relax if they wanted, for a few hours until they were moved into permanent residences. Nearby was a reserved toilet block. All of this was explained to them, as they progressed from one place to another.

Most settled down to sleep, drained of energy after the stresses they had undergone.

The question of what to do with their small guests had been generously resolved by the PM himself. Being a fairly wealthy man, he had bought a small cluster of holiday homes at the unpronounceable address of Neuadd Cross, in the hamlet of Ponthirwaun, in the county of Ceredigion, which were located several minutes away from the base.

One of the detached Grade 2 houses was used by himself as a holiday retreat and to host regular visits to the base, and the others belonged to his daughters Sharon and Julie, although they hadn't been told about these acquisitions on their behalf. Currently, these two other houses were being furnished by local companies, ready for occupation by the children, and by staff recruited from the base, who would act in multiple capacities as wardens, cooks, counsellors and educators – just as they would if they were parents with children, at home (which in these instances, they weren't).

It was a secluded place, easy to secure and patrol.

In a few hours, they were being roused by a posse of cheerful adults, who had been given these roles vital to their development. After a break for another meal, they returned to their dormitory, in time to see rails of cloths lined up, ready for them to choose items for everyday wear and outings. Shortly after, they were to be taken to their new homes.

Apart from their large, black eyes and sharp wits, they were now indistinguishable from other children. This was also about to be remedied.

Whilst her companions being relocated to Claude's hamlet, Pollyanna was the centre of attention at the base, midday, when she would normally be relaxing in her classroom.

Claude and Alice were in the room, sitting with her, and Claude was asking, "Pollyanna, would you mind if I got a specialist to look at your eyes, such as an Ophthalmologist?"

"What's that?"

"A qualified specialist in eyes. I want to find out how different your eyes are from those of humans."

"Okay."

"Good, I'll take you to him. There's one here, at the base. Put your dark glasses on; I don't want you frightening the natives!"

The ophthalmologist was using, amongst other tools, a slit lamp and biomicroscope to inspect Pollyanna's eyes, individually.

"Mmm...apart from the all-embracing black membrane where the sclera (or white of the eye) would otherwise be, the eyes are functioning normally. There's an iris but it's barely visible, a cornea and a lens, behind the thinnest part of this substitute sclera. Is this a genetic deformity? I've never seen anything like it before."

Claude replied, "Yes, it's exceedingly rare. Can it be remedied?"

"I don't want to be cut" Pollyanna yelled, her body stiffening.

The ophthalmologist ignored her. "I'd like to get an Ocularist to take a look. The solution that springs to mind is 'a scleral cover shell prosthesis'."

He looked at Pollyanna with a smile and explained, "This is designed to be worn over the existing discoloration." He stared at her fixedly and said with relish, "Or it could replace this horrible black thing permanently, unless you feel squeamish. Either way, it is fitted in minutes, young lady, painlessly. My advice to you is: let the true colours of your eyes shine through!"

Claude met up with Alice and his new, favourite junior geneticist, Katie, to explain the situation to them, adding, "I should think the greys developed this black eye membrane naturally, to protect their sight against exposure to harmful rays, sometime over the millennia they've been around. With the speed that our medical knowledge is expanding, a simple, longer term remedy could soon be found."

Katie promptly replied, "I think I have the answer: we could modify the OCA2 gene in all the affected chromosomes, to modify the black sclera inherited by the black-eyed children!"

After she'd gone, Alice pouted, "I could have told you that!"

Claude said, "I know, but there's nothing like seeing other, rising stars emerging, is there? Anyway, you should be concentrating on Bob. He's so keen on you it's distracting him from my work!"

Claude had reason to feel pleased; the children, or those who were left of them, had been rescued and were being readied to play their part in the development of the human race.

Now, he could look forward to settling accounts on behalf of Sharon and David.

§ 22: Natural Order Is Restored

This part of the story is for all those who have an interest in things esoteric, like the intimate vagaries of Genetic Engineering.

The specialists amongst the greys had recently been provided by the humans with the Type B mutant strain, which was specific to the ammonia breathing hybrid that had been designed to take their race back to its reproductive roots.

They had examined the mutant strain in depth, and had found most of the locations where the human geneticists had embedded strands intended to distort the growth patterns of the embryo. These mutations, if not found and remedied, would have had a devastating impact on the growth of specific parts of the desired adult grey.

The precise consequences were revealed by enhanced acceleration of the growth of a specimen hybrid embryo, injected with the mutant strain. They found that the hands were going to be very strong, the arms long and muscular, and the supporting shoulders more than capable of carrying the trunk of the body, for prolonged periods.

In contrast, the legs would be short and spindly, much like those of a Kangaroo's original front legs, which in the real world could only be used as feeble arms; they were in fact totally disproportionate, measuring less than 12 inches long. Neither were the buttocks anything to write home about, being weak and flabby, like two, small wobbly jellies. It was a stroke of good fortune that the sexual organs were facing the correct, opposing directions, or was it?

Realisation set in that the end product of this genetic nightmare of a mutant creation would have to walk on his or her hands, and suffer excreted body waste landing on the head from above, front and rear. Before this possibility was revealed, they had been anticipating the arrival of normal, separate sexes!

The residual problem lay not in the very subtle modifications to rectify the mutations, but elsewhere. Each time the greys scientists achieved a modicum of success, the mutations reproduced themselves automatically.

Somewhere elaborately disguised and hidden, lay self-reproducing mutant strings of DNA code that searched for changes being made to the original DNA structures and re-instated them. It was like searching for umpteen needles in a haystack, with millions of places to search that seemed to be innocent, on the surface.

Happily, the provided sample of mutant strain was being kept separate to the independently developed ammonia breathing hybrid, which was going to be the greys' model for their future survival.

It was crucial that they were kept apart, but why had the humans gifted this sample to them knowing that they, the greys, could never allow the original hybrid and its mutant strain to meet? The threat of this 'firewall' not proving effective was a worry.

Timed to perfection, another meeting of the top cupula was breached again. The image of the solemn middle-aged female human wearing a uniform once more materialized in their midst, looked pointedly at Number 1 and stated: "*Sharon and David are not your playthings. This is the last warning we will give you. Put them back together again, in their correct bodies, or you will have no future hybrids to look forward to! You have been warned!"* The image rippled and vanished.

Number 1: *"How do they do this?"*
Number 2: *"Does it matter anymore? They've outsmarted us."*
Number 3: *"Yes! Recall the gruesome twosome heads on a platter and put matters right."*
Number 4: *"I don't trust the humans. They might infect our original hybrid anyway."*
Number 5: *"For once, we have to employ mutual trust."*
Number 1: *"I have a way to gain that trust. Recall the two humans for corrective surgery."*

Claude had returned to London, but phoned Bob and Alice excitedly, on a conference call line. "The greys have capitulated! They are providing a craft to collect Sharon and David, and undo the mischief they caused, no strings attached."

Bob asked cautiously, "Do you, can you, trust them?"

Claude replied, "Yes, they've handed over engineering drawings and a fully functional version of their faster-than-light-speed power unit. This will truly get us to distant stars.

"They've also reluctantly given us their deflection shield technology, to prevent our craft being damaged en route to these distant places. Now Bob, you can appreciate why I need to you to come back to the Potty Development Centre and confirm that these marvels of technology are the real McCoy, before Sharon and David return."

Bob replied, choosing his words carefully, "You do appreciate that I'll need help? The best I can get is available at The Skunk Works belonging to Lockheed, if that's alright?"

"That's okay with me, provided we all share the knowledge acquired."

Bob spoke to Alice, "I'm afraid I've got to go away for some time on urgent business. It involves new technology we've been gifted and I'm a key player in this. I'll miss you terribly, and Pollyanna." They hugged each other before parting, with her starting to kiss him on the cheek, before their lips met in a moment of tenderness and desire.

"I'll miss you too," she said, as they parted for a while.

As a result of this act of rapprochement between the two races, deep apprehension was being felt by Sharon and David. They were being transported back at breakneck speed to the twin star system of Zeta Reticuli, which is located a distance of some 39 light years from Planet Earth. There, they were to undergo a complicated operation by a top, resident team to transfer their heads between their existing bodies, and reverse the operations conducted by the original greys' medical operatives, in an act of unwarranted malice.

It was considered essential for the twin operations to be successful, in order for the greys' own future to be safeguarded with the smooth launch of a new breed of hybrids that would allow them to revert to traditional methods of reproduction. Their present evolutionary path had led them up a blind alley, where they were now social outcasts who had no children being born naturally, and no method left to them of ingesting food other than by rubbing liquid proteins on their bellies.

The method they had to resort to for excretion of their body waste was equally unconventional by anyone's standards.

It was a taboo topic, in polite greys' social circles, where stenches could be generated unawares at the most inopportune moment.

They also lacked the qualities of compassion, love, tenderness and understanding, which was why they could be cruel on occasion, since they didn't possess these sensitivities.

Conversely, open warfare and religion were also beyond their comprehension, and they fully understood why the human race was cooperating with them to breed this 'lust for logicised vengeance' out of their own, emerging race. It was an early, survival instinct that was no longer of value in the present age, as these 'new kids on the block' sought mental maturity.

Sharon and David were led, trembling with fear, into the presence of the medical team that had been assembled for the task, and were mentally sedated as they lay down on the bare, metallic slabs. Vocally silent, with their minds sharing their accumulated skills, the surgeons delicately separated the heads from the bodies along the original, faintly visible seams, while maintaining the blood flow to allow all the vital organs to function undisturbed.

Swiftly, they re-attached them to the correct male and female bodies this time, and at top speed re-connected all the discs, tissues and ligaments, with the aid of a small army of micro robotic creatures, each performing its own, dedicated routines very precisely.

When the two patients awoke, they were in a highly sanitised small ward, containing them alone, gratefully breathing their own oxygen-rich atmosphere. They felt drained of energy, which they began recovering as greys of indeterminate sex tended their needs and fed them with bland, vitamin rich food.

"Get away!" David snarled at one inquisitive grey, who was no more than 3 feet tall, who had lifted a corner of the sheet covering him, and was trying to find out where it was best to insert a bedpan under his backside. "I' don't need the blasted thing yet!"

He looked at Sharon and commented bitterly, "You've got a lot to answer for, Wifey! My 'bone' is aching like mad!"

She returned his stare and replied starchily, "No doubt you'll allow it plenty of time to recover. There's more to marriage than you lead yourself to believe. there's also marital duties to perform.

"Congratulations!"

"What'd you mean?" he asked her, wondering what she was suggesting.

She put her hands behind her head and said with a broad smile of satisfaction, "I'm pregnant! Count you're lucky stars that you don't have to carry the product of my efforts for the next eight months!"

What she would never admit to was suffering down below from 'Thrush', a yeast infection, usually caused by a fungus called Candida albicans. This is often associated with newlyweds.

They were discharged within days, Sharon being anxious to get away from her hosts in case they tried to kidnap her baby.

David didn't think that was a likely event, having picked up 'vibes' that their previous bad behaviour would make that possibility unlikely.

David's reasonable assumption was, "*Who, in a sane mind, would want our offspring to sire their own race, after what we and The Inlooker did to them? They've got bad memories of us.*"

There was a noticeably louder humming noise coming from the space craft they were in, on their return journey to Planet Earth than there had been coming, and the stars outside were being passed in a constant blur.

It wasn't until they slowed down, just before entering earth's atmosphere, that they could see where they were, and the pilots began to monitor the landing routine.

Their arrival was unexpected, occurring as soon as it did, and when immigration officials realised they were dealing with the PM's haughty 'Goddaughter' as she claimed herself to be, wheels were set in motion to alert the press and then the PM, in that sequence of priority. They were driven to 10 Downing Street in an unescorted potty, and marched into the PMs Inner Office, to be greeted with great enthusiasm by Claude and Pat. Sharon lost no time in announcing her pregnancy.

"That's great!" said Claude, emotionally. "Isn't it wonderful, having a child at the age of 59!"

"Oh my Aunt Fanny!" said David, rolling his eyes, as Sharon looked shocked.

"What'd you mean, 59? I'm only 47!" she demanded to know, while Gloria covered her face with her hands, to hide her embarrassment.

"You ninny!" Gloria said, dropping her hands to stare at Claude in despair.

Claude tried to deflect their attention by looking at her neck. "Would you look at those scars, they're hardly visible! That's skill that is!

Sharon looked at herself in a mirror and burst into tears; the scars were indeed faint, but there was a slight, reddish infection either side of them.

"That's nothing, it's to be expected; it's probably a common reaction," Claude surmised, unhelpfully.

He turned to David and asked, "Can I see yours?"

"No chance, not while you're so undiplomatic! How many wars have you started recently? Come on, let's go," he said to Sharon, marching off.

Sharon asked, "Where to? We've got nowhere to stay, and why are you trying to boss me around?" David stopped in mid-stride.

Trying to recover the initiative, Claude blurted out, "We've bought you a detached house in West Wales. It's the ideal place to recuperate. Stay there as long as you like! It's yours!"

Gloria intervened, "Er Claude, haven't you forgotten something?"

Realising he'd made another bloomer, having lodged the black-eyed kids there, Claude tried to remedy the situation.

"Or there's the Nag's Head pub not far from it. We'll put you up there for as long as you want. In fact, it's up for sale, and I'll back you if you wish to put in an offer. A good living you'll make there, and it's very near Cenarth Falls. It's worth checking out, thoroughly."

Sharon replied sharply, "Where's that, if it's to be called home? Is it really called the Nag's Head?"

She decided that nothing would be gained by further exchanges and said, resignedly, "Look, we'll take up that offer, seeing as it's the only one now on the table. If you could write down the address of the first place you mentioned, so I know where it is?" What she really meant was, "*So I know it really exists!*"

"Good!" Claude replied, hastily writing it down on a piece of paper and handing it to her. "I'll get you a four seater potty, so you, Sharon, can spread out on the back seat! You can mount it in the back garden, here."

Regaining her appetite to be argumentative, she replied, "I've not had the baby yet! Or are you implying I've put on weight? Are you having another dig at me?"

David tried to intervene, "Guess what? My skin condition's been dealt with. I no longer have it!"

Sharon looked at him snootily, "Come to think about it, I never felt a skin condition when I was in your body! Were you having me on, just to air your residual bad temper?"

He flapped his arms in exasperation, cursing silently.

Claude looked relieved when an aide arrived, and gave him some eagerly awaited news.

He said, "Hey, let's not quarrel! Your potty awaits you, madam! Go and mount it!"

After they left, Pat, who was in charge of Gloria's body for this overdue visit, sighed, "Oh Thomas, you and Sharon never have get on. Things don't change much, do they?"

A few weeks later, Bob reported back to Claude. "Everything's fine. The faster-than-light-speed power unit performs superbly, as does the deflection shield."

"Excellent! Now we can upgrade our fleet of deep-space craft."

"I suggest we contract the work out to Lockheed and British Aerospace, as a joint venture. I'd like to be released for a while, to get back to Alice and Pollyanna."

"Sure. I've got to spend some time with my other daughter, Julie, and see how she's doing." Claude vowed not to repeat the same mistakes as he'd made with Sharon. "It's a long time since I've met up with her and her family."

"Incidentally, as regards my other family, Sharon and David; the operation went well with the greys, and they are now in their correct bodies. She's having a baby, you know!"

There was a pause while Bob digested this fresh information. With his head cocked on one side, he asked Claude, "By my estimation, this means that she inseminated herself?"

"Sort of," Claude replied dismissively, "But not quite. She was using his body at the time, to um... energize the process."

The greys' cupula was simultaneously holding its own investigation on the handling of the issues revolving around the two mutant strains.

Number 1: *"How did the humans know when to intervene, with this female of theirs issuing warnings to us?"*

Number 2: *"Yes, the timing was perfect. They seemed to know exactly what we were doing, and when we were doing it."*

Number 3: *"It was as if they were watching us!"*

Number 4: *"I have thought about this, and come to a conclusion."*

Number 5: *"Which is?"*

Number 4: "*That this Inlooker was amongst us, monitoring us, from within.*"
Number 1: "*That would explain the strange feeling I have had that I am not always on my own, but am being accompanied! This is a worry, since it means that they could easily have merged the Type B mutant strain into the Type B hybrid DNA structure without hindrance, using me as their agent!*"
Number 2: "*That is a strange coincidence. I too feel that I have been accompanied! But whenever I check, I am on my own, without memory of a strange being occupying part of me.*"

Number 6: had arrived on the scene and now announced,
"*Which is why we are here!*"
It pointed to its companion, Number 7, who had entered the Cupula Chamber with it.
"*We are here to replace both of you, Number 1 and Number 2, on charges of espionage and sabotage. Until your innocence or guilt can be established, you will be barred from high office, and you will assume temporarily our numbers 6 and 7. Go now to Inquisition Room 1, for interrogation.*"

After a period, when the cupula held another of its regular meetings.
Number 3: "*What has happened to Number 6 and Number 7?*"
Number 1: (the new Number 1) "*They have been liquidized. A pity really, because they could have been spared that death. We now grow food and rear animals for meat, like the humans do, and*

could have shown compassion to them. This 'food' is eaten by our fast growing hybrids."

Number 4: "*What is compassion?*"

Number 2: (the new Number 2) "*Compassion is the quality of forgiveness. It is a human quality that our hybrids are demonstrating in abundance.*"

Number 3: "*We don't have compassion. Where did our hybrids get it from? This is a frightening development! Have they been contaminated with a modified Type B mutant strain?*"

Number 4: "*Number 1 and Number 2; have either of you had the feeling that you are not alone, that someone is with you?*"

Number 1: (the new Number 1) "*I confess to nothing!*" *Neither should you, Number 2, if you value your continuing life!*"

Number 4: "*The fact that you are thinking in a fearful way suggests that an exterior force has also infected you! It was probably The Inlooker! I have checked with all the other numbers in this cupula, and none of us has these human frailties.*"

History repeated itself when:

Number 6: (the newly appointed Number 6) arrived on the scene and announced,

"*Which is why we are here!*"

It pointed to its companion, the newly appointed Number 7, who entered the Cupula Chamber with it.

"*We are here to replace both of you, Number 1 and Number 2, on charges of espionage and sabotage. Until your innocence or guilt can be established, you will be barred from high office, and you will*

Sharon and David were already lodging at the Nag's Head Inn and Restaurant. It was downhill of the main village of Abercych, on the northern border of Pembrokeshire, and facing the fast flowing river Cych.

"What'd you think of it?" David asked, laying back on the deep, sumptuous double bed. "I find it very tranquil myself."

"Very nice, but it needs a dollop of money spent on it, to bring it up to a decent standard," Sharon replied, assessing it as its prospective owner. "These bedrooms have been modernised, but there aren't enough of them for my liking. As for the pub itself, it's a bit dowdy, but it does seem to be attracting a lot of regulars. It could be worth a look at the accounts. Let's go and have breakfast."

They'd both washed and dressed, before laying back down on the bed, to watch the flat TV; this was on top of a chest of drawers on the opposite side of the room. They locked the room after exiting, and left by a flight of steel steps mounted on the outside of the property. "I don't like this," she said, "It's been bolted on as a safety requirement. I bet it's a dash when it rains around here, as it must often do, in wet West Wales."

As they walked into the pub's snug bar, using the side under the exterior steps, one of the staff, a smiling, older lady approached and led them to a table, already laid with place settings. "Would you like the full, Welsh fried breakfast?" They both nodded, as she invited them to tuck into cereals and milk while the main course was being fried. In minutes, a large pot of hot coffee was put in front of them, with triangles of toast in a silver rack.

The lady owner was doing the cooking, and said, "It'll be ready in ten minutes, for the duchess."

She had latched onto this nickname from the guests' married name of Duke, and was of the opinion that Sharon was the boss in the marriage, from her airs and graces.

The 'duke' himself was a down to earth sort of guy, but he didn't look as if he suffered fools gladly, so she kept a respectable distance from him. He had the most amazing pale blue eyes, like she'd seen in photos of Steve McQueen.

"*Killer eyes they are,*" she reckoned.

The potty they'd arrived in was parked slap in the middle of their large, unmade car park, which had annoyed her at first, but she didn't like to ask them to move it, in view of their status as prospective buyers.

"That was superb!" David said after clearing his plate.

"I agree!" Sharon said. "When we finish upstairs, let's head off and find this house I'm supposed to own. I'll give Claude a ring, so he knows where we're going."

Within a quarter hour, they were picking their way between the pools of water in the car park, with Sharon complaining, "Bloody dump! This is one thing I'd fix if I were to buy this place, as well as that stupid name! I reckon we were put up here because my father thinks that's what I am!"

David wisely kept his opinion to himself, but thought, "*I think it should be rechristened 'The Bloody Nag's Head'!*"

The potty was given the address by Sharon, confusing its guidance system by her bad pronunciation of *Ponthirwaun* as 'Poncy one'.

The biological chip at the heart of the control system had decided from the outset that it would be better to keep a respectful distance from its current occupants, in particular from the one named 'Sharon Duke'.

When this confusion first arose, the chip tried to clarify matters by asking, "Excuse me, but I cannot find anywhere local that is called *Poncy*. My search reveals that a *Ponce* is defined as an effeminate man, or someone who lives off a prostitute's immoral earnings. That is not what you meant, was it?"

To a suppressed chuckle from David, Sharon frowned and looked around the rim of the potty, trying to find who or what was addressing her.

"Who's that?" she asked imperiously, having failed in her search.

"This is Miss Chip," the biological chip replied, pompously. "I control the mind of this potty. Please answer the question, or spell the name you are seeking."

Sharon cursed under her breath, replying, "It is spelt *P O N T H I R W A U N*. Is that clear enough for you?"

After a short pause, Miss Chip confirmed by saying, "Yes, I have found the destination. Please improve your diction in giving future instructions."

David was in stitches by this stage, until Sharon glared at him.

"There's no way I'm getting into an argument with a stupid machine!" she decided, and wisely stayed silent.

"Your modicum of self-restraint is appreciated." Miss Chip relayed dispassionately, brain to brain, using telepathy. *"I will take you there forthwith."*

They flew above the tree tops and poles carrying cables, using the exact route they would have followed if they were on the road itself. At the brow of a hill, they veered off to the right, where they flew above a narrow lane leading back down the slope of the hill. Occasionally en route, there were short wider sections allowing traffic to pull in and wait if oncoming vehicles were encountered.

Dark grey, slated roofs came into view further down, sheltering on the lower slopes of a valley, with a security barrier and cabin to one side, preventing access via the lane. A beam of light focused on the potty, and a warning was issued to the potty's chip for them to land at a nearby helipotty pad, adjoining the security barrier.

A stern looking, uniformed guard approached as the potty settled on its struts and its occupants dismounted. He looked at his records and compared them with the two, expected guests, before giving them a welcoming smile.

He pointed in the general direction of a cluster of large detached houses. "The property you are seeking is the second on the left, facing the lane leading to the interior courtyard. Enjoy your visit!"

With her nose stuck in the air, Sharon asked, "What if it was raining; would we be expected to walk then, as well?"

The guard frowned, looking puzzled. "No, we would have provided you with a buggy. But it's not raining, so what's the problem?"

"There isn't one, so never mind!" She was still in 'enquiry mode', after her inspection of The Nag's Head, and unaware at times of how aloof her attitude could appear to be, to strangers.

She and David looked around and were impressed by the quality of the restored houses. "Tastefully and sympathetically done!" was her stated opinion.

As they approached, the main door was opened by a male in his late twenties, wearing a track suit and a welcoming smile.

He came forward to embrace them in turn, saying, "Mr and Mrs Duke? Please come in and enjoy our hospitality. It's so nice to meet you, and to thank for allowing us the temporary use of your home."

They crossed the threshold and were shown into a large room on the right, with sunlight streaming in through its wood-framed windows on both sides. What drew their attention was not the room itself, the ceilings of which were authentically wood beamed and the floor laid with large slag-slate slabs, but the thirteen young children sitting squat-legged and facing them.

"Good lord!" murmured Sharon, as her and David were taken aback by the large, totally black eyes surveying them, emotionlessly.

The spell was broken when, with a chorus of high-pitched voices, the youngsters greeted them, "Hello Sharon, hello David. Thank you for allowing us to stay here, and sorry if we are a nuisance!"

Without ado, Sharon responded by sitting on the floor in front of them, her legs crossed and posture relaxed, before answering, "It is my pleasure to see you all here, safe and sound. I hope you are enjoying yourselves?" David sat next to her, fascinated by these strange, young creatures.

"*Where do they come from?*" he wondered.

As if on cue, they startled Sharon and David by using their minds to communicate their story of group escape and survival with pictures and commentary in the most thrilling of ways, as if it was just an adventure story - which in a way it was, told this eager way.

Sharon suppressed her emotions as best she could, only the tears forming in her eyes showing how she felt.

She decided to respond, in kind, and as best she could she mentally related to them her tale, of the cruelties inflicted on her and David at the hands of their creators, the race of greys that had spawned them.

She realised that this cold and callous race of beings would have dispensed with the children if given the chance, and her heart went out to them. She also felt more kindly disposed towards her father, Thomas, now that she knew how cleverly he had dealt with the threats presented by the greys.

The children gasped as her story unfolded, and when it ended they rushed forward to surround her and David and hug them as equal victims, with staff watching bemused at the sudden bonding, unaware of what was being relayed, confidentially.

After things had settled down, the kind young man who had welcomed them on arrival came into the room, gave a clap to draw their attention, and said, "Come on, let's have something to eat with our visitors." The other track-suited adults helped to carry in trays of food and drinks, to lay on the large table at the far end of the room.

Afterwards, the children started to show another side to their nature, while relaxing around Sharon, who sat with them once more on the floor.

One of the girls had asked for sheets of paper, and started folding one of them, Origami style.

"What's that you're doing?" Sharon asked her, "and what's your name?"

The little girl replied, "I'm making you a coronet. Look!" she said proudly, holding it up for all to see. "And my name was Number 11.1, but we decided I should be called Laura!"

"Put it on your head!" she ordered Sharon, saying excitedly, "See, it's fit for a duchess!"

Sharon wondered, "*How clever can these alien-bred children become? Did Laura read my mind or did she make the connection from my married name of Duke?*"

Slightly later, she noticed one of the boys mischievously picking up a scoop of clotted cream with a teaspoon, and flicking it at another boy. What startled her was the sudden stop of the scoop, mid-air, with no one near it, until the boy at whom it was aimed allowed it to continue its journey into his mouth. He swallowed it, with his eyes closed and gave a satisfied burp.

Another of the three girls was presented by one of the boys with a half-full plate of jam tarts. The others giggled as she reached for one of them, and they all slid away from her outstretched hand, huddling at the far side of the plate.

They were constantly playing tricks like these on each other, until it became late afternoon, and it was time that 'Aunty Sharon' and 'Uncle David' decided to leave.

"Will you come back and see us again?" the children asked, jumping up and down eagerly, in anticipation.

"Yes, of course we will, soon!" Sharon replied, while David looked at her with a smile, pleased at the softening of her attitude.

They said their goodbyes to the children with kisses and hugs, before formally shaking hands with the beaming staff and taking the short stroll to their waiting potty.

The minute the potty ascended, Sharon burst out crying, and held David tightly. "I hope that our baby, when it is born, never has to face the types of ordeal that we and those poor children have had to! Life can be so cruel at times!"

David replied, "You know, I like this part of the country so much, with its relaxed way of life. Perhaps we should consider settling down here? The way I earnt my living is fast disappearing, and no one wants to buy second-hand cars anymore; potties have put an end to that way of travel, once and for all!"

Sharon replied, "Yes, it is nice here. As the world population decreases, it will get more rural in places like this, and I think this area is ripe for tourism to blossom. Eventually, my future house will be handed over to me, although it will not feel the same when those lovely children vacate it.

"If Claude is willing to provide the funds, perhaps we could draw up a plan to reform The Nag's Head and settle in for the duration? I have had my fill of travelling, as you can imagine!"

§ 23: Another Reunion In The Offing

Sharon had regained her conscience. She finally wanted to settle down in Cardiganshire (Welsh *Sir Aberteifi*), also often signposted as Ceredigion, and enjoy the fruits of her father's largesse. She could hardly think of him now, without his sharing the presence of Claude in the overall scheme of things. Thomas Beckon may have been the real driving force in matters of state, but it was always in Claude Broadbent's persona. This 'Inlooker' thing was bizarre.

On the spur of the moment, Sharon decided, "*I've got to clear my debts.*" What was uppermost in her mind was her credit worthiness, or rather the lack of it. She and David had waltzed off to America when the potty craze began to take over as the main type of transport, and their second-hand car business looked like it was going to fail.

She phoned up the leading credit rating agency and, heart beating fast, asked to check what debts were on her and David's formal records. To her pleasure, they had all been cleared years ago by an anonymous benefactor. She was debt-free, and could contemplate a future that included plans for a desirable business like The Nag's Head.

It was obviously her father's doing, and she phoned up Claude to say a big 'thank you'. While they were speaking, she took the opportunity to mention her memorable visit to see the black-eyed children, about whom she was gushing in her praise.

She also told him how knowledgeable they were about their creation and upbringing by the aliens, and the gratitude they felt for the help provided in their escape from probable death.

Claude paused before replying, "My close friend and confidante Bob is returning to the base near you, at Aberporth. Why don't you contact Alice, the head of the team of geneticists at the base, and arrange to meet them both? She is someone he is very fond of, and has a ward called Pollyanna. I think you'll find that Pollyanna has a special bond with the black-eyed children. I'm sure they'll all be delighted to see you."

Sharon intended mentioning a duty that she really wanted to perform. Being mindful of the possibility of the call being monitored, she said, "Claude, after I hang up, I'm going to call my sister Julie and bring her up to date with what is happening in my life, and therefore in hers too."

There was silence the other end.

Sharon asked, "What's up?"

Claude finally answered. "I've just ensured that this line is scrambled. I'm afraid I've been remiss in keeping in contact with your sister and her family. She knows nothing of what has been going on under my new identity. Could you brief her, in advance of the situation? As far as I'm aware, she thinks I'm dead! It'll soften the impact."

Sharon pondered the situation and replied, "No, it's up to you to do that! How could I possibly explain all that you've been up to, or that mum is by your side and still alive as a resident spirit? No, it is your responsibility so don't be a coward!"

He reluctantly agreed, and gave her Alice's contact number.

Before she put the phone down, Sharon said quietly, "Thanks again for all the help you've given us. No matter who you become in future, always keep in touch."

The call ended.

Claude called an aide and asked her to make enquiries about the neglected Julie and her family, and provide details about their current circumstances.

It was soon reported that she and her husband Oscar were in good health. She was still running the original, specialist garment business, which was ticking along nicely in its niche share of the eco market.

It was also reported that her children Tam, Keats and Hazel were in their teens and doing well in their education. Tam was now in sixth form.

Claude wondered, "*Where did she get the name 'Tam' from? The only Tam I know is from the famous poem 'Tam O' Shanter' by Robert Burns. It is about a farmer called Tam who is chased by the scantily-clad witch 'Nannie', dressed only in a 'cutty sark', an archaic Scottish name for a short nightdress.*"

The problem was that Julie was never a problem child, and Claude (that is to say, Thomas) had always felt relaxed about her behaviour, even into adulthood. That was why he had left her to her own devices, but this had become tantamount to neglect in recent years, and bringing her back into the fold was going to be awkward.

An idea sprung into his mind, and he made an arrangement that might help to overcome this obstacle.

There was a knock at the door, which Julie answered. She and her family were living at her deceased parents' house, Thomas's favourite abode, and it brought a lump to his throat, standing there at the entrance to what he couldn't help regarding as his own property.

She stood there looking at him with a puzzled expression, until she recognised him.

"Good heavens! It's you, our Prime Minister, isn't it? I remember seeing you at my mother's funeral! And didn't you come to my father's as well? Come in!" she said, inviting him into the hallway. "Would you like a cup of tea, or a coffee?"

"Coffee would be fine, if you wouldn't mind."

"If you come with me into the lounge and sit in one of the comfy chairs, I'll go and fill a percolator. Will Java be to your taste?"

He nodded, fiddling with the folder he was carrying and looked around the room with appraising eyes. Nothing much had changed; they always had similar, if not complementary tastes in furnishings. The style of furniture was still traditional dark wood, but the walls had been freshly repainted.

She came back into the room, carrying the full percolator, a sugar bowl, a jug of cream and two small coffee cups on saucers, with dainty spoons. The style of serving was to his liking, and one he had employed regularly, in his previous incarnation.

They sat either side of the empty fireplace, in quiet contemplation as they sipped their coffees together. Claude broke the silence by asking, "How's the family? Is everything okay?"

She nodded, asking, "And with you? Is the country running well, under your leadership?"

He looked at her carefully, ignoring the question, and remarking, "You've hardly aged over the years."

"Thank you!" she said, looking pleased at the compliment. Looking at Claude more keenly, she judged him to be somewhat stiff and restrained in his posture, as if he was on edge; handsome and slim too in a way that many women might find attractive, with a polished accent.

He handed her the folder, saying, "I want you to read this. It's quite thick, and it describes events over the period before and since your parents 'passed on'. It is illuminating, and I am going to take a stroll around the garden while you are absorbing its contents.

"Hopefully, it will bring us close together, but it could drive us apart. Whatever the outcome, remember that I am telling you now that I love you and your family, will forever love you, and am deeply sorry for any upset I may have caused you in the past. When you call me back indoors, I will answer any questions you wish to raise."

She looked up as he rose and walked into the back garden, her brow furrowed at trying to interpret what he had said, then she began reading the intriguing autobiography that had been retrieved from a vault in Hatton Garden.

A quarter hour later, Julie came out to look for him. He was standing in the shade of the arbour that he had erected many years ago in the centre of the garden, tenderly scooping a pink rose in his hand and wafting its scent under his pointy nose, with his eyes closed, reminiscing.

She asked him, in a determined way, "Would you mind answering some questions?"

"Fire away," he said, opening his eyes and sitting on one of the two stone benches he'd once positioned there, in the shade of the arbour with its climbing roses.

She sat on the bench opposite, and so the questions flowed. They included:

"How did we set up the clothing business?"

(By recruiting an army of home workers to sew the garments, and renting a unit on an industrial estate near here, to supervise and coordinate activities, and package the finished products. Is that what you meant?)

"What was the main garment and what purpose did it best serve?"

(A long robe with cowl, to keep a person warm in a cold room. The rise in electricity costs was foreseen as motivation for people buying the robe.)

"Which retailers did we approach to sell the garment?"

(Liberty's, Harrods, Selfridges and other upmarket stores in London.)

"Describe the vehicle we used to market the garment, when we travelled around the country?"

(It was a gleaming black Ford Estate.)

"How did you acquire the cash funds to finance the spin-off business venture that made you famous?"

(By syphoning off the accumulated surplus cash in the garment business. I haven't told you this before, but I also stole money from rich strangers in London. I could be unscrupulous in those days!)

"Where was the new venture located?"

(In a unit next door to the garment assembly unit, near this house.)

"Who was your business partner and best friend in that venture?"

('Call me Bob', who came from Lockheed's Skunk Works in the USA.)

Then it got more family orientated.

"Describe some of the more memorable holidays we went on?"

(*Paris, repeatedly, and Orlando.*)

"Tell me of the gaffs you made, when buying clothes for us as children?"

(*Brown patterned dresses, identical, that you and your sister hated because they were identical!*)

"What questions did I always ask when we started off on holiday?"

(*When are we going to get there? How long will it take? Then, 'I want to go toilet', after we started a long drive.*)

What hairstyle did you and mum insist on giving me, when I was six years old?"

(*A bob cut above the neck, just like Twiki the robot, in the TV series 'Buck Rogers in the 25th Century'. 'Biddy Biddy' we used to say to you, just to aggravate.*)

"What action did you take when Sharon upset you, before we drove on a trip abroad, by sea, to Belgium?"

(*I tore up the tickets, and mum had to sellotape the pieces back together.*)

"When we stayed at an apartment in Paris, what was the creature that kept following you around the dining room, every time you moved?"

(*It was a huge flatfish in an aquarium that kept following and staring at me wherever I went or sat!*)

Julie stared at him dumbfounded, before bursting into tears and rushing over, to hug him.

"Dad oh dad, how could you ignore us for so long?"

Tearfully, he explained, "There was so much to be done in such little time. Believe it or not, I achieved an unimaginable position of power. I still occupy it, and will give you glimpses of understanding. *But*, and it is a big, big *but*, I could never have involved my family, or you would have been abducted and tortured.

"The same applies to Sharon, who suffered that fate but was rescued. Speak to her and see what she went through. We have lost time and need to make it up. I want to meet Oscar, Hazel, Tam and Keats and get to know them."

He waited a while to give her both the opportunity to recover her composure, before saying, "Please accept the gift I am about to give you. I have bought each of you girls, my grown-up daughters, a detached house. They are next to mine in a hamlet in Cardiganshire, West Wales. I'll email the details to you, in the hope that you can pay a visit there and meet some unusual youngsters.

"Only then will you begin to comprehend what has been done, for the sake of humanity. Since you won't be able to stay at the house for the time being, I've arranged for you to be put up for a week or so at one of the guest cottages near where Sharon and David are staying."

Meanwhile, Sharon was phoning Alice and introducing herself as 'Claude's goddaughter', saying that she was hoping to meet her and Pollyanna, at Claude's bequest. This claim to be his goddaughter was getting to be a trend, since it avoided complications.

If the truth was told, it would be difficult to explain that she was really Thomas Beckon's daughter, whose spirit resided in Claude Broadbent, the Prime Minister, who did his bidding as his 'puppet master'. It was a hardly believable way to introduce oneself was it?

However, Bob was with Alice at the time of the call, and knew exactly how to explain to her the complex relationship between Thomas and Sharon. He gave her the thumbs up to inviting Sharon and David to visit them that evening, suggesting the time and date with sign language.

Alice looked at Bob and confirmed with Sharon, "Yes, would this evening be convenient, at 6pm?" After she put the phone down, he told her that Sharon was Thomas's daughter and explained exactly how he operated as a strange referred to as 'The Inlooker'.

"Got it!" she said, breezily.

"Just to make sure, recite what I've told you back to me," he urged, which she did precisely.

"That's great!" he confirmed, relieved. "I'd underestimated you. No wonder you're a leading geneticist! Is Pollyanna alright for clothes? We want her looking her best."

That evening, Sharon and David dodged the pools of muddy rain water in The Nag's Head roughly surfaced car park, mounted the potty and were whisked at low level, up hill and down dale, to Bob's cottage. There was no overt sign of activity at the Aberporth base entrance as they flew past it.

They were greeted at the cottage door by Bob and Alice and ushered into the warm interior, where Pollyanna waited by the burning low-stacked wood fire. She gave a well-executed curtsy and said politely, "It's a pleasure to meet you, Sharon."

Sharon was pleasantly surprised, and replied formally, "The pleasure is all ours, Pollyanna. May I introduce my husband, David?"

She gave him another curtsy, saying, "It's a pleasure to meet you as well, sir. I understand we've got something in common!"

Adopting the same style of making introductions, David contained his mirth as he kissed the back of her hand and asked her, "To what are you alluding, young lady?"

She replied solemnly, "Why sir, I am referring to the close encounters we both suffered at the hands of the alien race called 'the greys'."

Sharon whispered to Alice, "I could eat her all up, she's gorgeous!"

To Pollyanna she said, "Well why don't we find a comfortable place to sit down together and relate to each other our experiences?"

"Willingly!" Pollyanna said, pulling her by the hand towards some armchairs, placed by the front window and beckoning David to follow them. All three of them sat down and, at Sharon's bequest, Pollyanna opened proceedings by telling them how she was created by the greys as a hybrid, in accordance with a treaty signed between the humans and this race of aliens, who would otherwise have invaded Planet Earth forcibly.

She went into some depth about her upbringing by the greys, and eventual abduction from them by a snatch squad recruited specially by 'The Inlooker'. She told it in an excited way, with Alice charging in and adopting her, as her ward.

When she had finished, Sharon told her how she and David were abducted by the greys, because of their suspected relationship to 'The Inlooker' and how their heads were separated from their bodies and transported around the greys' universe, to prevent them being recaptured. Pollyanna gasped in horror at their plight, putting her hands to her mouth, her eyes widening in shock.

Sharon omitted the part where she and David had their bodies switched, when The Inlooker managed to get them released. Neither did she mention the parts of the story where the greys were threatened with genetic mutations to their own, separate race of breeding hybrids, since she didn't consider it appropriate to frighten the girl unnecessarily.

She didn't want to upset her digestive system either, with the hosts finishing their preparation of the evening meal, and looking in their direction with anxious smiles.

"Yuck!" Pollyanna exclaimed, pulling a disgusted face. "How could those little beings behave so abominably?"

Sharon examined her face closely, and asked, "If you are a hybrid human being, in origin, how come your eyes are normal? The rescued children I met earlier this week have totally black eyes!"

At a light clap of the hands from Alice, who wanted them to sit at the table, Pollyanna got up from her armchair and replied, "I've had an operation to replace the original scleras with new ones."

As they reached it and went to the chairs indicated by Bob, Alice whispered to Sharon and David, "By *scleras* she means 'the whites of the eyes'. The originals were membranes that covered the whole of the eyes and were meant to protect them from harmful rays on other worlds."

Pollyanna hardly surprised Sharon by showing that she too, like the other children, had telepathic abilities, and relayed a message to her, *"Yes, and the others are going to be operated on, just like me! Aren't we lucky?"* She gave her a big wink.

Conversation flowed easily during the meal, with Bob filling in many of the gaps in Sharon's knowledge of her father's activities as The Inlooker. He updated them on the development of the 'potty', regaled them with tales of the biological chip at its heart, and made them laugh with stories about the early days when the 'Have-nots' tried to impede progress.

Alice looked at him with admiration, and Sharon couldn't help but notice there was considerable fondness between them. When Bob had gone to bed later in the evening, Sharon asked Alice if she felt attracted to him.

"Oh yes!" she replied with a contented smile. "He's asked me to marry him, and I've said yes. Would you like to come to the wedding? We were going to invite you before you leave. It's next week, I'm afraid, if that's too little notice."

"No, that's fine," Sharon replied. "We're in no rush to leave the area. Who's giving you away?"

"My brother Steven. Neither of my parents is still alive."

As they were on the point of leaving, Bob came downstairs and said to Sharon and David, "I've had a message from Claude. He says to tell you that Julie and her family are coming to the area in the next few days, to see her house and meet people. It looks like a big reunion is in the offing for all of you!

"He also says to tell you that something unforeseen has come up, and delayed his return to Aberporth by a couple of days but no to worry."

What delayed Claude was a significant development of in exopolitical relationships. By 'exopolitics' is meant a direct logical extension of conventional politics to the interplanetary theatre. The actual events are outlined as follows.

The greys' cupula had convened an extraordinary meeting, to discuss things which had immediate repercussions.

Number 1: *"Do you remember that hybrid embryo that we injected with the mutant strain, and whose growth we accelerated?"*

Number 2: *"No I don't remember it."*

Number 1: *"Are you sure? Its hands and shoulders were very strong, and its arms were long and muscular. In contrast, its legs turned out to be short and spindly, measuring less than 12 inches in length."*

Number 2: *"I do NOT remember it, and even if I did, I would deny it. It was nothing to do with me. You can take any blame on your own. Why, what happened to it?"*

Number 1: *"Nothing; that is the problem. It should have been terminated and liquidized but one of my predecessors forgot to issue the order to terminate its existence."*

Number 3: *"Why is that a problem? How do we know it wasn't you that forgot to give the order? Surely it is in hiding?"*

Number 4: *"It is not in hiding, not a bit of it! Do you not see the entertainment viewing canals? It is appearing everywhere, standing on its hands and making our citizens laugh by ejaculating its bodily wastes over its head. It is amusing, so I understand!"*

Number 5: "*What! Our citizens have a sense of humor now? Is it widespread? Have most of us been infected by this human called The Inlooker?*"

Number 2: "*Yes, that appears to be the case. PLUS, the latest news is that we have been expelled from The Federation of Aliens!*"

Number 3: "*Why?*"

Number 2: "*For trading our faster-than-light-speed power unit and deflection shield technology in a deal with the humans, in order to stop them contaminating our own ammonia-breathing hybrids. The humans were offered membership, and the condition for their joining the federation is that we are expelled.*"

Number 6 poked his head around the chamber entrance, saying,

"*Number 1? Where are you going? We want to send you to Inquisition Room 1, for interrogation.*"

That was the reason for Claude being delayed; the Planet Earth representative and treaty signatory with the greys was Claude Broadbent, the Prime Minister of the UK.

Julie, Oscar and the three nearly grown-up children arrived by potty in Cardiganshire and made an eager beeline for their future holiday home at Neuadd Cross, in the hamlet of Ponthirwaun.

They knew that the black-eyed children were in temporary residence, but were not bothered. Julie was a compassionate person who practised yoga; she had a laid-back approach to life and they sought to emulate it, most of the time (it has to be remembered that three of them were teens!).

Anyway, a cottage near those occupied by Bob and Alice had been provided, in acknowledgement of the PM's regular presence at Aberporth base.

It was pretty much the same path as trodden by Sharon and David, except this time the first venue was Julie's house, in which the black-eyed children had been ensconced. This was done for convenience sake, in order for the family to see the place they would be occupying, very soon.

On meeting them, the first thing that Julie remarked on was the eyes of the assembled, bobbing-around children; they were no longer totally black, and were adorned with 13 pairs of see-through plastic goggles.

One of the jovial track-suited attendants told her, "They've all had remedial eye surgery, and are wearing them for protection."

"I'm not surprised!" Julie said, noticing one child flicking a blob of something at another. "Better safe than sorry!"

Checking their faces more closely, Julie said, "The irises are brown, albeit with the eyes generally larger than normal. I was warned what we were in for, but now it's difficult to tell the difference between their eyes and those belonging to normal, human children."

As they were being introduced, Julie noticed that the children were wearing name badges, for ease of identification. The attendant explained, "We allocated their names here; the kids were referring to each by numbers, which was strange."

One of the girls approached Julie and asked her, "Please Julie, was it your sister, Sharon, who came to see us recently?"

Julie nodded.

The girl, Lula, asked, "Did she tell you how she was abducted by the aliens?"

"No, she didn't! Could you tell me?"

The other children went silent and sat on the floor, cross-legged.

"Yes Julie. Really horrible it was! They cut off her head and David's head, and sent them in a space ship all over the universe, to show off to other aliens."

There was a big "Oo!" from the other children, who pulled disgusted faces.

"How did they escape?"

"They didn't! Her father negotiated their release with the aliens, *and* helped us to escape as well, I think!"

"Thank you Lula," Julie said, as the girl joined the others. She whispered to Oscar, "I presume they reattached the heads to the bodies!"

A boy named Rob asked her, "Are you going to the wedding?"

"Whose wedding?"

"The one between Bob and Alice. Sharon and David are going!"

"Then we probably are as well. No doubt there'll be an invite waiting for us at our cottage."

There was a repeat performance of childlike behaviour in front of the visiting family, who took it all in their stride and enjoyed the carefree antics they witnessed.

One curious incident caused slight consternation; this was when one of the youngsters, a boy named Llewellyn, who was about the same age as Hazel, strode up to her and brazenly expressed his love.

Initially, there was general merriment when this occurred, but Hazel and her impetuous beau locked eyes in a way that unsettled the onlookers. They realised that both were behaving in a serious manner, and that she was returning his declared high-octane affection with equal intensity.

As Claude was to tell Julie later, "These youngsters that have come amongst us are the way forward. They have unparalleled skills and talents and will develop a fondness for us, come what may. My advice is, don't intervene for the moment. Wait and see what he is like, and we will psychologically profile him and the others. My opinion of Hazel is that she is like you: talented and level-headed. I know you will not rush to premature judgement."

As the family were leaving, after farewells were exchanged with the thirteen children and their attending staff, Julie asked Oscar and her youngsters, "What do you think of the house?"

The universal response was, "Smashing!"

"Yes, it's great!" she replied, holding hands with them as they walked away to mount their potty.

"To our cottage, Miss Chips!" she ordered the hidden biological chip, who responded sweetly, "As you wish, Mrs Wilde."

No sooner had their potty touched down outside the cottage and they had all dismounted, than another potty landed; they espied Sharon rushing to get off it and greet them, with David trying to keep up.

They embraced warmly, and Sharon gushed, "Let us help you with the luggage. As soon as you've unpacked and settled in, let's share a pot of tea, or coffee if you wish. We've got a lot of catching up to do!"

Julie entered the living room and noticed a sealed, ornately addressed envelope on the dining table. She opened it and said to Oscar, "It's our invite to Bob and Alice's wedding. I'm looking forward to meeting them!"

§ 24: Guests Versus Unexpected Visitors

The following days had flown by, with Sharon and David, and Julie and Oscar enjoying a shared spirit of bonhomie. Her sister gasped as Sharon fully related her travels through the greys' universe, and marvelled at 'The Inlooker's' shrewd ability to intervene and rescue her and David.

They were over the moon at the news that Sharon was expecting a baby, and laughed fit to bust when she confided in her sister – out of David's earshot – the circumstances of how it had happened.

"I can see the bump!" Julie commented, looking closely at her sister's belly.

When David re-entered the lounge, he looked at them as they started looking at him and sniggered, so he asked, "Why are you looking at me like that? She's told you how we had the baby, hasn't she?" His suspicions were well-grounded.

In contrast, Julie and her family had been left unscathed, although there were emotional scars left by the presumed deaths of her parents, and the subsequent revelations - by the prime minister no less! – that Thomas and Pat still lived, albeit in someone else's bodies (Claude's and Gloria's)! *And* they had a baby brother who had been christened 'Thomas Claude Broadbent-Beckon'!

They took Julie's teenage children to a local beauty spot, Cenarth Falls, which was inland from Cardigan Bay, where they could splash through the shallow pools as if they were much younger. They also went to Poppit sands, in the same coastal area, where they could swim off the endless expanse of beach in the mouth of the estuary of the River Teifi. These were on the many sunny days they were enjoying at the time, although the weather could be unpredictable.

They had yet to meet Bob and Alice, who initially kept their distance to allow the two families to catch-up on past events, and who then took an unannounced last minute break with Pollyanna to a destination unknown. The children were disappointed, since they had heard so much of this strange, likeable girl with special abilities.

"I'm afraid you'll have to wait for the wedding to meet her," Julie told them.

During this period, the 13 alien-bred children had been moved to a new destination, leaving Sharon and Julie's holiday homes vacant and cleared of temporary furniture, ready for them to furnish and move in.

At Claude's expense, they swiftly chose their furniture and fittings from local shops in Newcastle Emlyn, which straddles the River Teifi, and deliveries soon began.

Sharon was proving reluctant to give up guest residency of The Nag's Head, and had made a bid to buy the inn, after seeking Claude's backing for the deal. This was agreed with the current owners, who agreed to stay on for a month or two while Sharon settled into her new home a short distance away, and after the legal formalities had been completed. She already had previous experience in the pub trade and possessed the necessary qualifications and experience to begin as soon as possession was gained.

Curiosity having overcome her, Hazel asked her mother, "Where have the 13 children been moved to?"

Julie replied, "When I asked, I was told that the base was looking after their best interests." Knowing that this would lead to further questioning, she continued, "This means that military regulations apply, and the children qualify to go to a private, residential boarding school to be educated and to pass national exams. Before you ask, I don't know where it is at the moment, only that it is not far away, and Pollyanna will also be going there."

Hazel further asked, "Where will they be staying during their home visits?"

Julie explained, "The arrangement is that volunteers at the base have agreed to adopt them, as members of their existing families. Pollyanna, for example, will be staying with Bob and Alice.

"*And*, before you ask, NO, I am not having that young man who says he adores you anywhere near us, unless under constant supervision. What was his name: Llewellyn?"

"But mum...!"

"No buts! You will abide by my decision, young lady."

The evening before the wedding day, there was an informal get-together at Bob's cottage. This was attended by Alice, Katie (one of her team of superlative geneticists), Jeremy (Katie's boyfriend, also a geneticist, who Claude didn't particularly like), three of Bob's buddies from the Lockheed 'Skunk' works, Julie and her family, and Sharon with her husband. Also attending was a minister from The Church of Wales, wearing a dog collar; he would be officiating at the ceremony tomorrow.

Bob assumed responsibility for making the introductions, to ensure everyone felt at ease. He left Pollyanna till last, as she had to be coaxed into the limelight after hiding for most of the time behind Alice.

"Hello everyone, so pleased to meet you!" she said, waving meekly to them as she came into view.

They stared at her for a while, murmuring their greetings, as Julie's youngsters went over and surrounded her. Shyly, she responded to their questions and the ice began to melt.

"Hello Tam," she said, looking at him keenly for the first time. "Why did they call you Tam?"

"I dunno for sure," he replied. "It has something to do with an 18th century poem by Robert Burns, with somebody in it called Tam o' Shanter being chased by a scantily clad witch."

Pollyanna replied, "Well I'm no Cutty Sark!"

Keats intervened, "Who is Cutty Sark?"

Pollyanna explained, "Cutty Sark is a short skirt or petticoat, not a person. It is a reference to the comely witch who was chasing Tam."

Julie, who had overheard the exchange, asked her, "How did you know that?"

Pollyanna turned to look at her, saying "I honestly don't know, but if you have read the poem, then you are my source!"

She pouted cutely and continued, "I am no Nannie either, but I would like to be Tam's Kate, when I am old enough."

Julie's knees nearly buckled, and she left the group to rejoin Oscar, wanting to explain the significance of what had been said.

"You'll never believe what she just told me?" so she went ahead and told Oscar the story, adding, "Nannie was the short-skirted witch chasing Tam on his nag of a horse named Meg, and Kate was his wife. In effect, she said how she'd like to be our son's wife when she gets older. The child is wise beyond her years! She's also a telepath, with mind-reading skills!"

Tam himself had become tongue-tied, and was clearly bewildered by Pollyanna. He didn't know what to make of her, and was overawed by her assumption that they had a future together. It didn't seem to his mother, Julie, that he disliked the prospect, seeing the contented smile he was trying to suppress.

Oblivious to what was going on around him, Bob tapped the side of his nearly empty wine glass with a spoon, to attract everyone's attention. When they became silent, he began his speech.

"Dearly beloved, we are gathered here this evening in your presence, ready to witness the marriage between myself, Robert Keller and Alice Smythers."

He grinned when he saw many of the guests getting concerned, and wondering if the ceremony had been brought forward.

"Don't worry, especially you vicar, nothing will happen until tomorrow. That was my silly way of borrowing from your speech, in order to grab the attention of all of you.

"What I really want to do is say a few words of welcome on behalf of myself and Alice, and thank you for joining us on this happy occasion. We took time out to ask my two grown-up children and their families to attend the wedding, and they will be here shortly.

"I am also fortunate to have three lifelong buddies with me, and wish to introduce them; they are Teddy, Jed and Wilbur, who graduated with me and also worked alongside me at The Lockheed Skunk Works." He gestured in their direction, and they all smiled, bowed their heads and raised their beer glasses in acknowledgement.

He continued, "I am equally fortunate to count amongst my friends the Prime Minister of Great Britain, who should be arriving soon. He will be acting as my best man, which is a tremendous honour. I would ask all of you raise a glass in toast of the wonderful woman who has decided to become my wife. Cheers, my darling Alice!" having said which he led the toast in her honour.

The Reverend Bennett looked flabbergasted, as he asked those around him, "Is the PM, the Right Honourable Claude Broadbent no less, attending in person?"

"Indeed he is!" Sharon interceded, joining the circle around him and added, "I'm his goddaughter Sharon."

About half an hour later, Claude walked in with Gloria by his side, preceded by two of his ex-special services bodyguards and with two others following. With a smile, he walked up with Gloria to the minister and introduced himself and his wife, saying, "I understand you are going to be officiating at the wedding ceremony tomorrow? May I say what a pleasure it is to meet you!"

He then made a point of approaching Bob direct, and congratulating him and Alice on their forthcoming nuptials. "Yeah, as if it's a surprise to you, the king of matchmakers!" Bob replied, warmly clasping his hand.

Claude grinned, and was on the verge of replying when another bodyguard came up to and whispered a message to him. His face remained expressionless, as he said, "I've been informed that I have visitors, and I'm afraid that they require my attention for at least a few hours.

"This means that the next time I'll probably see you all will be at the wedding. Please excuse me for now, and rest assured I'll not be late, come what may." He asked Gloria to mingle in his absence, especially with Sharon and Julie.

He nodded to Bob and Alice, and waved to his families, who looked puzzled and disappointed at his imminent departure. Before he left, Claude confided to Bob, "I'll speak to you as soon as I've dealt with my visitors."

Bob joined the other guests straight afterwards, and announced, "I'm afraid that Claude has been called away on a matter of state, but will be with us tomorrow. I have no doubt that all will be explained in due course."

The rest of the evening passed uneventfully, although Keats attempted repeatedly to question Bob's pals about what they did at Skunk Works. No matter how hard he tried to prise information from them, the polite refrain from each one was always the same: "I'm afraid I cannot answer any questions about our work. It is a top secret black project."

Keats was obviously thrilled at that response, since it hinted at the mystery surrounding the place, with the implied UFO connections that he had read about. Even at an early age, he already knew all about Ben Rich and his deathbed confessions; Teddy, Jed and Wilbur had guessed this, and were amused to play along with the boy's inquisitive nature.

Claude's Unexpected Visitors

Claude had headed outside, feeling angry at the interruption to his attempted reconciliation with his family.

He stopped suddenly when he saw that his visitors had chosen to meet him *in the flesh*, without wearing protective garments and helmets.

There, standing together, were six greys, with hundreds behind providing what appeared to be moral support. Searchlights were trained on them and they were ringed by troops armed with automatic weapons.

Overhead was a fleet of stationary space craft, waiting for negotiations to commence. No doubt, much higher in the heavens, craft from the Planet Earth space fleet were also keeping watch, in case anything untoward occurred.

The major in control of the troops marched towards Claude, saluted him and said, "Major Clegg reporting for duty, sir. I am awaiting your orders, sir!"

Claude replied dryly, "Oh really? Clegg is it? Hard luck about the name but there we are, blame the parents I say! You can tell your men to stand down and go away, but *you* can stay, to act as go between me and the high command at the base.

"This branch of the race of aliens called the 'greys' have made a long, long journey to see us, and could overwhelm the lot of you without having to raise one of their long, spindly fingers, if they wanted to. You and your heavily armed force could be lying unconscious on the ground by now.

"I can tell you categorically, their intentions are peaceful."

He had confirmed this by reading the aliens' minds, whilst still attending his social gathering.

"It is obvious to me that they are in dire peril, having decided to make a personal appeal *in person, without breathing apparatus and protective clothing*. I think that they can only do this for a limited time, so let's hear them out. I will communicate with them by mind."

He had no idea how they managed to breathe earth's atmosphere, apparently unaided, presumably for short periods. Perhaps they used a filter of some type, or encased their heads magnetically in an invisible force field rich in ammonia?

Major Clegg interrupted his train of thought by asking, "Do you mean you will communicate with them telepathically, by using your mind sir?"

"Shut up for once, Clegg!"

"Sorry, that was rude of me; there was someone else I was thinking of, not you, when I said that, telepathically."

Clegg responded, *"Oh, I see.* I'm getting the hang of this now."

Poor Major Clegg not only looked similar to that wretched, insufferable man he'd endured for so long as a deputy, but he also sounded like him.

Claude focused and started the meeting by asking,

"What do you want Number One?"

Number 1: *"Asylum and protection. Your 'Inlooker' has no doubt informed you that we are vulnerable."*

Number 2: *"Yes, ever since he adjusted our DNA structure we have begun to share your frailties."*

Number 3: *"Yes, we feel fear."*

Number 4: *"Yes, we are outcasts, under threat of attack from our kin on other worlds we inhabit."*

Number 5: *"We are frightened. We need shelter. Please will you help us?"*

Number 6: *"Too many of us have died already, and I don't want to become the next Number 1 to die in rotation."*

Claude continued,
"How many of you are there?"
Number 1: *"The same again as you see here, plus 50 more. The rest are no more, since we haven't reproduced for a time that is beyond comprehension."*

Claude asked,
"Why do you distinguish between yourselves and the other 50 you mention? Why did you do that? Not that I mistrust you, but…"
Number 6: *"If you insist, I will get them here now."*

Without waiting for a response, traction beams shone from some of the fleet of spacecraft hovering overhead, and transported down 50 beings, who were totally different to the greys. They looked similar in appearance to the 'black-eyed' alien-bred children already at the base, but there were also young adults of both sexes amongst their numbers.

Claude studied them and asked,
"These are the ammonia-breathing versions of the hybrids you are breeding?"
Number 6: *"Yes, they are. If you like, I will demonstrate them copulating?"*

To illustrate their good faith, he gestured anxiously to two of the adult hybrids, the female of which lay on her back with her legs apart, while the male clumsily and energetically tried to impregnate her. They were breathing hard and heavy in Planet Earth's nitrogen and oxygen rich air.

Claude looked alarmed and shouted out loud, "No, there's no need to prove it, I believe you!" The female looked luscious to him, and he had to suppress his own desire for her, as he too joined involuntarily in the heavy breathing.

He relayed:
> *"Yes, we will take you in, Number 6. I will arrange for the base here to accommodate you on a new level that we are tunnelling out, and you can adapt to your own needs. It is Level 7."*
> Number 6: *"Very good. Did you like the performance that Abba and Abe gave for you?"*

Claude paused before asking,
"Why do their names both begin with the letter 'A'? Is this a naming convention you are following?"
> Number 7: *"Yes, we started with the letter 'A', but have now moved onto the letter 'B'. It is very restricting. Is that why the Americans also use numbers to identify their offspring? Do they have a 'Bubba 1' and 'Bubba 2'?"*

Claude replied,
"Maybe, don't worry about it. We also recognise many of our children by sight and sound. I'll explain how that works later."
He pondered the possibility that they might inadvertently use obscene or graphically descriptive words in their naming of the hybrids.

As an urgent task, he politely instructed Major Clegg to advise the base commander of the need to accommodate the greys in the newly dug level 7 and help them to make it self-sustaining in atmosphere.

"Tell her that these are new allies that are essential to our future survival," he told him.

He also made arrangements to secretly ship the new, now proven fully reliable mutant alien DNA structure to the other worlds in the greys' empire, to ensure they too were infected with human characteristics.

He logicised, "*We can't have our new friends being terrorized by their own kin, can we? Solving that will be the top priority for Alice's team, when she returns from honeymoon.*"

He commanded the newly appointed liaison officer, "Off you go to the base, Major Clegg, to smooth the way for our unexpected visitors."

Number 1: "*We want you personally to escort us to the base, not your subordinate.*"

Number 2: "*Yes, now we know the way you humans act, we don't want any cockups or disobedience coming from a bolshie high command at the base.*"

Number 6: "*I must say Number 2, your command of vernacular English is improving by the minute!*"

After further thought, realising that his social evening was about to be absolutely ruined, Claude reluctantly agreed, sighing, "Oh very well. You'd better come with me Clegg, to stiffen the resolve of the base commander."

He ordered his potty to be brought to him, and was soon on his way, followed by a most menacing fleet of alien craft that looked identical to his potty, plus a couple of huge, monolithic blocks that looked totally unaerodynamic.

"*What's in them?*" he wondered.

Sally, the Aberporth Base Commander, was purring. A brunette in her thirties, she had a slim, well-honed figure and sultry manner towards the prime minster of her adoptive country. After the primary exchanges, which consisted of attempts by her to wheedle more funds out of the PM, Claude had told Clegg he could push off, and they were alone.

Sally continued, "Yes of course Claude, you know full well we can accommodate these 'visitors from afar'. It was you that initiated the building of level 7 for this precise reason. If I may congratulate you on your foreskin... Oops, I mean foresight! You anticipated this eventuality remarkable well. When are you going to take me for lunch?"

She pressed a button to give the office privacy, got up from her side of the desk, and sat on it his side, as he leant back to admire the bare, bronzed thighs she was exposing. A vison of the naked female hybrid lover came into his mind as he rose to the occasion, and began acting out his fantasy with Sally, who by now he had stripped naked from the waist down.

"God, you're delicious!" he said, sucking tantalisingly at her neck.

"I'm amazed you've got the energy left, after Gloria 'has done' with you each day!" she replied, kissing him feverishly.

"Where there's a willy there's a way!" he answered philosophically, as he thrust at increasing speed and reached a noisy climax with her.

She patted his bare, muscular bottom as he went to pull his underpants up, while he remarked, "You wanted lunch. Aren't you satisfied with the smoking ham baguette I've given you?"

She laughed as she slid down from the desktop to retrieve her knickers and skirt.

"Naughty hot pants!" she quipped. "Sod it! Shall we do it again?"

Outside, the armed, helmeted guard heard nothing and said nothing, discretion being the better part of valor (if one equates caution with courage).

In the meantime, having received approval to proceed, the bulk of the greys had descended from their smaller craft and were making their way to the 7th level. They were going there to assess the extent of the 'blasting out' still left to do and to assist with the manual work associated with completion.

The few compatriots they had left on the surface were gathering around a huge monolithic transporter, as it landed briefly in front of the base and lowered its cargo ramp.

Out of it flowed a convoy of formidable, cylindrical drilling machines, which noiselessly floated into the main vehicle entrance of the base, to descend by cargo escalator to the lowest level, where they would use laser-derived technology to blast through solid rock in record time.

Once unloaded, the monolithic transporter sealed itself and ascended noiselessly, to be replaced with the second transporter, which was loaded with equipment to provide the greys with a breathable atmosphere and to construct general living quarters. This consignment was intended to make the 7th level habitable and self-contained.

The transporters headed back to their USA base in Texas, which had been virtually emptied of personnel and was now running a 'skeleton' service pending ultimate transfer to Aberporth. This was a coup for Claude.

There was not a single human visible to witness these remarkable events, as this strange breed of colonists was added to the population of Aberporth. Be that as it may, the latest technology cameras were dotted around in the hope that no magnetic interference would block their transmissions.

Scattered around the world were bioscientists who had been tasked with finding alternative food sources for beings whose staple diet had been rich in adrenalin soaked blood, sourced from humans and animals.

At the crack of dawn on the day of the wedding and feeling absolutely worn out, Claude returned on his potty to Bob's cottage. To his relief, he could see a light on in the kitchen, and knocked on the door. Bob answered, relieved to see him, and invited him in to sit down and tell him what had happened.

Claude said, his speech slurring, "The mission to accommodate the greys has been a success."

"You look shagged out," Bob said to him, unaware that this was a condition induced by the base commander's demands.

"Have a shower, put your head down for a few hours and enjoy a power nap. You're in no fit state at present to act as my best man! I'll arrange for your dress-clothes to be collected from your house in Neuadd Cross. That is where you've stored them, isn't it?"

He looked at Claude, who had already fallen asleep in the chair and, decided to leave him alone. He'd seen him recover his energy after a brief nap like the one he was taking now, and was confident he would be as spritely as ever, given the necessary time.

Yes, it promised to be a grand occasion, his wedding to Alice.

§ 25: Wedding Guests Are Entertained

The following morning, the guests walked towards Mwnt Church, romantically sited above Mwnt beach. It is a very small building with some parts of it dating back to the 12th or 13th century. Used originally as a medieval sailor's chapel of ease, it gets its name from the nearby prominent, steep conically shaped hill (Foel y Mwnt).

The Flemings unsuccessfully invaded this part of Wales in 1155, at this exact coastal spot, and much blood was spilled that day as they were slaughtered.

The beach itself has been rated as one of Europe's top ten loveliest hidden beaches, and the guests were diverted by Teddy to look at it from the cliffs, before they entered the church, where the minister could be seen entering with a large group of children dressed in white vestments with starched, frilly collars.

Looking down, they could see that someone, probably Bob, had traced in the sand the bold message *I LOVE YOU! BOB.* Claude's two daughters dabbed their eyes when they witnessed this expression of the bridegroom's love.

Sharon grasped David's hand and said to him, "That's the type of thing you did, on our wedding day!"

"Did I?" he wondered, trying hard to remember.

Keats looked down, vainly hoping to find the bones of the ancient invaders, which were reputedly washed up at intervals, but not recently.

Tam wondered, slightly fearfully, if his initials might one day be there, in the future, instead of Bob's.

Hazel had a similar vision, with Llewellyn in mind. She dreamt, *"That's a long name to trace. Perhaps he'll abbreviate it to Loo!"*

On resuming their short walk to the church, they all heard the sound of a vehicle being driven towards them.

"Look, Bob's driving!" Wilber exclaimed, pointing in the direction of a large, green tractor with enormous black tyres, where Bob could be seen through the windscreen of the enclosed cabin, sitting at the steering wheel. There were two white ribbons attached to the bonnet from the handles of the cabin. He stopped the engine, and took care not to dislodge them as he descended to join the group, looking dapper in his dress suit with tails and shiny black shoes.

"Hi folks, nice to see y'all!" he declared with a beam, looking energetic. "Let's get inside, out of the wind!"

The church was as small inside as it looked outside, although there were 13 children standing facing them in short rows, one side of the altar, where the minister stood. Teddy judged the kids to be all of similar ages, perhaps 11 years or more, and similar in build and hair colour.

When Sharon entered, preoccupied in talk with David, she noticed an unexpected visitor sitting in a pew on her own; it was Rose, her daughter sitting there, with a welcoming smile as pretty as a picture and wearing a short, floral dress that emphasized her slim figure!

"Hello!" she mouthed to her mother, whose eyes moistened as she rushed forward to embrace and smother her with kisses, leaving red lipstick on her cheeks.

"Careful mum, you're covering me in slobber!" she said, pouting, and trying to dab it off with a tissue.

"Slobber? Slobber? I'm no dog like Ellie!" she retorted; Ellie was the name of their most recent pet dog, that had died not so long ago. "Be grateful to your old mum that she loves you so much! When did you get here?"

"Last night. I'm staying at the Nag's Head."

"Well I never! We've been staying there ourselves, for a while. What'd you think of it?"

"A bit run down, but the room's very nice, and the breakfast is huge! Claude booked it for me"

"How thoughtful of him. It may be near where we settle down as a family. I'll tell you more about later. You *are* coming to the reception, I hope?"

"Of course!"

"Then we'll talk all about what's happening to us later!"

There was plenty of space remaining in the church to accommodate all the guests, including the families of Bob's two adult children and their families, which numbered nine in total. He rushed over and embraced them, kissing all his five grandchildren before taking his position on the front right-hand side, to await the bride's arrival.

A keyboard had been hired for the occasion, which Oscar had volunteered to play, and he kept them all amused while he played various religious tunes, with slight variations on the originals by jazzing up the beat.

They didn't have long to wait, before Oscar began pounding out Mendelssohn's Wedding March, as Alice appeared at the church door, with her holding her brother Steven's arm as they walked slowly up the aisle. She looked radiant in her simple white wedding dress, which emphasized her slim figure. A veil covered her blue eyes, while she purposefully looked at everyone directly, smiling as she passed.

A few paces behind, Pollyanna walked holding a posy of flowers, wearing a long, plain white dress and attracting admiring glances from the congregation.

Alice stopped in front of the minister and raised her veil. Bob took a few paces to stand next to her, while Steven and Pollyanna moved back to stand either side of Claude's wife, Gloria, who smiled and placed her hand on that of the young girl.

The ceremony began with the minister welcoming the congregation, and then reading an introduction explaining what Christians believe about marriage. Afterwards, he asked the congregation if there was any reason why the marriage may not lawfully take place, and the 'tying of the knot' began in earnest.

Barely noticed, the choir began chanting in the background. It was almost Gregorian, and added a new, mystical dimension to the ceremony.

"Where on earth did they learn to do that?" Jed asked Wilber, in a whisper. "It's spooky!" Even the minister looked startled, but relaxed when he realised how tranquil it sounded.

The ceremony went exceedingly well after that, and concluded with a resounding cheer when Bob kissed her.

The choir burst into Handel's Hallelujah Chorus with gusto, stopping immediately upon the minister beginning the formal registration of the marriage, on the other side of the altar. They then resumed their restful chanting in the background, as the guests sat down and listened, many with their eyes closed restfully.

After the ceremony, as soon as Bob and Alice made their way down the aisle, Oscar played a lively version of the Wedding March, but stopped when they exited; he was in a rush to join his family before the church emptied. Only Teddy stayed-put, no doubt to settle any outstanding matters with the minister and perhaps to congratulate the choir.

Most of those who had attended the ceremony began gathering in groups outside, waiting for guidance on what to do next, while the minister locked up the church as the young choristers stood in a huddle apart from the others.

Some adults noticed that Wilber was ushering them all, from afar, to come to the bay. Claude and some bodyguards were already there, waiting on the clifftops overlooking the secluded Mwnt beach. They spread out to join him, standing in bright sunlight with gentle breeze fanning them, under a blue sky, with fluffy white clouds passing overhead.

Making room for Bob and Alice, they all looked down to see what had been traced in the sand; it was the message *I LOVE YOU! BOB*, while a local youngster had added *I DON'T*, and was being chased away by one of Claude's bodyguards, shaking his fist at him.

They all laughed, but stopped suddenly as a large pod of dolphins swam rapidly into the bay and began playfully leaping around. It was an unexpected treat, seeing these large marine creatures gambolling about, with their pups emulating them.

Some noticed that the children in the choir were standing at the back, and could not see what was going in, so they signalled to them to come and watch as well.

They all moved to the front, and were joined by Pollyanna, watching the dolphins in a single group.

"They must be those black-eyed kids we've heard so much about," Wilber speculated. Sharon confirmed this.

She also noticed that they were starting to spread out, holding each other's hands while closing their eyes and reciting their hypnotic Gregorian chant. The next thing they did horrified her, and she tried to scream but couldn't.

In unison, the children stepped forward into space, with the onlookers starting to shout a warning. However, Claude put a finger to his lips, warning them to keep silent, being totally composed in his attitude.

The youngsters did not plunge down the cliff face, but gradually lowered themselves as if they were on a cushion of air. There were gasps of amazement from the adults, while their own children acted as if they had witnessed a commonplace occurrence.

The poor minister didn't know what to make of this and started praying, until Claude explained who and what the children really were. He concluded by saying to the poor man, "Even the Catholic Church has accepted the existence of aliens, so who are we to judge if these children are good or evil? In no way are they the Devil's spawn!"

Down below on the beach, the bodyguard who had been chasing the local youngster stopped in his tracks, as one of his companions contacted him to say what was going on, as did the lad himself. They both looked agape as the children floated onto the beach, still holding hands, and walked steadily over ridges of raised sand and pebbles to the water's edge, where they fanned out into a single row and began making rapid clicking noises to 'speak' to the dolphins.

These agile 'creatures of the ocean' responded by dancing rhythmically, and leaping in pairs with their pups following, and pushing themselves onto the beach for patting by the children before wriggling back into the deeper water.

Teddy commented to Bob, "This is one hell of a show they're putting on!"

Jed said, "Yup, and it's all in your honor!"

It finally finished with Claude saying, "That was better that any firework show! We ought to get mammals like these released from the water circuses they appear in, and back into the wild. It's not right for them to be held in captivity."

Unusually, the children broke ranks as the dolphins were leaving, and raced competitively back to the paths that led to the clifftops, panting as they reached the wedding group.

"I'm the winner!" a few of them claimed, rushing up to Bob to confirm which of them was first. Pollyanna was with them and gave Alice a hug.

When she also came and hugged him, Bob asked her, "Why didn't you go up the same way you went down, by levitating?"

She shrugged her shoulders and replied, "We've only recently managed going down, and weren't sure how to do the same thing going up. Anyway, it was fun having a race!"

He thought, "*They've been rehearsing this party piece, how interesting!*"

They walked back towards the tractor, where Alice removed her shoes for Bob to help guide her up into the cabin and sit next to him. Within seconds, he started its engine, waved goodbye to everyone and motored off to their cottages. They had to change into casual clothes, ready for the reception being prepared nearby.

Sharon asked Julie, "Where's Pollyanna staying, while they're away?"

Julie responded, "With me, Oscar and the kids, in our holiday home."

Sharon said, "You sound doubtful. Do you have a problem?"

"Not really, except that Tam and she have a thing for each other, and I'm not sure it's advisable. She is lovely though, really lovely."

"If they get 'ants in their pants' for each other, it will be the devil's own job to keep them apart. Still, there's years before you have to face that prospect."

"Yeah, I know, but I'll have to keep a close eye on them, especially her, seeing how she can levitate like she did on the cliffs. Heaven knows what she'll be capable of as she grows up!"

Seizing the opportunity to approach Julie and her family, Claude and Gloria walked over to them and made formal introductions, before whispering to Julie, "Keep addressing us as Claude and Gloria, but remember we are you are your parents, Thomas and Pat. As soon as we can, we'll get together and talk openly."

Gloria looked at Oscar and their three children, and commented with sincerity, "You all look so lovely, bless you!" before tweaking the youngsters' cheeks and making them blush.

After a short time of socialising with them, Claude said, "If you can make time for us, we'll pop around to your house tomorrow evening, say at 6pm?"

They agreed, and Gloria said, "Now we've got to make our peace with Sharon, so we'll wish you goodbye until later."

Claude and Gloria walked over to Sharon, who was watching, waiting anxiously to be given their turn as a family.

Claude gave her a kiss on the cheek and shook hands with David.

"Well, we've finally got round to getting to know each other, again! Did you enjoy the ceremony, and are you settling in well, at your new properties?" He was alluding to The Nag's Head as well as their holiday home.

Sharon replied, "Yes we are settling in, and can't thank you both enough for your generosity. How lucky we are, to have such *God*parents!" She sarcastically emphasized the word *God.*

"Hush girl!" Claude hissed. "I don't want you blowing the gaff!"

David looked puzzled and asked, "Does that mean the same as *spilling the beans?*"

"Yes!" Claude hissed again, briefly looking annoyed before flashing his trademark smile around. "I'll see you both at your place, tomorrow afternoon, say at 3pm?"

Gloria whispered to Sharon, "What are you two like? Try to get on with each other, and I'll get Thomas to behave himself!"

A swoop of potties sailed into view, to transport the rest of the group to the cluster of cottages built directly over the Aberporth underground base. Within minutes, they landed softly near a marquee that had been anchored to the ground, near the cottages where Bob and Alice lived.

They dismounted to admire the view of the rugged coastline, before wending their way to the marquee. They could see catering staff from the base laying tables, arranging chairs and scurrying to and from a series of vans to collect food and drinks.

A uniformed member of the catering staff stood on the right of the open entrance, ushering them to enter.

Inside, they found Bob and Alice standing to the left, waiting to welcome them as they passed.

Beyond, both sides of an informal aisle, stood two waiters and two waitresses, smartly attired in black and white uniforms. They held trays filled with flutes of sparkling champagne, and red and white wines in shorter glasses.

A separate tray held a selection of soft drinks for the teetotallers and youngsters.

Beyond, a jazz trio on an elevated platform came into view, initially tuning up and then playing a softened rendition of Glen Miller's String of Pearls.

Gloria commented, "Delightful, simply delightful!" as they checked the seating arrangements from one of the layout charts dotted around the marquee, and went to their allotted places, as indicated from the place cards above their table mats.

It was the start of a long, convivial day that stretched into the evening as the food was served at the round tables. The formalities concluded with speeches by Claude and Bob's buddies from America and a well-judged reply from Bob, who commented on Keats inquisitive nature, and wished all present a safe, healthy and prosperous future.

Darkness descended, and the trio ended the evening by playing a rasping Louis Armstrong style version of, *'Ain't you got no homes to go to, it's getting mighty late!'*

They all trailed outside, under a cloudless, slightly chilly star-lit sky, as Bob looked upwards and commented on the flashing lights of aircraft silently landing and taking off at Aberporth base.

He remarked to Claude, "There's a lot of things happening there tonight. No doubt, it involves the 'visitors' that you told me about earlier?"

"Yes, it does. Not to worry! It is all under control, and was anticipated. This universe is a diverse place, and I think we are establishing a foothold in it."

Bob had other, more pressing matters on his mind of a personal nature, and accepted that Claude would use his special abilities on behalf of Planet Earth, without needing his assistance.

"Take care," he urged Claude, shaking hands, as his chosen craft landed, while Alice and Pollyanna left her cottage, their luggage following on cushions of air.

"Look after everyone while we're away."

Bob and Alice were going by potty on a 'honeymoon', while the two families from his first marriage were staying at his and Alice's cottages for the duration. They would remain there, while the newlyweds and Pollyanna would transfer to a nearby cottage that had been refurbished and in which their household goods had already been moved.

Claude considered it would be a pleasurable duty to call on Bob's families in a couple of days' time, as one of Bob's closest friends.

The 13 alien-bred children were staying with their adoptive parents, scattered within easy travel distance of the base, since it was the summer holiday period away from boarding school. They were also given every opportunity to socialize as a group, with personnel from Aberporth base acting as daytime carers.

Gradually, at this stage of their upbringing, they began opting out of group activities, since they were integrating with their new families and starting to enjoy their new, independent lifestyles.

It was now the day after the wedding, and Claude was staying in his own holiday home, alongside those occupied by his two daughters and their families. He felt rejuvenated after a full night's sleep, and escorted Gloria the short distance to Sharon's home at the agreed time of 3pm.

A sudden downpour had threatened to soak them, and they were in a rush. He had put on an all-weather jacket with its hood up and was holding a golfing umbrella over Gloria's head, to protect her and baby Thomas, wrapped in a Welsh shawl, who she was carrying.

On arrival, while the three of them huddled in the open porch, he furled the brolly and rapped the brass knocker to attract attention. Sharon opened the door with a welcoming smile, caught sight of the gurgling baby, and held out her arms to take him.

"Aw, what a little cutie!" she gushed, cuddling him tightly and enjoying the baby milk smell she detected on his breath. "Just fed him, have you?" she asked. Gloria nodded and said, "Yes. He's your little brother!"

Sharon looked up sharply, and Claude decided to strike as this golden opportunity presented itself to elaborate on matters.

"Well not exactly," he explained. "In one sense he's your brother, but in another he's not!"

Gloria looked at him with murderous intent, guessing what was coming next.

Sharon rolled her eyes in exasperation and said, "You'd better come through to the lounge and tell us what you mean."

Rose rushed over to embrace Claude and Gloria as they entered the room, and David approached as well, more formally, to say, "Thanks for the present of the house. It's beautiful and we are deeply touched by your generosity."

Standing by the door, Sharon asked, "What would you like to drink?" They chose what they wanted, while Sharon passed the baby to a delighted Rose and Gloria went off to help her.

Having dealt with the question of refreshments and everyone having been served, Sharon impatiently asked Claude, "Now, what did you mean? Is he my brother or isn't he?"

Realising that he had to be careful and precise, Claude explained the situation as he saw it.

"You do understand that we, Thomas and Pat, occupy the bodies of Claude and Gloria, as guiding spirits?" They all nodded, but he wasn't sure how much Rose already knew about this key fact, so he asked Sharon, "Have you told Rose about me, as the Inlooker?"

She said, "Yes, I have, and you don't so much 'guide' as 'control', do you?"

"That's not quite true, but I'm digressing. The fact is that baby Thomas Claude Broadbent-Beckon is a product of Claude's and Gloria's reproductive cells, not ours.

"We may have instigated the act of love–making, and fully enjoyed it with Claude and Gloria's *physical* participation, but the only part *we* played was through their senses.

"Ergo, there is no direct relationship between us, the resident spirits and this lovely infant boy. To put it bluntly, Rose contains our DNA structure, the baby doesn't."

Sharon asked, "To be blunt in my reply, you were in control of their bodies and are trying to make it seem that your involvement was minimal. Far from it, *you* were controlling the situation! Doesn't that make you parasites?"

Claude spluttered indignantly, "No, certainly not! Unlike a parasite, I feed off no one, nor do I drain the person whose body I occupy. What I actually do is take a person to a higher level of prominence, one they would never have achieved without my assistance.

"I prepare them to play a new, far more important role in society, and to cope mentally with the demands that will be placed on them. Then I hone the body that I occupy temporarily, and remove any residual deficiencies with Nano technology so that they enjoy a longer, healthier life than they might have done otherwise.

"Afterwards, when I have vacated their body and their own life resumes, I remain on call for any help needed in resolving matters they encounter.

"I do these things purely to help mankind. Do these goals bear any resemblance to the actions of a parasite?"

She asked him, "How many times have you taken over another person's body?"

"Personally? Only once, of any concern" Claude lied. "And that was to become the PM of a country in dire need, and to influence world matters before we got into trouble with extraterrestrials. I did what was necessary to ensure our survival."

Sharon looked at him suspiciously, her interest perking up when he declared, "I am considering one more spell of 'occupancy'. This may involve a certain President of the United States, who is currently underperforming, and who..."

Sharon interrupted, raising her hands with her palms outstretched, "Don't even think of doing it! Don't intervene ever again, just because you feel it's justified. Your twisted logic goes against the spirit of free will.

"Can't you ever be satisfied with the concept of reincarnation that you claim to believe in? If you are right, your spirit will be reborn any number of times, so why the rush to move from one body to another before you age and die naturally?

"What is the value of wanting to live forever, you and mum? Won't you regret it, when all around you die off naturally and you are still roaming the earth, on a journey that never ends?"

Suffering the impact of this moral bombardment, Claude checked his watch and said, "Good heavens, it's time for us to go across and say hello to Julie's family! Are you coming with us?"

Sharon retorted, "Mmm, you know you're in the wrong, don't you? Come on then, let's be off to Julie's and listen to what she has to say."

"*Oh Lordy!*" Claude thought, fearing he was in for another ear-bashing.

"Hi Julie!" Claude said, making his greeting sound contrived, as she opened her door and welcomed them all in. It didn't help that Sharon was glowering as she walked past, and Gloria didn't look too pleased either, even though she was holding the gurgling baby.

It didn't take long for the same subject to be raised in front of Julie and Oscar, after the children had been asked to go and sit for a while in their den.

After hearing both sides of the argument, Julie cast her vote by saying, "I have to agree with Sharon. Carry on like you are doing, and you and mum will end up looking like my grandchildren, when I'm in my dotage. All this gallivanting around and body-hopping will do you no good, in the end!"

To Claude's relief, Gloria chose to intervene, and protested, "Hi y'all! This is the real Gloria speaking, who shares my body with your mother Pat. Her presence, alongside mine, has been a great comfort to me, especially with helping to bring up baby Thomas. She's also taught me different types of intercourse."

The others took a deep breath, wondering what was coming next, only relaxing when Gloria continued, "Like having social intercourse." Then she lost trace of the theme by saying cheerfully, "Anyway, Pat's husband, Thomas, had a nice arse like Claude's, and I love 'em both to bits!"

The same voice continued, but with a different way of talking. "This is your mother Pat now speaking. Can you all hear me? Good! I think you owe a debt of gratitude to my Braveheart Thomas, who has achieved many things in his life. I number amongst them the replacing of our transport system with potties endlessly flowing around us. He has also introduced the ODD party that now governs us democratically, better than we've ever been governed before.

"He's also significantly reduced the size of the world's population without artificially inducing any natural catastrophes, and he has opened dialogs with extraterrestrials.

"We are now members of The Federation Of Aliens. Didn't know those things, did you, or had you forgotten them in your attempts to belittle my husband?"

Sharon shook her head, waggled her finger at Claude and asked, "Your achievements speak for themselves. However, if what you say about your method of operating is true, why hasn't Claude made his voice heard? You won't let him, will you?"

Claude lowered his head and sighed; what Sharon had said was true, and he didn't want to let the real Claude Broadbent pitch in and have his say, because the man was so limited in his abilities.

Fortuitously, baby Thomas chose that precise moment to bubble-fart.

"His nappy needs changing!" Said Sharon, leaning over towards Rose, and wrinkling her nose in disgust. Until then, Rose had shown no inclination to hand him over to anyone else, and was tentatively squeezing his saggy, padded bottom.

"Then do it!" Gloria and Pat demanded, both speaking at once, using the one voice.

Claude had retreated to the kitchen to get some peace, and also because nappy changing was not a skill that he had ever wished to acquire. He was sipping a wine glass half-full of Châteauneuf-Du-Pape and not appreciating its superior qualities, when Tam entered carrying a thick folder that he recognised immediately; it contained the autobiography of The Inlooker, which he had loaned originally to Julie.

"So your mother's given you that, has she?" he enquired glumly. "Have you read it?"

"Yes," Tam replied, "and I think I've inherited your gift."

"Prove it!" Claude said sharply, glugging at his wine.

Julie entered the kitchen, carrying the baby, which had resumed its contented gurgling.

Tam closed his eyes, clenched his hands into fists and concentrated hard.

The baby stared at Claude in an appraising way, gave a wink and said, "Hello foster father, or should I also say, grandad!"

Claude re-joined the others in the lounge, his arm over Tam's shoulder, and made an announcement.

"I've come to a decision. The reduction in the world population should stabilise within the next six hundred years, and two births per family should start becoming more widespread over that time span.

"I need to spearhead the process, and will therefore remain in Claude's body for most of that time. Pat will stay by my side, with Gloria for company during the same period. My death will come when I exit Claude, accompanied by my darling wife Pat, and we float towards the bright light that beckons most of us on natural death.

"I have a natural successor, whose identity will remain known to only a few, and will be guided by me in his moral behaviour."

Sharon looked vaguely relieved, as she said, "Yeah, and Tam had better behave himself more than you did when you started in the City of London!"

§ 26: Spiff Tracey, Private Eye

[*This person will feature in other books in the series*]
There was one person, a stranger, that Claude had singled out as worthy of his special attention. His known name was Spiff Tracey, and he had chosen a career as a private investigator.

He was actually well qualified to undertake this role in life, having served as a uniformed police officer in Los Angeles before being rapidly promoted to the rank of detective and solving in record time a multiple murder case that had baffled all the seasoned plain-clothes officers who had investigated it.

He had cut a swathe through the ranks, gaining rapid promotion before unexpectedly resigning to set up his own agency. He was an outstandingly handsome young man, with a distinct, offbeat personality that appealed to Claude's own eccentric sense of humour.

His awareness of this unique hombre came when he started returning his hired potties outfitted with garish trimmings and interiors painted in Banksy-style graffiti paint.

"*Who is this freaky guy?*" he asked himself, and made his own investigations. He read his career record and was impressed. How he laughed when he read that Tracey had resigned from the police department, with the official reason given that he '*Disliked having to push Vapour Rub up his nostrils to prevent his sense of smell being ruined by the pungent odour of death.*'

"I want this man on my payroll," he instructed the head of his security team, and arranged for him to be provided with his own four-seater potty, on permanent loan, with the open proviso, "No need for it to be returned until the employment contract is cancelled by either of us, with one month's notice required.

"Tell him I want him to investigate the possibility that giants roamed the world from ancient times until at least the 17th century, and were wiped out by the American Indians. Let's see what he makes of that brief," he concluded, positive about the outcome.

Are any of you aware of a TV series called 77 Sunset Strip, which was aired in the late 1950s to the early 1960s? The series took a look at how private detectives work in Los Angeles, based out of an office located at 77 Sunset Strip. It featured a character called Edd 'Kookie' Byrnes, who bore a strong resemblance to Spiff, in Claude's opinion.

The catchy tune that went with it contained the lyrics,
> *77 Sunset Strip,*
> *77 Sunset Strip,*
> *You meet the highbrow and the hipster*
> *The starlet and the phony tipster*
> *You meet most every kind of guy and gal*
> *Including a private eye!*

Spiff had adapted these for his own use, as follows,
> *Spiff Tracey, private eye, boom boom!*
> *Spiff Tracey, private eye, boom boom!*
> *He meets the highbrow and the drifter,*
> *The star struck and the wallet lifter*
> *He meets most every kind of gal and guy,*
> *The Milky Way private eye!*

and regularly sang them when using his potty.

It has to be said: the reference to The Milky Way private eye was pure baloney. Spiff had never even been to the moon, even though his potty was capable of taking him there, so the reference to 'The Milky Way Galaxy' was codswallop, moonshine, claptrap, call it whatever you choose.

The same brand of negative thought applied to his sidekick, who was a huge woman referred to as 'Chewbacca', the fictional monster from Star Wars. Those who knew her said, unkindly, that she had the body of a Russian lavatory attendant and the attitude of a Suma wrestler. To her credit, she didn't mind being called 'Chewy', but that was only because she thought it meant that the men found her attractive enough to want to 'chew' her.

Her true role was to protect her boss, Spiff, from the overt attentions of his fan club of female admirers, who got all swoony when he was around. Those less knowledgeable thought she was his girlfriend, believed the relationship was kinky in the extreme, and debated his true sexuality.

Upon receiving his first brief from Claude, entitled, *'Investigation Into: The Giants Who May Have Roamed the USA'*, Spiff studied the Mission Statement, consulted the internet, and made some notes on his tablet.

"A piece of cake," he commented, and shouted, "Chewy, lift off!" to advise her that they had a case to complete.

She had been using his walk-in shower and was standing there wrapped in a towelling robe; it would have fitted a 30 stone man, whose build approximated to hers. Spiff glanced at her and said, "I'll give you ten minutes." He knew that being shacked up next to her on his potty would turn it into a spa, if she didn't dry herself adequately.

As they mounted the two front seats of their potty, Spiff waited for an event to occur. This part of the procedure, where she got on it always fascinated him; he expected the potty to sink slightly, but that was an impossibility, since it was held rigidly at a fixed height by gravity.

Chewy glanced across to admire his classic features and asked him, "Where are we going, oh golden master?"

Oblivious to her charms, Spiff stuck a strip of Wintermint chewing-gum in his mouth and replied, "Chew a plaithe not far from here, in a shtate called Massachusetts, in the county of Hampshire near a shmall town called Goshen, where a giant ith rumoured to be buried in an underground chamber."

Chewy replied, "You can be a thilly thod at times. Try thpeaking in future without yer mouth full."

He took the gum out of his mouth, stuck it on the control panel, and fed the destination coordinates into the biological chip, Chippy.

In a female voice, it replied, "I see that your diction has improved. Thank you Chewy, for putting him on a self-improvement course of remedial articulation."

With a smile, he reinserted the gum, closed his red velvet side curtain to keep the sun out of his eyes, put his Ray Ban Aviator sunshades on and leant back with his eyes closed, to pass the journey in meditation.

Minutes later they landed, so he leant further back to pull his side curtain open and attach it by its golden, woven cord to its brass hook stand.

They had set down in a fairly level area that had been cleared for an archaeological dig, in the centre of which was a large, diagonal area of freshly turned earth.

Retrieving a pair of gumboots from the foot well in the rear, he put them on in place of his brown leather brogues. He also collected some items laid across the rear passenger seats; these included a rake and a spade, and finally a piece of equipment with a handle and wheel, that looked like an updated version of a metal detector.

It was quite sophisticated, and Chewy asked him, "What's that?" as he turned it on and it began making a high-pitched sonic whistling chime.

He ran the wheel over the patch of loose earth in a panning motion, and studied the flat screen at the top of the handle. With a knowing grunt, he finally replied, "This gives me a 3D view of what's underneath the ground, to a level of up to 9 feet, if it's mainly earth."

He pressed a transmission button and turned off the device, commenting, "Hey my little beauty, my little cutie, what we see reveals a family tree!"

"Are you talking to me?" Chewy asked, hopefully.

Sorry but no, we've got elsewhere to go," he replied, reaching in his pocket and scattering some small, shiny items around. Afterwards, he used the spade to embed them in the soil and then raked the ground.

"Let's be off into the big blue yonder."

Carefully, he stacked the three items on top of the protective blanket across the rear seats, and got in the front, waiting for Chewy to join him.

"Where to next?" she asked.

To Goshen Town, to disseminate false information about potential fracking operations in the area, and thence to Springfield to spread the rumour farther afield."

"Which area do you have in mind?"

"Ah, you get right to the heart of the matter, don't you? I will hint at *this* area, for one."

They stopped off at a local bar in Goshen, mainly to have a coffee but also to talk cheerfully about the local prospects for fracking, seemingly oblivious to the outrage they were causing.

"You don't mean close by The Goshen Tunnels?" asked one incredulous local, who looked as if he was going to launch himself on Spiff, then changed his mind when Chewy loomed up over him.

"I sure do!" Spiff said, looking into space.

The barman charged them well over the odds for their drinks.

On leaving, with a hostile crowd following, they got on their potty.

"Where to next, before I get vexed?" Chewy asked him.

"Springfield, the local big TV and radio stations, after I've announced to them our imminent arrival in the area, as the bringers of good, business tidings."

Immediately outside town, Spiff ordered the potty to land in a secluded forest clearing. He dismounted, opened the nearest rear door, and reached for the clothes holder suspended behind the rear seat. There, he wet flannelled his armpits and neck, dried himself and changed from his casual clothes into a formal shirt, tie, suit and shiny black, Cuban-heeled shoes. Finally he combed back his shoulder length, wavy blond hair and admired himself in a small mirror on a concertina stem, fastened between the two rear seats.

The journey resumed as Spiff gave directions to the nearest broadcasting station, where they landed on a vacant helipad. He made his way to reception and was escorted to the studio, to be interviewed.

Chewy listened as her boss broadcast the most outrageous of fabrications, and did the same again at another station later on.

"Yes," he confirmed at each location, "Western Massachusetts is going to be targeted for intensive fracking, with a pipeline planned to be laid across sacred ground." In front of the outraged interviewers, whose incoming phone lines were becoming jammed, he cheerfully brought out a blurry image of a colossal skeleton, about which he said, "This has been found and recorded this very day, near Goshen, using an advanced radar detector."

He emphasized, "This prize specimen will be excavated and preserved for posterity, in the very near future, I can promise you that much!"

Spiff knew that attempts had been made to dig at the site already, but officialdom had always stepped in and prevented it, much to the frustration of the archaeologists.

At the end of the long day, they returned to their potty and headed home, with Spiff quipping, "Now off to bed, to rest my weary head!"

They heard nothing the following day, but the day after that, Spiff's cell phone nearly took off as it vibrated across his bedside cabinet, repeatedly bellowing, "Dive Dive Dive!" as if it was a submariner's emergency warning. Spiff grabbed the phone before it fell off the edge, and listened to the automated message.

Chewy had burst in, hoping to catch him in the nude, but was disappointed when she saw what he was doing.

"What's up?" she asked.

"We've got a bite in Goshen!" he replied cheerfully. "We leave in half an hour."

Well within the hour, they landed alongside the Goshen Tunnels site, where all seemed to be pristine in the main, diagonal excavation site. They both dismounted, and Spiff knelt down with his tablet on his lap, as Chewy looked over his shoulder.

He accessed an application that summoned the Nano robot cameras that he had scattered around previously and dug into the ground. The speck-sized cameras gathered in front of him, with only a few stragglers left as they emerged from little mounds after scratching their way to the surface.

The tablet screen burst into action, revealing in small panels what had happened the night before, but only selecting the best shots of the activities that had been witnessed. Far from being a haven of rest, the dig had been scene of turmoil!

"Wow!" they both exclaimed.

"Would you look at the size of those monsters!" Spiff said excitedly. "This is the bizz!"

There in front of them stood two scantily clad humanoid beings, who towered over the North American tribesmen who were gathered around at a distance, holding torches. Spotlights stood on the perimeters, and in the near distance, a petrol-driven generator could be heard running.

The others needed to keep their distance, to cater for the mounds of earth being piled up by the giants, who were using enormous shovels to clear the diagonal area. At barely thigh height, they stopped digging when a clanging noise was heard.

One of the giants waved across to in a specific direction, and the tribesmen made room for two more giants to come through and join them.

"They all look to be about 12 feet tall, and the other two are women!" Spiff said.

They watched spellbound, as all four leant down with their knees bent, and easily slid a monumentally large thick stone slab to one side.

The onlooking tribesmen started chanting and dancing in a circle, as a slightly shorter skeleton was reverentially lifted up from the tomb beneath, and was wrapped in a ceremonial, embroidered shroud. It was lifted onto a litter and carried away by the tribesmen, while the giants set to work restoring the emptied tomb to its original condition, piling earth on top and pounding it down.

"Heavens above, that took them no time at all!" Spiff exclaimed, shaking his head in amazement, as the site was cleared and they all left.

"That wasn't what I expected to happen," Spiff said, "I reckoned it was going to be The Smithsonian Institution that would do this, not giants themselves!"

Chewy said, "I thought they wus all dead!"

The following night, in the early hours of the morning while he was fast asleep, Spiff received another, "Dive Dive Dive!" call that almost made him jump out of skin. He picked up his phone, listened intently and called Chewy, before showering and diving into casual clothes, for a prompt lift-off on his potty, with her by his side.

They landed a short distance from the Goshen Tunnels site, keeping out of view by skirting a forest clearing, and walked towards the lights illuminating it a few minutes away.

In full view, a team of men in casual clothes were digging away the top soil covering the previously excavated stone tomb, while two women in white overalls were supervising, holding clipboards and taking notes and photographs with cell phones. Spotlights again helped show what they were doing, flooding the site with almost daylight conditions.

Spiff took some photos of his own, with the flashlight set to the 'off' position, and then retraced his steps, with Chewy, back to the potty, to make some calls of his own. The first was to the police department at Goshen, where he spoke by phone to the desk and asked, "Are you aware that an archaeological dig is taking place at Goshen Tunnel, to remove ancient bones?"

"No," was the terse reply. "Who are you?"

"I represent the Massachusetts Archaeological Society (or MAS for short), acting in accordance with NAGPRA, or the North American Graves Protection and Repatriation Act.

"It is my submission that, prior to the beginning of an acquisition project, any individual, group or organisation conducting archaeological research under the auspices of the MAS is encouraged to submit a proposal to the Project Review Committee that we have established. This group, whoever they belong to, has not complied with our requirements and will be disposing of artefacts, illegally.

"Unless your department acts immediately, it will be held accountable for this presumed illegal activity.

"This warning is also being relayed to two broadcasters in the next few minutes, and will become public knowledge. Do you realize the consequences?"

There was a grunt of confirmation the other end, a reference number was allocated, and Spiff ended the call.

The additional calls were made as pre-warned, and all were also transmitted to another number, for formatting as text and issue to Claude.

They comprised an ongoing record of the progress that Spiff was achieving.

Spiff and Chewy crept stealthily back to the site, and watched as the police swooped on the unsuspecting team, who argued furiously with them as they were led away in handcuffs. When the site was abandoned, Spiff went over to the empty tomb, saw that the stone slab had been pushed to one side at an angle, and threw into the empty interior a few pieces of ancient cloth that he had bought from the local 'Mashpee Wampanoag Tribe'. Realising that the site wouldn't be deserted for long, as the public responded to the broadcasts, he and Chewy scarpered home on their potty.

During the following days, Spiff was entertained by the volatility generated between the broadcasting stations and their listeners, most of whom were siding with the Mashpee Indians. It seemed to be the case that The Smithsonian Institution had initiated the dig, without anyone's prior permission, and were suspected of doing so to hide evidence that 'Giants Once Roamed the Earth.'

Once such proof had been found, from the traces of ancient clothes still remaining in the emptied tomb, the institution was in serious trouble. The Massachusetts Archaeological Society was demanding that the major finds they had already removed be returned forthwith. Of course, this was not possible, since the tomb had been emptied beforehand.

Spiff handed over his report to Claude, who became absorbed in thought as he read it, saying, "Well done! I like the way you uncovered the fact that giants still exist, and highlighted the cavalier way that the Smithsonian Institution has behaved. This man who was its first curator; do you think he was personally responsible for destroying all traces that giants once co-existed with humans?"

Spiff replied, "It looks that way. He was a Czech immigrant, with a name, which is pronounced (so I'm told) Alesh **Hurd-leech-ka**.

He pointed out the relevant entry in the report, headed Aleš Hrdlička and the picture below, adding, "He was elected in 1903 and served in that capacity for a long time."

"There exist meticulously recorded accounts of giants being found in tombs and mounds the length and breadth of our country, supplemented with eye witness reports by people alive today.

"Others are based on oral stories passed on by one generation to the next. This type of story-telling should not be discounted, because the Eskimo Inuit tribe helped modern explorers to resolve an enduring mystery: what happened to the ships belonging to Sir John Franklin's expedition in 1845 that was attempting to find the Northwest Passage above Canada?

"Inuit hunters provided the last real clue of what happened to the expedition. After all the other reported sightings, hunters said they had seen a set of 'white man's footsteps in the snow', much further south of King William Island, bordering Queen Maud Gulf, with a gangplank lowered from a wooden ship stuck fast in the ice. The story was relayed in this fashion until it reached the ears of modern explorers.

"In 2015, Canada announced the discovery of a Royal Navy vessel, which turned out to be HMS Erebus, which disappeared in the Arctic nearly all those years ago. It was identified from the ship's bell."

Claude closed the report. "Highly commendable. Do you have any idea where the giants are now?"

Spiff replied, "Naturally! Do you want me to tell you?"

"No!" Claude said. "I don't want this information to be shared. They could become extinct, if their location becomes known.

"I see places like the fortress town of Mycenae in Greece in a new light, and the temples in Malta and Gozo. Those huge stones *were* placed in position by giants!

"Keep it in a secure place, in case they need to be unleashed, and let me alone know where that is. Their numbers must be encouraged to grow!"

THE END

But see Addendum

Addendum

Reference 1. Basis for Decapitation Story

Location. Near Tehachapi, California
Date: 1919
Time: night

While hoboing across the country Mike Childers spent what he thought was a night in the woods near Tehachapi. When he awoke and set off on his way, he discovered that the year was 1934 and America had passed into the Great Depression.

Childers made a small media splash as a modern day Rip Van Winkle but was never able to discover what happened to the fifteen years he'd lost. It wasn't until 1990 that the decrepit Childers began to have nightmares that hinted at forgotten memories. Having seen Dr. Denton Schaeffer on a tabloid talk show about repressed memories, he mailed Schaeffer a description of his experience and dreams (along with his collection of journal articles and news clippings about him from the mid-1930's).

Schaeffer interviewed and hypnotized Childers on thirty occasions before Childers' death in 1995 and was able to uncover a vivid tapestry of dark and horrifying memories in which Childers was taken beneath the ground by chattering alien creatures who surgically removed his brain and transported him to alien realms.

The most disturbing part of this case is the medical evidence that Childers was subjected to extensive and inexplicable cranial surgery sometime during the 1920's.

Reference 2. The Black Eyed Children

http://www.dailystar.co.uk/news/latest-news/402988/Terrifying-plague-of-black-eyed-GHOST-children-around-the-world

A PLAGUE of black eyed child ghosts was seen in Britain and across the world, sparking fears of a spook invasion.

Reference 3. Alien Shot Dead by Police

http://www.ufocasebook.com/ftdix.html

One of the airmen on duty was a Sgt. Jeff Morse (pseudonym). The state trooper told Morse that a Fort Dix MP was pursuing a low-flying object that had hovered over his car.

Then a small being with large head and slender body appeared in front of his car. The MP had panicked and shot the alien several times with a .45 automatic. The being had fled over the fence between the two bases, before falling and dying on the deserted runway.

Morse and his colleagues found the body lying on the runway. As they followed routine procedure and roped off the area of the crime scene, as other blue beret forces unfamiliar to Morse and his companion took over. Morse was relegated to a back-up role, but could see from a slight distance what was happening.

The only other anomaly that Morse attributed to the presence of the body was the **strong smell of ammonia** in the cold night air, and, I note here that the same odour has been present at other crash sites.

Reference 4. The Solway Firth Spaceman

http://www.bbc.com/news/uk-england-cumbria-27391210

On 23 May 1964, an off-duty fireman from Carlisle, Cumberland named Jim Templeton, took photographs of his five-year-old daughter while on a day trip to Burgh Marsh. Templeton said the only other people on the marshes that day were a couple of old ladies sitting in a car at the far end of the marsh. Templeton stated, "I took three pictures of my daughter Elizabeth in a similar pose – and was shocked when the middle picture came back from Kodak displaying what looks like a spaceman in the background." Templeton insists that he did not see the figure until after his photographs were developed, and analysts at Kodak confirmed that the photograph was genuine.

Templeton said he was visited after he published the photograph by two men dressed in black, wearing sunglasses, who refused to show their identification. They said they worked for the government, **and only referred to each other by the use of numbers**.

Reference 5. Did Giants Roam the World?

http://www.6000years.org/giants.html
What do fossil records show? Well this is where things get interesting. Giant ancient humans would fly in the face of evolution. It would show that we have actually **devolved**, not **evolved**. Since the 1800's, there have been many written accounts of giant human fossils having been found. Additionally, very large tools have been found, which only very large people could have used.

http://bucklinsociety.net/bucklin-family-history/william-bucklin/nine-mens-misery/
The Nine Men's Misery monument marks the place where on March 26, 1676, nine Rhode Island soldiers, including Benjamin Bucklin, were killed by Native Americans in King Phillip's War.

One of the skeletons was dug up and was of extraordinary size. By the fact of it's having a double set of teeth, it was recognized as that of Benjamin Bucklin (Buckland), of Rehoboth.

A must read:
http://grahamhancock.com/dewhurstr1/
His new book, The Ancient Giants Who Ruled America, meticulously chronicles the missing giant skeletons of one of the Smithsonian's greatest cover-ups.

Other accounts include:
The most amazing discoveries in California were on Catalina Island. In the 1920's, this island was owned by the Wrigley Chewing gum family, who hired Professor Ralph Glidden to conduct a series of digs on the island under the direction of the Catalina Museum.

What they found made headlines around the world, only to be written out of the history books less than 10 years later. For over 50 years the proofs pertaining to these discoveries were vigorously denied by the University of California and The Smithsonian, but in 2011 it was finally admitted that the evidence for these finds had been locked away from the public in the restricted-access evidence rooms of the Smithsonian, along with detailed field reports and hundreds of photos.

The Paiutes, a Native-American tribe indigenous to parts of Nevada, Utah and Arizona, told early white settlers about their ancestors' battles with the ferocious race of white, red-haired giants. According to the Paiutes, the giants were already living in the area.

According to the Paiutes, the red-haired giants stood as tall as 12-feet and were a vicious, unapproachable people that killed and ate captured Paiutes as food.

The Paiutes told the early settlers that after many years of warfare, all the tribes in the area finally joined together to rid themselves of the giants.

The mounds are scattered throughout the Midwest from as far south as Tennessee stretching northwards into Wisconsin, westwards to Oklahoma, and eastwards into West Virginia. Excavation of most mounds has unearthed many artefacts and the remains of average-sized humans.

But older mounds have been discovered containing the skeletal remains of giants...giants with red hair.

Archaeologists cannot deny that the mound builders are real. What they deny are the things sometimes discovered inside the mounds.
Over the past century and a half it's been revealed again and again that some of the mounds - and the small pyramids - are the burial grounds of huge men often eight feet or taller that had a very sophisticated culture. Some of the giants have been found wearing intricate leather armour and have been buried with swords. One such giant was found near Spiro Mound in Oklahoma during the 1930s.

The most credible stories of giant skeletons were concentrated in the Appalachians, Cumberland Plateau and Ohio Basin. They were typically found in graves lined with stone slabs or field stones, known as the Stone Box Grave Culture.

In 1821, 7-feet tall skeletons were found in stone lined sarcophaguses in a White County, TN, burial area.

In 1754, George Washington was colonel of the Virginia Colonial militia. When hostilities broke out with France, he supervised construction of Fort Loudon in Winchester, VA.

Labourers digging the fort's foundation uncovered a cemetery of 7-foot skeletons and what appeared to be Native American artefacts. The skeletons were viewed and reported by Washington. It is not known what happened to them.

During 1918, archaeologists discovered over 10,000 Neolithic artefacts in a Nevada cave. Many seemed too large to have been made by standard sized humans. A male and a female skeleton were also found. The male was said to be 8-feet tall. The skulls are on display at the Humboldt County Museum.

Don't forget, if you want to contact the author you can do so via

www.terrytumbler.com

Have a good life.

If you would be so kind, please leave a review on Amazon!